Willi Gallagher Mysteries
by Kat Goldring

ALL SIGNS POINT TO MURDER

DEATH MEDICINE

Death
medicine

�-symbol ✳

Kat Goldring

BERKLEY PRIME CRIME, NEW YORK

DEATH MEDICINE

A Berkley Prime Crime Book / published by arrangement with the author

PRINTING HISTORY
Berkley Prime Crime mass-market edition / August 2002

Visit our website at
www.penguinputnam.com

ISBN: 0-425-18580-X

Berkley Prime Crime Books are published
by The Berkley Publishing Group,
a division of Penguin Putnam Inc.,
375 Hudson Street, New York, New York 10014.
The name BERKLEY PRIME CRIME and the BERKLEY PRIME CRIME
design are trademarks belonging to Penguin Putnam Inc.

PRINTED IN THE UNITED STATES OF AMERICA

10 9 8 7 6 5 4 3 2 1

ACKNOWLEDGMENTS

Thanks to all those interesting folks who have strewn blessings upon the first book in the series, *All Signs Point to Murder*, and have helped launch this second one in a magical way. These include my agent, Carol McCleary of the Wilshire Literary Agency and my Berkley editor, Kim Waltemyer, both ladies with strong *Ant Medicine*.

Thanks and love to Aunt Norma and Uncle Steve Stevens and Aunt Betty Williams. All will be glad to see this second book come out, seeing as how it proves I've got the perseverance of the Scotch-Irish Bogle clan blood still strongly influencing me, too.

To friends from California to New York, from The Great Lakes Regions to the southern tip of Texas, a hi howdy and a thanky y'all to each one for your encouragement. Especially those Sister-friends, Claudia, Peggy, Shirley and Elaine.

For those wonderful workaholics at the bookstores who set up opportunities to introduce Willi, Quannah and the Native beliefs as well as other beautiful mysticisms of the world to folks, thank you *muy mucho*. For interviews, reviews, publicity shots and generosity of time spent on these, I offer a *gracias* to our media folks. Two in particular, one a former student of mine, seasoned reporter and now *compadre* in teaching, Derik Moore, along with an up-and-coming student in the journalism field, Kirby Jackson. They wrote the first generous-hearted article.

Thanks and warm hugs to all these "behind-the-scene" folks. You've made this pathway so fun and magical.

Pilamaya ye, pilamaya ye.

K'eya Kimimila Win

(Butterfly Turtle Woman)

Kat Goldring

CHAPTER
I

"IT'S so cold, I could spit ice cubes. If, of course, a lady indulged in spitting," Willi Gallagher muttered into her cell phone.

"I'm going to be in major trouble if I don't get out of Austin this morning," she went on. "Held up one day by a blast of ice through the city. Another day in the hotel while the roads cleared."

Aunt Minnie continued to just listen patiently on the other end of the line.

Willi rubbed her temple. "Talk about a screwed-up schedule. If I'm not in time for that seminar, the superintendent will have my scalp at half-mast." He was always teasing her about her volatile heritage of Comanche and Irish blood, but she figured his German roots might be just as fierce if he didn't get his way. The beastly weather didn't know the meaning of *enough*.

"Well, dear, there's only so much you can do. Now you'd better get going or you'll miss your train." And Aunt Minnie abruptly hung up.

Willi's troubles were bad enough, without her favorite relative—Aunt Minnie—shutting her out. Willi sighed. No matter. The battery was low and wouldn't last for another half minute

She glared at the morning newspaper. And now *he* was in town. The lead article entitled "Texas Ranger Lassos Drug Lord" carried a color photo of Quannah Lassiter. The reporter even got the double *n* correct. There he was, exuding strength and calm confidence if not downright arrogance. She glanced again and tried not to notice his smooth bronze skin, black hair and those . . . those dark eyes that seemed to see right through her.

She gazed at the caption and photo. Smartly dressed even with his ponytail and Stetson. If he changed that hat for a war bonnet, he'd sure enough look like a war chief. She knew he spoke Lakota, for he'd taught her a few phrases here and there in an effort to get her to embrace her own lineage. The wind grasped the paper, and she had to hold it tightly.

The article said Lassiter was due out on the afternoon train, which was why Willi now stood in front of the station to leave on the midmorning Amtrak. And she had the uneasy feeling someone was following her. Sometimes when that happened, one Special Investigator for the Texas Rangers lurked nearby. Perhaps her uneasiness was just that infernal sixth sense of hers, that damnable intuition that often kicked into gear to warn her of impending disaster.

Wind beat like a huge tom-tom against the train station's roof to create an eerie cadence. Goose bumps rose on her arms. She shivered. Although inside there was a crowd waiting for numerous train departures, only three other passengers stood between her and the warm haven inside the station.

Yes, Elba had said Willi would be smothered in white, soft white. Willi pushed dark tendrils of hair underneath her red scarf before she again peered over her shoulder at the other waiting passengers. Maybe she should have listened to Elba Kachelhoffer, one of two sisters who were her neighbors. Professed white witches with hearts of gold, the two often predicted the most uncanny things with their crystal ball and tarot cards. Willi smiled. Probably those were just trappings, things folks accepted more easily even though eccentric. If Elba and Agatha had just said they were psychic, folks would call them crazy. With the trappings in place, they were merely eccentric. What else had Elba said?

Be in trouble with the law, too.

No way. She'd be out of Austin before Quannah and his badge even thought about leaving his hotel room. With a fist she pounded the article. First, get out of Austin. Second, avoid forgetful, insensitive Lassiter, who never had shown up for a summer Pow-Wow as he'd promised.

It was bad enough the man could practically read her mind, but worse, wherever he went, disaster followed. Of course, *he* insisted her curiosity got them into danger. Unreasonable man. Well, she had no intention of seeing him again, so that problem wouldn't arise.

The crowd surged toward the various tracks. She wouldn't have to stand in the cold much longer. The man in front of Willi stopped and pointed. He said, "That there woman in the white fur. You recognize her?"

"Well, I'll be. BeeBee VanBauer. She's the Republican running against her ex-husband for state treasurer."

"Got that right, ma'am. Uh-oh. More trouble getting out of that limo."

"Who's in the limo?" she asked, stretching her neck.

"The congressman himself, looks like, ma'am."

"Odd coincidence—VanBauer on the same run as BeeBee. Well, I hope they're in separate cars at opposite ends of the train."

The man said, "Don't think it's coincidence, neither, not with that BeeBee. Ain't no real politician, but she's good at grabbing the publicity any way she can. That woman done threatened many times to do away with him, and what you want to bet she wasn't talking about beating the old boy out in the race. Can't no state in the borders beat Texas politicians for entertainment, no ma'am."

"I'm sure they'll behave civilly if they cross each other's path."

"Maybe so, ma'am."

A fiendish wind howled and swirled underneath her coat. Beside the train station door, a cadaverous potted bush pierced her sleeve. She jerked the cloth from the thorny hold.

"Well, blast and damn." Threads unraveled from the torn spot. The ends of her crimson scarf flapped wildly like a Thunderbird's wings. She sighed. Such thoughts would never have entered her mind before she knew Lassiter. Wolf Medicine. Hummingbird Magic. Thunderbirds. *Damn you, Lassiter, get out of my head.*

She pulled open the station door and kept her weight against it until she struggled her bag inside, then let the wind's momentum close it behind her. Serenity engulfed her for a moment as if she'd stepped into a bear's quiet den, the bright wings of her scarf settled, and she drew a steadying breath.

She sat on a bench, removed her scarf and pulled out a compact. Black, curly wisps escaped from her French braid. She fixed the loose ends and touched up her makeup a bit.

The Amtrak's arrival boomed over the loudspeaker. Willi headed back outside on the train track side. A woman swathed in fur stumbled against her, not apologizing with nod or word, and strode in front.

Willi slipped on an icy spot, but got her balance and her determined-teacher persona took over. She sidled past the ermine, looked boldly at the woman and resumed her place in line.

"Oh," she gasped. The pushy woman was BeeBee VanBauer. At the moment she looked mad enough to skewer Willi with a handy icicle.

A feral howl of wind wound its way underneath the Amtrak. Willi's neck hairs stood on end. She grasped the straps of her purse and makeup kit.

The fur-wrapped BeeBee tried the defensive tactic of the injured party. "Well, of all the nerve. Did you see what that—?"

"Really," a silver-haired woman said. "You brought it on yourself. I did not appreciate your huffing past me, nor obviously did this young woman." With that admonition, a petite yet elegant figure moved in front of BeeBee.

"I am Catherine Noble." She presented a gloved hand to Willi. "Don't people like her make you want to invest in cyanide for the protection of civilized society?"

Over the popping and flapping of her red scarf, Willi yelled, "Glad to meet you, Catherine. I'm Willi Gallagher. You may have a point about the poison." She studied the glowering clouds. "Right now I'm more concerned about those. Have you ever seen such a storm in Texas?"

"Once. Up in the Panhandle area, though. Quite unusual in central Texas, I'd think. I hope we won't have any trouble clearing tracks through to Fort Worth."

A whirlwind of ice blasted, stinging Willi's eyes. The stiff wind pushed against her back, and when Catherine lost her balance, Willi grasped the older woman's elbow.

"Thank you, Willi. Are you headed for Fort Worth, too?"

"Almost. Nickleberry."

Willi finally reached the platform. With the help of the porter, she assisted Catherine onto the train and stepped into the entrance where the few people chose upper or lower, right or left sections.

"Which way?" inquired Catherine as she pulled her scarf off. Her bangs were crimped in ringlets. The rest of her hair was in a perky little flip ending just below her ears.

"To the right, I think."

"You go ahead. I'm so slow on steps," Catherine said. Her starched, white blouse with a silk rose at the throat set Catherine apart from the few passengers, bleary-eyed mouth breathers, who shuffled up and down the aisles.

Catherine, now two steps below, asked, "In Austin on business?"

"Yes, business, in a way. I came for the Democratic fundraiser. It wasn't quite what I'd hoped for. More partying than real work accomplished. And you?"

"An appointment with a Republican congressman and a couple of the Democrats." Catherine smirked and in a lower voice said, "Fools. Everyone of them are arrogant fools who ought to be shot."

"You won't get an argument from me."

Nodding, Catherine said, "I'm a representative from a Fort Worth group of retired teachers. We're hoping to convince the state powers not to pass the new teacher retirement bill and to change the insurance coverage. It'd make paupers of us all."

"I've taught for ten years. I'm ashamed to say I wasn't even aware of such a bill being considered."

Catherine patted Willi's arm. "All things in their time. You've got your hands full with learning about the internet, illiterates, gangs and pregnant teenagers. Heaven knows what else."

Willi climbed to the upper level and turned right. "My super isn't a tolerant man. His worst peeve is tardiness. His second one is *me*. This train better get to chugging down those tracks soon."

"Whatever," Catherine asked, "happened to the crowds?"

A steward, *Uzell Speer* emblazoned on his badge, approached them. "Perhaps best you ladies be deciding about going on or taking a later train. Others, they done been going. *Only a handful left now on this train. About ten or so.* What you think?" He sneezed and coughed into a handkerchief. "Be pardoning me with this beginning of a cold."

Willi tilted her head to hear better. She spoke Spanish and some German—a few words of Lakota, but his accent didn't fit any of those languages. She frowned in concentration.

Uzell said, "I think the tracks not be looking clear on up the way. Be delays, maybe. Maybe not." He pushed some pillows into a bin at the head of the stairway. "In fact, we be uncoupling most of the cars here." He frowned. "This passenger, a sleeper, the diner—those be left with us."

She placed his accent in a category and smiled. His soft Jamaican patois, tinged with just enough twang, indicated he was an islander relocated in Texas for some time. Uzell, still sniffling, marched away, stifling the sneezes in his handkerchief.

"Oh, my," said Catherine. "I don't have money for an overnight stay. I believe, young man, I'll take my chances."

Willi said, "I'm sure the Amtrak authorities wouldn't let the train leave the station if there were any *real* danger. The airlines weren't having problems an hour ago."

BeeBee VanBauer brushed past Willi, threw her fur coat across three seats and declared, "You! Steward! Watch this while I'm gone. They're holding the train for another fifteen minutes of interviews." She bumped into Willi, cutting her off from Catherine Noble who, like a dove, had nestled in a seat across the aisle from the territory annexed by BeeBee.

Great Hades, now the VanBauers' political monkeying for the media would delay the train. Willi put both hands on her hips and opened her mouth to protest, but a voice from behind stopped her.

"Well," Congressman VanBauer, stroking his thinning hair, drawled in a media-trained voice, "the trip home won't be dull." He smiled across Willi's shoulder at his ex-wife and stepped closer, blocking Willi between him and BeeBee.

Willi tried to sit, but BeeBee made that maneuver impossible. "Would you excuse—?"

BeeBee hissed across Willi's other shoulder. "No, not a bit boring with a nasty bit of goods like you aboard, darling. Nauseating, but not boring."

Willi tried again. "If I could just get out of—?"

VanBauer narrowed his eyes, but allowed a crocodile grin to spread across his face. "You can avoid the nausea, BeeBee, if you just don't look in any mirrors."

"You loathsome excuse for a man," BeeBee said. "By the time this campaign for treasurer is over, the whole state will know you for what you are."

"Maybe," Willi said, twisting, "you two might converse better if I could get out of the way and—?"

Congressman VanBauer leaned over Willi's shoulder. His hot breath hit her cheeks.

Willi blinked. The least the man could have done was not eat garlic for breakfast.

He said, "But, dear BeeBee, my life is an open book. No hidden woman, no unlawful activities, no ugly skeletons. You'll have to come up with something else. I left you for one reason only. You're a marble-hearted bitch, BeeBee. And some of my constituents, like this lovely lady, are right here observing that fact."

"The . . . uh . . . lovely lady," Willi said, "would sit down if one of you . . ."

BeeBee shifted to a more aggressive stance by thrusting herself forward.

Willi, arms locked to her sides, looked up at the ceiling. With her torso sandwiched tightly, she tried to get one leg back far enough to ease down into a seat. Sweetly, she said, "Oh, look. Here come some photographers. Guess they'll want photos."

BeeBee stretched her lips into a smile, turned on her seal skin boots, and sauntered toward the dining car, which left Willi in an awkward, pigeon-toed position. Congressman VanBauer palmed his hair and retreated toward the sleeper.

The train lurched. Willi stumbled a few feet backward, where she fell into a seat and onto another passenger.

"Oh, I'm *sorry*." She tried to scramble off the man, but he held her around the waist.

"Good morning, *Winyan*. I was wondering when we'd find each other again."

Willi's heartbeat cantered like a skittish colt's. "Lassiter?"

CHAPTER
2

WILLI forced her heartbeat to slow to a gentle trot. "Let me up, Lassiter."

"Certainly, *Winyan,* just don't fall on my Stetson. It's new. You demolished the last one, and—"

"I what?"

She scrambled out of his lap and stood facing him, both hands on her hips. Okay, she had to deal with his presence, had to convince him he didn't rattle her every time he stepped into her life, and while she was at it, she had to make herself believe it was mere imagination that made her heart race. "I don't recall—"

Folding his arms across his chest, he nodded. "—with a baseball bat."

"That wasn't your hat I—"

He looked at the ceiling and grinned. "Come to think of it, you used an upswing and got me right between—"

"Nevertheless." Willi blushed, got her breathing under control and placed her hands behind her back. "If my aim had been better, I'd have hit that hard head of yours."

"To think the Great Winter Wind—*T'ate Waziyata*—blew us into each other's arms again is truly frightening."

Willi moaned. Great Hades. "Well, Tater's Wazooty can just blow you back to . . . to—"

With a look on his face indicating he was dealing with a slow Moe, he said, "*T'ate Waziyata. You* can shorten it to *Waziyata*. And I'm not complaining. You landing in my lap is much better than the baseball bat."

She ignored the playfulness in his voice and got practical. "Doesn't look like we're going to get home on time, does it?"

"Things happen when they happen, *Winyan*. Why be so worried?"

"I have a seminar to present, and I'm not exactly on my super's list of favorite folks to be kind to."

Quannah grinned. "You have no control over this situation other than how you choose to react."

"Thank you for that bit of philosophy. I'll remind you of it next time you can't catch a crazed killer. Guess the petty concerns of a small-town teacher seem of little importance to someone who just brought in a drug lord."

"Not at all. Nothing wrong with commitment unless it becomes an obsession you can't turn loose of when necessary. Your superintendent would be lucky to have a campus full of dedicated ones like you, and I've always respected my mother and others who chose the path of the Wolf."

"The Wolf?"

"The teachers in the tribe."

She shut her eyes to try and recall a distant dream vision, one of two wolves beside a lake. It wouldn't quite come into focus, and she frowned.

"Gallagher?"

"What?"

"I meant it, really."

"Thanks." She blinked and sighed. She was fine, just fine, and she would live through the trip without making a fool of herself in front of this self-assured, overrated lawman. She took a deep breath and changed tack. "You're headed for Nickleberry, too, I guess, to visit Sheriff Tucker."

"Yes, Uncle Brigham promised he wouldn't get me involved with any local crime this time. If you don't get off the train there, he might be able to keep that promise. How about you going north another city or two?" Quannah laughed, his infectious grin spread and the twinkle in his eye invited her to join in.

Giggling, she did.

"Impossible man. The newspaper said Big Chief Lassiter was due out on the *afternoon* Amtrak."

"Can't believe everything you read, Gallagher. I don't think there'll be another train for a couple of days, and I didn't care to stay in the capital. After I turned those *waglulas* in, some lowlifes got the itch—the one that makes them want to count coup on one lawman."

"You're in danger? Here?"

"It's good of you to worry, Gallagher, but don't. Everything's fine."

Infuriating man to think the concern was for him, not for her or the other passengers aboard if someone came gunning for his happy ass. Willi frowned. "What do you mean, another train won't leave? I didn't hear any report like that. Why won't another train leave?"

You'll be smothered in white. She shook her head to dislodge Elba's prediction.

Uneasiness slid along her spine, slowly like the slick rot of mold on spoiled cabbage. "This train *has* to make it through, right? There's not a possibility of it stopping and staying in Austin, surely?"

Narrowing his eyes, he picked up his black Stetson with four feathers—two each of raven and falcon—shifted over to the window seat, and peered out. "Uhmmm. *Waziyata*."

He stared hard into her eyes before tapping his chest and said in a quiet voice, "In here. You know, too. Many elements have come together. For one, *T'ate*, the fierce spirit wind of *Waziyata*, the North. Did these two not speak to you outside the station?"

Willi wiped her palms together. Damn the man, he was inside her head again. "That wind pounding on the roof? Sounded like your whole tribe beating drums."

"Things happen in their own time. I couldn't, for example, make it back to take you to the Pow-Wow because I was stuck up in Montana on a case and—"

"That never crossed my mind; I don't care if—"

He smiled and continued. "Many things have converged and all for a reason."

"Many? What else?"

He stuck out his bottom lip, slowly drew it in and sighed. "Perhaps a better question might be *who*?" He saluted with two fingers placed to his hat brim. "Believe I'll stretch my legs."

"Wait a minute. Are you talking about the VanBauers?"

Quannah sauntered away without answering.

"Annoying man. Capture my interest and give me no answers. Irritating." She'd not get her nose stuck in matters that didn't concern her. Blue Blazes, she'd just pretend he wasn't on the Amtrak and make an effort not to encounter him again.

Checking her watch, she was surprised to find that the train was more than two hours behind schedule thanks to the VanBauers' media-grabbing little hearts. But at last, a reassuring rumble became a steady click of iron against iron.

"Great. Goodbye, Austin. Hello, Nickleberry," she muttered to herself and settled in for the journey.

In her hometown, she would definitely find ways to avoid Quannah Lassiter along with the conflicting emotions roiling within her. But he wasn't, as she'd imagined in the station, the instigator causing her uneasiness. That *feeling* of some pending catastrophe still lurked. Thank you, Elba, for the warning about *trouble with the law* and *being smothered*. She glanced around.

Catherine Noble, asleep, really did look like a dove with her head tucked underneath one arm. She moaned in her sleep.

Willi knew *she* wouldn't be able to enjoy a wink of sleep anytime soon. She got up anyway and walked to the bin of pillows, brought one back and plumped it up on her headrest. Still, she couldn't settle down. She wandered into the next car, peered outside for a good ten minutes and finally traipsed back to her own car and passenger seat. Her mind kept playing around the problem of one lawman's appearance on the Amtrak.

She touched her palms to her hot cheeks. He could be chasing down Mexican *cucarachas*, Carolina boll weevils or Alaskan moose for all she cared. She scrabbled in her purse and pulled out a small stone, clutched it in her palm and closed her eyes.

"Tunkasila," she whispered.

Her Teaching Stone—a small rock from the sacred Black Hills referred to as the Grandfather, the *Tunkasila*, by the People—still worked its magic. Calmer, she sighed. Light blinked off the stone. She smiled at the gift Lassiter had given her, then stared out the glazed pane.

The wind of the North—*Waziyata*—screamed in fiendish agony like a hundred spirits of massacred Comanche. Yes, Waziyata howled, then wheels shrieked against metal, the car pitched and leaned into the curve, swung back, steadied and moved onward . . . but so . . . damned . . . *slowly*.

That feeling she'd had in the station of being watched, returned. She peered over her shoulder, shuddered and clutched *Tunkasila* to her heart.

CHAPTER
3

RUBBING the back of her neck, willi shivered.

This internal conflagration was for the crows. She needed other folks to talk to so she wouldn't concern herself with the VanBauers' melodrama, wouldn't think about who might be after Quannah, wouldn't drift off into those daydreams often acted upon. She headed toward the diner. She'd strike up a conversation with someone or, failing that, indulge in one of her favorite pastimes, eavesdropping. She got up, held on to the passenger chair in front of her for balance, and was about to head toward the diner until she peered closer at BeeBee's ermine coat.

"What in the world?"

She quickly glanced over her shoulder before she reached around the seat to touch the glaring spot upon the white collar. Dried, it was dark as burgundy wine.

"Blood?" Willi whispered.

No. Absolutely not. *Don't even think it.* But she'd clearly seen the ermine when BeeBee had rudely passed her in line. There'd been no stain, nor had there been when BeeBee threw the fur across the seat. Perhaps while Willi had wandered from car to car, BeeBee had returned for her coat and somehow spilled something on it. Sure. Probably BeeBee VanBauer would be in the diner with the other passengers. Willi grabbed a mystery novel from her bag, squared her shoulders and sauntered in that direction.

Waziyata whistled and moaned outside the diner windows, too. She edged down a narrow aisle between booths with tables bolted to the walls. Covered with red-checkered plastic cloths, the tables seemed less glamorous than she'd expected. Past the eight dining booths was a lounge seating section. She sat in a swivel chair with a high back, which she carefully turned three-quarters around to view the occupants.

BeeBee was nowhere in sight. A tiny worry worm niggled its way into Willi's thoughts. The woman wasn't the type to leave an ermine coat—even one with a stain.

Congressman VanBauer sat in one of the plush chairs, his legs crossed in a fastidious manner, and he brushed a flattened palm against what remained of his silver hair. Relaxed, he seemed to be exactly what the tabloids called him—the Renaissance Man—intelligent and passionate about arts and commerce.

Willi leaned her head back, the better to hear VanBauer and a younger companion. Percentages and hidden taxes were bandied about between the two. As far as she was concerned, nothing could be duller or safer.

VanBauer said the younger man's name.

She shifted to hear better and opened her eyes wide. Had she heard correctly? *Elvis?* VanBauer called the other man *Elvis?*

To better observe them, she swiveled her chair around a tad more. The man, pomaded hair gleaming blacker than India ink, grinned in a sure-enough-Elvis-one-sided curl of lips.

Willi pursed her own generous lips. Elvis was probably twenty years the junior to the Renaissance man. No, she decided with that feminine intuitive jump she never questioned. He was even younger, barely twenty-seven if a day.

The clink-chuga-chuga-clink of the train escalated as Austin yielded to open farmland and ranches outside the city. Well, at this speed it'd be a good twelve hours, possibly more with this weather, before she'd reach Nickleberry. Quannah was right. She had no control over the situation except in how she was going to react. For the moment, she chose to just enjoy events and folks around her.

VanBauer and Elvis pulled out papers and, leaning closer to each other, lowered their voices.

Damn it, she couldn't hear a thing. She tapped her foot on the gray carpet, swiveled her chair back around and stared at her book, *Cooper Street Girls,* a mystery by one of her favorite authors.

The Jamaican train attendant-cum-waiter came by. "You be requiring anything right this minute?"

She squinted to see his name tag again. Uzell Speer. That seemed such an ugly name for someone as beautiful as the young Jamaican. Admittedly, *beautiful* wasn't an adjective she'd apply to any male; yet it suited Uzell.

Close-cropped hair, dusky lashes that curled like wisps of smoke to touch the wide lids over chocolate eyes.

"Well, actually, yes."

"Golden pecan coffee? It be a special favorite of the ladies—"

"No, thanks. Have you . . . have you seen Mrs. Van-Bauer?"

"No, miss, I no be seeing her in the diner."

"She was wearing a white fur—"

"Yes, miss, but here she not coming today, what you think?"

"Perhaps for a glass of wine? Maybe someone else served her a glass of wine because, you see, there's a stain on her coat, and—"

"Miss, I being very sorry, don't you know?" He pulled out a handkerchief, rubbed his nose and stifled a sneeze.

She sighed and smiled at the lilt of questions at the ends of his soft-spoken statements.

"Thanks, anyway, Mr. Speer."

"You be calling me Uzell. Mister not be suiting this fellow, what you think?"

"Uzell, then. I . . . I have some cold tablets in my makeup bag if you'd like to try them."

"No, miss, not while I be working, but when I be sleeping later, maybe." He made his way to the end of the lounge.

The look on VanBauer's face took her breath away. Her scalp prickled, and she searched for the cause. Like a predator waiting for his victim to come closer, the congressman narrowed his eyes.

Her heart flip-flopped. Oh no, he'd heard her questions about BeeBee. Maybe *he* was responsible for his ex-wife's no-show in the diner, and maybe he didn't *want* the fact of her not being present advertised.

As Uzell approached him, the congressman's glance turned as hard and cold as the ice crusting the diner windows.

Why would VanBauer stare so . . . so . . . viciously— yes, *viciously*—at the train attendant? *She* was the one who'd brought up the subject of BeeBee.

A sickly smile boding no good for the steward spread across VanBauer's face. He snapped his fingers.

Uzell, tray in hand, paused. Only a millisecond passed before he moved in response toward the congressman and Elvis.

Willi sat up straighter as if the tension noted in Uzell's shoulders had spread to her. The air crackled with energy.

What was going on here? She moved one seat closer. An uneasy thought pushed its way to the edge of her mind. Such curiosity had catapulted her into trouble many times over, often endangering her life. She stifled such nonsense along with Elba's admonition, *Curiosity killed the cat,* and leaned a bit closer.

Uzell's young, halcyon face seemed to crumple. He offered, "May I be getting you gentlemens any refreshments?"

"Ah," said VanBauer and chuckled. "Old friends like us. We're not going to stand on ceremony, are we? Act as if we don't know each other?"

Uzell stiffened his back. His cocoa skin deepened in color as if someone had added fresh coffee to a weakened drink, but he said nothing.

Willi let out her breath.

A tall, gangling fellow dressed in typical rancher's go-to-town garb, stood in the car doorway. Well, things were getting more interesting. Who in the heck was that?

With a hand touched by the swollen joints of rheumatoid arthritis, he adjusted a battered hat the color of wheat spattered with a few well-placed spits of tobacco. He smoothed his yellow-gray locks as he placed the hat, pulled his pants up over his beer belly, and entered.

VanBauer nodded at him in a dismissive manner as if to say, *I'll handle this*.

The man halted and said, "Fine by Royce Droskill, Mr. VanBauer, fine by me. If it's private *bidness*, ain't a hair on my chin that's gonna wag. Just glad to do my job, but when you see fit, sir, when you see fit." Droskill nodded at Willi when he sauntered toward the dining booths up ahead. VanBauer palmed his hair back again.

Willi smirked at him and that decidedly snobbish and egotistical little habit, one she'd never noticed him indulging in on television. Probably, Elvis or Droskill or one of the congressman's other minions kept cue cards before him. *Don't pat yourself. Stop preening.*

VanBauer sneered at Uzell. "Don't you dare turn from me! You came out of a gutter. I'll put you there again!" He rose from the lounge chair.

Elvis pulled him back. "Sir, someone could overhear."

Willi kept her sight glued to her novel.

"Perhaps you can settle this," Elvis said, "at another time and more . . . privately?"

"You're right. Of course, you're *quite* right." VanBauer waved both his aide and the attendant away.

Elvis smiled at Uzell. "What do you have?"

"There be soft drinks, coffee, liquors, tea. What you think?"

"I'll have a coffee. Black. You, sir?"

VanBauer capitulated. "Bring me a coffee, too. You *know* how I like it."

Elvis, smiling, said, "Make sure the congressman's has a dollop of cream on top and three spoons of sugar."

Uzell stepped away, nodding only to Elvis, and said, "Being just a moment."

VanBauer's cultured voice cut the air between them. "You say 'yes *sir*' to me." His face suffused with carmine.

Uzell peered back over his shoulder, blinked and left to fill the orders.

Peeking from beneath her lashes, Willi expelled her breath again. She'd have to learn better survellience techniques or have an oxygen bottle close at hand.

VanBauer's jaw muscles fascinated her. They produced a minute tic, and his stentorian breathing filled the lounge as if he were a snorting bull. If Elvis hadn't been present, maybe the congressman would have given free rein to his temper. Perhaps he already *had*.

Where in Hades was BeeBee?

Another attendant returned with the drinks for the congressman and Elvis. No more flare-ups in the foreseeable future with Uzell's absence, she moved to a table in the dining car.

The train eased to a stop in a town without even the amenity of a station, just a crossroads where three people, wrapped in heavy coats against the increasing chill and with suitcases in hand, looked expectantly at the silver streak hissing at their feet. They boarded and the Amtrak, leaving an unnamed town in the distance, picked up speed.

She tested the cold by leaning over and blowing on the window. Her breath created a haze.

Rubbing out the icy pattern, she leaned back in the chair and smiled. Try as she might, she could make no sense out of the Elba's last admonition. *Old folks and hanky-panky? Murder without teeth?* Feeling even more depressed about having to eat alone, she was about to leave when Elvis arrived just as the Amtrak stopped and let those three bundled passengers off in a no less desolate place than where they'd boarded. Three others also departed, leaving only seven passengers on the train. She wanted company to draw her out, make her forget one bloody stain, and help her figure out where BeeBee VanBauer could have gotten to on what remained of the Amtrak cars. *How could she get lost among only seven folks?*

A black curl cascaded across Elvis's brow, much as his namesake's had on stage.

Willi said, "Looks like we're the only ones hungry. Sit with me, please."

"Thanks," he said, brushing the seat off with a napkin before sitting. His Olgivan suit, elegantly tailored, fitted him well and his manner indicated he knew the fact. Yet, to her, his self-knowledge was neither pugnacious nor overtly offensive. He was simply assured of himself and his station in life. His DeArman cologne, gold cuff links and styled hair added to the effect. "Elvis is the name."

She roused herself. "Willi, Willi Gallagher, and you're Elvis . . . ?"

"That's the only name I have on driver's license, checks, charge cards."

"I see," she said although she didn't quite.

"Elvis, *the Elvis,* was my idol. The only real joy I knew as a teen revolved around an Elvis impersonator who let me perform with him on stage." He laughed comfortably at himself. "Perhaps it made too much of an impression. As soon as I could, I legally got Elvis as my name."

"Ever regretted the change?"

"No, never. My name is the only flamboyant aspect of an overly conservative personality."

"I've been accused a few times of being overly anxious . . . and . . . curious. You'll probably think so, too." She frowned, pushing a vision of a stern-faced Lassiter to the dustiest corner of her mind. He'd not approve of her meddling, but just a few simple questions couldn't cause any problems surely.

"Why's that? You have a cousin-slash-friend-slash-reporter who needs an inside tidbit for the local paper, and you want to ask something about the congressman's personal life?"

Willi laughed. "Yes, in a way."

"He wears boxer shorts, his favorite TV show is only on the reruns and he hates spaghetti. Can't get the hang of the spoon technique."

Willi raised an eyebrow and smiled. "Interesting, but I really wondered about BeeBee VanBauer. I haven't seen her since the train left the station."

Elvis set his fork beside his plate and wiped his mouth with the napkin. Half a minute ticked away before he quietly said, "You know, *that's* not good."

"NO, that's not good," willi said, "and neither is this." She cleared a spot off the frosted window to peer outside. The Amtrak shifted slowly into a curve. "I've taken this trip a dozen times. We usually stay on the straight tracks, not ever taking these twists and turns. Something's wrong."

Where was Quannah? And BeeBee VanBauer? Willi's heart missed a beat, and she jumped up and scrambled down the narrow aisle between the tables. Quannah came from the other end of the car. When they met, she placed a hand on his chest. "We're taking a wrong—"

"I know, Gallagher. Can't be helped. Big wreck up ahead and such deep snowdrifts you'd think we were in Montana instead of Texas. Good weather for Snow Snake."

"Snow Snake? I don't like snakes."

"I'm talking about good weather for the game, Snow Snake. Just a long, feathered rod when sent spinning along the snow and ice, lifts at the decorated end like a snake rearing and leaves a track."

"Doesn't sound like a sport either of your two plains tribes would indulge in."

"Sure. The Sioux played with bone sliders, but they borrowed it from the northern tribes, who used feathers on the end of long, polished rods—the sliders. Brave that could sail his rod or Snow Snake the farthest won. Iroquois had the best varia—"

"Excuse me, but do I need to know this now? Couldn't you—?"

"Try to make polite conversation with the woman and she interrupts. Anyway, the Iroquois raced small wooden canoes down trenches that had been trodden into the snow of a hillside and then watered."

"I bet you'll get to one of those philosophical points of yours *soon*, right?"

"See? You read my mind. Lots of *bets* went down on those competitions, but not the kind of bet I'd want to make on this train. The ice is what caused the earlier accident."

"But we're heading west, and if I remember correctly, the only places near this part of the tracks are old ghost towns, and that puts us another day's travel from Nickleberry."

"True. Get your things from the other car." He stared at her feet. "Thank Great Spirit you wore sensible boots. We're going to have to walk up a hill." He turned sideways to allow her to pass by.

"Lassiter?"

"Get a move on, Gallagher."

"But . . . BeeBee's missing."

"Mrs. VanBauer?"

"Yes, and there's blood on her fur coat."

"You're not imagining things again?

"Absolutely not."

"Maybe there is another type of Snow Snake slithering around, one that seems innocent but is damned dangerous." His intense stare bored into her.

Her scalp tightened and goose bumps collided with each other on her arms. Damn the man. Why couldn't he just come right out and say things rather than go through his Indian lore? He *knew* exactly why he was telling her about that game, and she was supposed to seek the inner balance—as he called it—and figure it out. She just knew BeeBee's disappearance wasn't a game.

He said, "You get your things. I'll look for Mrs. VanBauer. We're all to meet outside the train at the stop. Another half hour maybe. By then one of us will have found the lady."

Quannah headed toward the booths, encountered Uzell, caught in another paroxysm of coughing, and waited. When Willi looked back, Quannah knit his brows. Uzell shook his head, obviously giving Quannah the same information she'd received. She reached the passenger car. Only the fur lay in the seat. Hell and damn.

A woman in high heels stumbled toward her. "God, isn't this awful?" She resembled a white-faced mannequin, long legged and pencil thin, makeup a mask, not an enhancement. Red-orange hair hung sleekly against her cheeks, the left side cut three inches shorter than the right. "God-awful," she repeated. "Do you have an extra pair of shoes by any chance? I came so totally unprepared. God, where are my manners? Ivon. Ivon Paulklin."

Willi glanced at Ivon's feet. Those boats would never fit in anything Willi owned. "Sorry, no. Perhaps Catherine does." She leaned across the aisle and nudged the curled-up figure. While Catherine rubbed sleep from her eyes, Willi explained the situation and helped get Catherine's bag from the overhead rack. Catherine dug out a pair of scruffy house shoes, probably even a size smaller than Willi's.

"Have either of you," Willi asked, "seen BeeBee VanBauer?"

"No," Ivon said. "She and her ex are the last ones I wanted to meet this trip. Thanks for the shoes, Mrs. Noble. I'll have them cleaned at the hotel . . . if there is a hotel wherever they're taking us." She pulled on the fuzzy house shoes, smashed down the heels, and slip-slapped down the aisle to the next car.

Uzell, a thick coat thrown over his Amtrak blues, took their overnight bags. "These we be putting on the cart with the other luggage." His burnished bronze nose, now a bright red, testified to the increasing discomfort of his cold. "Don't be leaving your fur coat, miss."

"It's not mine," Willi said. "It's the one I told you about earlier, BeeBee VanBauer's."

"Yes, the man in the black hat be searching for the lady. Also the congressman's secretary and bodyguard, they be searching, too, what you think?"

Catherine Noble, chirpy now that she was fully awake, said, "See? Everything will be fine. Let's get wrapped up."

Willi pulled on her red scarf. The Amtrak slowed even

more to move ponderously around an icy curve that seemed to take an eternity to complete. Scrambling on top of the ermine coat, she peered outside. She pictured BeeBee's body frozen and wedged between the cars, then envisioned her mangled beneath the train's iron wheels. Just as her imagination locked onto that picture, a voice intruded.

"Let's go, Gallagher. Conductor and the train employees have already made one trip with half the luggage."

"We can't leave the train without Mrs. VanBauer. Maybe there's another type of Snow Snake, some slithering slimeball whose done—"

"Shouldn't have ever mentioned Snow Snake. You can wrap your imagination around less than a dust mote and build what amounts to Devil's Tower."

"Devil's Tower?"

Never mind. Anyway, we found the lady."

Willi sighed. "Thank goodness. Where?"

"Doesn't matter. Let's go."

"Is she . . . is she alive?"

"Yes, Gallagher, she's fine. What have you been doing, *Winyan,* dreaming up even more catastrophes?"

"Certainly not."

BeeBee rushed toward them. "There's my baby, oh baby, oh baby."

Willi blinked. *Baby, oh bab—*?

"Would you mind?" BeeBee asked. "Get up."

When Willi stood, BeeBee grabbed the white fur and wrapped herself in it. "Couldn't remember where I'd left my baby. I hope this Lillyville has a proper furriers to take care of this nail polish." She patted the red on the matted fur.

Willi sighed. "Nail polish?"

Quannah crossed his arms and arched an eyebrow. "Nail polish, Gallagher."

Quannah offered the support of his arm to Catherine Noble, who had to huff with the effort of keeping up with his strides.

Willi hefted her makeup case. She got her purse straps and makeup bag tangled, her scarf fell across her eyes and her coat belt got twisted with the scarf. Good heavens, this was like fighting her way out of a nest of vipers. She fumbled and fumed.

Uzell, chocolate eyes showing concern, approached and said, "May I be helping you? Here. Be setting the bag down and the purse." In a moment, he had her more or less together, and as if worried that she might do some harm to the car, he shuffled behind her. All the while he sneezed and coughed.

At the entrance, he helped first BeeBee and then Willi off the train. For a moment, Willi only sighed in relief. At least, she didn't have to stumble along beside Quannah. The chill wind soon invaded her coat and she shivered. Her red scarf ends flapped wildly. Uzell bent over to cough, finally caught his breath and signaled for her to go ahead of him.

She narrowed her eyes against the white upon white scenery. Hills and shrubs, hidden underneath a muslin turban of snow, wound upward. She followed the folks in front of her. First was the train conductor making his second trip by foot to wherever the authorities had decided they'd be safer than on the icy rails. Behind him were two attendants pulling a cart of luggage. One cart had already

been hauled through the landscape. Ah, there were
BeeBee and Quannah with Catherine.

Elvis helped Ivon Paulklin shuffle along in Catherine's
house shoes. Willi sighted the top of Congressman
VanBauer's head, slid, did a hop skip to regain her footing
and came to a stop beside him. She pushed her ebony
tendrils beneath her scarf. They escaped faster than she
could straighten them, bristling against her flushed cheeks,
and she gave up the struggle.

"How far?" wailed BeeBee. "My blood is like ice
cubes."

VanBauer's laugh came out as mirthless and hard as
the landscape. "That happened years ago, I assure you."
He halted, waited for his ex-wife to pass out of sight and
offered Willi his arm for support.

Slipping and sliding held little appeal, so she took hold.

"Just like the old biddy," VanBauer said. "Only one
with a fur, and the only one who complains. Even that
skinny, long-legged girl doesn't make a fuss, and she's
got to be frozen to the bone."

Willi shivered. "She borrowed those house shoes, or
she'd be shuffling along barefoot. How far to this hotel?"

"It's just up ahead," he said.

She missed her footing again and bumped into Quannah's back before VanBauer could help her balance. She
mumbled an apology.

Only a low growl came from the interior of his parka.

At last, she stood at the bottom of an icy incline and
stared upward. A winding stair of natural stone steps led
to a fearsome collection of spires and turrets above the
hotel. Willi whispered, "Just like the one in Hitchcock's
Psycho."

One end of the shingle painted with LILLY'S VICTORIAN ESTABLISHMENT hung by a chain a good six inches lower than the other side, which had been nailed in place. The broken chain clanked against the wall. Paint peeled from the window casings.

"Slowly," Quannah said. "We're in no hurry to break a leg."

"I wonder," asked Willi, "how many steps there—?"

"Don't count, Gallagher, okay? Just because you're superstitious doesn't mean everyone else is."

"Then there shouldn't be a problem with my doing a tally . . . unless, of course, there are only . . . thirteen."

Without mishap they reached the porch. When the train conductor stepped upon it, the wood creaked ominously.

"Should be fine," Willi said between chattering teeth. "Lots more than thirteen. Twenty-seven to be exact."

Quannah narrowed his eyes, but merely helped the conductor open the large oak doors. Welcome heat blasted outward.

"Howdy, one and all. Howdy. Come on in the house. I'm Jasper Farley. I'm the bellhop, the waiter and the general fact-*tote*-um. Hotel's been shut down for months, but what with the emergency and all, we'll make do. Here's the parlor." He pushed wide two doors on the right of the foyer. "Have you all a sit-down whiles I tote the suitcases upstairs."

"Uh, maybe," Quannah said, "you could use some help."

"Son, I'm only eighty-seven."

Quannah grinned and walked back outside with the conductor. Willi tried to follow, but he shut the door in her face.

Jasper Farley yapped while taking everyone's coats. "Miss Lilly Lee—she's the proprietress—lives on the home place, the farm, now. Poor girl. Turned a hundred and one last month, not more'n two weeks afore she broke her hip. Told her she shouldn't haul hay. She resides now at the old home place, the farm. Maybe I done said that." Farley scratched inside an ear, working his finger around really well.

Willi grimaced.

"Don't know," he said, "why that would make a never-mind here or there, though. Hot chocolate and coffee is out on the *buff-fet* yonder. Me and the conductor done decided you all needed warmth, room and food—in that order."

"How many hours," Willi asked, "will we be here? Is there a need to get all those rooms mussed?"

Quannah came in, brushed snow off his coat, handed it to Farley and crossed his arms over his chest.

Willi stepped back. Uh-oh, his Big Chief stance was not a good sign.

"What with the awful mess with the two-header collision coupled with the ice hazard, the Amtrak staff will move the train slowly along out-of-the-way tracks. We'll stay in Lillyville for maybe two, three days. Don't think anyone would wish to end up like the poor souls on those early-morning trains. Amtrak and Texas were just not prepared for this blizzard. Good news is the authorities will pay for the hotel and eats until safe passage can be assured. I think they're playing fair, folks, so let's make the best of this."

A hacking cough erupted behind Willi. "Uzell, you'll miss the departure."

"I . . . I be staying with permission. It being okay, miss."

Willi patted him on the shoulder. "Well, then, uh . . . Mr. Farley, is it? Perhaps you could get Uzell settled first. He's got an awful cold."

"Bold?" asked Farley. "Yes, you all are bold and brave to get out in this weather. Have you settled in a minute."

Ivon Paulklin, handing the house shoes over to Catherine, said, "God, the only human help here, and he's deaf."

Farley worked his finger inside his other ear. "Chef? Nope, but we got old Sam to cook and there's Odessa, the maid."

An ancient grandfather clock bonged out the hour in the vestibule accompanied by the chirping of a half-dozen cuckoo clocks. "God-awful cuckoo clocks. How appropriate." Ivon headed for the coffee.

Uzell Speer, despite Farley's request, picked up three heavy cases and trudged upstairs. His ascent was marked by numerous sneezes and sniffles.

Farley followed him. "Don't need no help. Young people don't pay no nevermind to their elders. Never have. Never will. Amazes me how folks don't never hear what a body says to them."

Willi grinned, hefted her makeup kit and entered the parlor. Weariness settled around her shoulders, so she closed her eyes a moment and fought the temptation to put her hands over her ears to shut out the voices, the bustle and hustle.

Catherine Noble minced down the hallway. Congressman VanBauer headed for a comfortable chair by the fireplace. The group acted like a bevy of wild quail, each

running as fast as possible for their own comfortable
hidey-hole. The scuttling feet stopped; the chimes ended.
Willi, left alone with the ticking clocks, searched along
the downstairs hall to find the ladies' room. After peering
in the mirror, she wished she hadn't. Faint circles underneath her blue-green eyes were less than flattering, and
her naturally curly hair, unbraided, tumbled in wild aban-
don across her shoulders. She fluffed the dark locks dry
with her fingers. Since a sofa was situated alongside one
wall, she sat and propped up her feet. Might as well give
everyone else a half hour to get settled. Even as spry as
Jasper Farley was, he couldn't expect to get everyone's
room ready simultaneously.

Hearing a particularly shrill cuckoo clock announce the
half hour, Willi went toward the stairs. She paused at the
door to the parlor. The scent of crackling firewood and
rich furniture polish wafted outward. Maybe she'd get a
magazine to take upstairs.

Congressman VanBauer still sat there, feet propped on
a hassock, jacket thrown across his legs. Tiptoeing so as
not to startle him, she walked quietly around the chair and
peered at him.

She gasped.

The front of VanBauer's shirt, suffused with fresh and
oozing blood, stuck to his chest.

Tentatively she reached out, but drew her hand back,
holding it over her pounding heart.

Most of the blood came from a gash in his neck, which
had left his head almost severed from his body. Tears
sprang to her eyes. She blinked. Another wound gaped
where a knife must have recently been plunged.

She opened her mouth to scream, but nothing came out.

Waziyata seemed to roar inside her head. She turned away from the sight, and her knees buckled. She caught a quick glimpse of the pristine world outside the window before her inner world turned gray, then black. Falling against something that lifted and supported her, she opened her eyes to stare at the rose-covered carpet.

"Bend your head down between your legs, Gallagher."

Quannah's voice broke through *Waziyata*'s screeching. "Damn, Gallagher, how do you always manage to do things like this? Thanks, *Winyan, pilamaya yelo*. Some vacation this is going to be."

CHAPTER
5

"AND what," asked Ivon Paulklin, "are we to do now? God knows, this wouldn't have happened if we could have stayed on the train. The Amtrak authorities are to blame." She clicked her bright orange lacquered nails together in front of Willi.

Willi concentrated on Ivon's red hair, one side lopped off inches shorter than the other, tried to focus on the Neiman Marcus suit, but she continually glanced toward *the* chair, the last resting place of Congressman Andrew VanBauer. Pushed into the corner and covered with plastic sheeting, it stood as a grim reminder that this room had hosted a murderer's violence only an hour ago.

Quannah had taken photos with Catherine Noble's camera. Old Jasper had been able to wash most of the stains from the rug while the investigator relocated the body. The cloying scent of carpet cleaner hung in the air when

Quannah returned none-too-happily to find the evidence all tidied up.

"Too early for recriminations," Elvis said to Ms. Paulklin. "It would have been extremely dangerous to go on. We're lucky to have found a hotel—any hotel in this remote area—to take us in."

Willi wanted to scream at everyone to shut up, but some dry devil kept her tongue clamped to the top of her mouth. She shied away from staring into anyone's eyes for fear of seeing the horrible deed somehow mirrored there. So, she sat, gathering the shreds of her world back into some semblance of order while those around her babbled on about their plight.

"All the lines are down," Elvis said. "Not much we can do, is there? The train is moving at a snail's pace knowing there's problems on the tracks. We can't contact the train or anyone else until the phone lines are repaired. Seems the cell phones are useless, too, for one reason or another."

"That," Ivon stated, stubbing out her cigarette as if she were destroying the last Amtrak employee, "is god-awful unforgivable. I have five—five packs of these with me. We're out here in the boonies where the lines will be repaired last, in an outdated Victorian monstrosity with three of the slowest dinosaurs for help, not to mention no cigarettes—"

"Shut up." Willi's words came out in a choked quiver. She stood, arms akimbo and tapped her foot. "A man, a person we knew, has been killed, his throat slit from ear to ear." Shutting her eyes a moment, she envisioned the rude, jagged cut, hardly the work of a trained surgeon. "Doesn't that mean more to you than a few discomforts?

Aren't you all the least bit worried by the fact you're sitting here with the killer? And secondly, these *dinosaurs* didn't have to take us in. They have been gracious enough to open this off-season, and seem to be moving their butts a hell of a lot faster than any of us."

Ivon tossed her head, which sent the straight red hair swirling before settling close to her cheeks. She lit up another of her Turkish cigarettes. "Look, finding Van-Bauer had to be god-awful, but that's no reason to get into a panic. The killer may be here. So? He got the one he wanted, the one everyone despised and the rest of us are safe."

"That's ridiculous. We can't read this creep's mind. He may just like the thrill of the kill or maybe has a thing for necks or . . . or half a dozen other reasons. And what do you mean by everyone despised him? Did you know him? Just what—?"

Ivon, eyes flashing, jumped up. "I don't have to answer any questions since I wasn't anywhere close to the jerk. How dare you imply that . . . Do you know who you're talking—?"

"Ladies, ladies." Quannah held up a hand, waved Ivon back to a sitting position, and stared hard at Willi.

Trembling, she sank to the sofa. "Now that we've placed the congressman . . . wherever one places the deceased in old hotels in forsaken Texas ghost towns, we have to"—Willi cleared her throat—"we have to do something. I'll be glad to help in any way that—"

"Not necessary," Quannah said, stepping nearer. "Droskill will help me, Gallagher."

Royce Droskill cracked his swollen knuckles and reached for his disreputable hat, which looked as if he used it for a spittoon—one he hit more often than not.

After a moment's hesitation, he took the stained relic off and placed it on the sofa beside Willi.

"This is a situation needs some taking care of for sure," he said. "Me and Investigator Lassiter and Mr. Elvis zipped the congressman in one of them clear plastic clothes bags and stashed him in cold storage—begging your pardon, ladies. Me and Lassiter can take care of any character roaming roundabouts here."

Willi tilted her head. She blinked and locked glances with Quannah. The man was doing what he did best, staring right through her, maybe delving into her very thoughts. Fine. She hoped he got one message loud and clear: *Do something. Quickly.*

"I'm so sorry, Willi," Catherine said. She smoothed her skirt underneath her as she settled on the sofa edge like a bird on a wire. "I'm so sorry you had to see. Oh, how terrible for you."

Quannah crossed his arms and narrowed his eyes. "Gallagher has seen dead bodies before, which makes me wonder why she had to go into a typical female fainting fit."

Willi opened her mouth to protest, but caught the mischievous glint in his eyes.

He winked. "But like I said, typically female. Anyway, to other matters." After he had explained about having to take a statement from each one and how he was going to go about doing it, he paused.

Willi spoke up. "Ivon and I agree about one thing. No outsider killed the congressman. Someone in this hotel did."

"Maybe," Quannah said, "maybe not, *Winyan.*"

Willi bristled. In shock or not, she was not going to let him run over her, not even for the sake of letting him appear to these people as being tougher than Bronco Billy's boot leather.

"There isn't any *maybe* to that fact, Lassiter."

Jasper Farley banged the door back with one shoulder, sauntered in, and offered her a plate of tiny squares of cheese on top of Triscuit crackers. "With such short like notice, these was the best *horse durfs* Sam could finagle together, but he's cooking up some mighty fine vittles for you all."

Willi sprang off the sofa. "Mr. Farley," she said, "we do not have time—"

"Gallagher, Gallagher." Quannah patted her arm, applied gentle pressure, stared into her eyes for a deadly flash, and released her.

Her resolve lessened, but straightening her shoulders, she said, "There's a murderer. We have to start—"

Quannah laid one finger across her lips. "The Ant."

"What—?"

"Be like *Ant*. Show a little patience, a little trust. Like Ant, we'll receive all the answers. That small one is good Medicine. *Lila waste. Lee-lah wash-tay.* Very good." He shoved a Triscuit in her mouth.

Willi clamped her teeth together and chomped. What in Blue Hades was he up to?

BeeBee VanBauer drifted into the room. She held a bourbon in one hand. With the other, she dabbed unconvincingly at her eyes. Elvis relinquished his seat and made her sit down.

BeeBee probably showed more emotion studying the stock market page. Her cheeks were bright patches, and both the dark circles and her lackluster eyes above them testified to the obvious strain, but no grief or compassion came from within their depths.

BeeBee sniffed, tried to speak, swallowed and tried again. "Who . . . who is in charge? Who is going to be responsible and take care of this horror? This must be cleared *immediately*. What would the media say if they got hold of this juicy bit of news? They'd do untold damage if the truth isn't discovered before we leave this hotel. I demand something be done. Now. *Now,* do you hear me?"

Willi smiled, waiting for Quannah to mention the Ant. She peeked from beneath her lashes at him in deep conversation with Royce Droskill. She tapped him on the shoulder. "Mrs. VanBauer wants to know—"

"Patience, Gallagher. Just a minute."

She smirked. "Oh, right—"

As he turned again toward Droskill, his ponytail shone like a raven's wing against his shirt. She wondered just how one did go about a scalping.

He and Droskill finished their Pow-Wow and Quannah approached BeeBee while Droskill spoke. "Mrs. Van-Bauer, him and me are in law enforcement, but I'm retired."

BeeBee nodded.

"Oh?" Willi sat straighter. "Then you, Mr. Droskill, would have more experience."

Quannah pulled out a badge identification wallet. "Thanks, Gallagher. I needed an opportunity to properly introduce myself. Not *Officer* Lassiter, *Special Investigator* Lassiter." He grinned broadly at everyone. "I'm part of a special undercover program, maybe temporary. I'm not sure at times the Rangers lay claim to this branch."

He placed his identification back in his jacket, winked and said, "Can't blame them. Their fathers hunted my kind. You know, the ones with the bows and arrows. Hard for some to believe I'm on the side of the law, maybe hard for some of you"—he peered at Willi—"to believe that, too, I guess."

She frowned, but inclined her head in a half-nod, which admitted defeat in consideration of his offer of truce.

A lopsided grin spread across his face and even reached his eyes.

What an infuriating man. *Get out of my head, Lassiter.* She blurted out, "Shouldn't we at least search the—"

"*Winyan,* think about *Tajuska*—"

"Is that Lakota for that blasted Ant?"

Still looking her up and down, he handed Catherine Noble a camera. "Thanks for the loan, Mrs. Noble. The department will reimburse you for the film I used at the crime scene." He looked like a dark wolf bending over to inspect a tiny bird.

"No, Investigator Lassiter, you keep the camera." Catherine reached into her purse and handed him two unopened packages of film. "Here. Take these, too. I won't be needing them, and you might."

"Thank you." Straightening; and with a nothing-but-business set to his face, he said, "Jasper Farley said dinner is about ready. I think we'll all be better for a hot meal. Afterwards, we can chat one-on-one."

Everyone filed past Willi. When Quannah tried to edge by, she slammed the door and, with finger to his nose, said, "Chat? The investigator-in-charge is going to chat? No problem, Big Chief Lassiter. After *horse durfs*, soup and salad, main course and dessert, we'll chat. And what in Blue Blazes do you think the murderer is going to do? I'll tell you. Whoever sliced VanBauer's gizzard and throat will be long gone."

He pushed her finger away and, with a hand on her elbow, guided her to the window. "The hotel, Gallagher, is locked up tighter than Fort Knox and has been since you found VanBauer. The storm has truly become an icy blizzard. See? There's no place for anyone to go."

The banked snow in front of the window barely left space to see out if she stretched her neck. Snow and ice blasted from a terrible and darkened sky. Wind vented its full strength against the building. A roof shingle tore loose, clamped wetly for a moment on the window, and was sucked away, flying into the maelstrom.

Willi whispered, "It's like that Snow Snake is without *and* within. Someone who seemed guiltless in our eyes has shed his skin for something evil. And . . . that white, clean snow seems innocent, but it's settling around the hotel, squeezing in on us and . . . and . . . *Waziyata* . . . is wild."

Quannah leaned close, lips near her ear. "Yes, *Winyan,* but no more wild or dangerous than the demented mind locked in this hotel." With one finger on her chin, he turned her to face him. "No hasty moves, Gallagher, promise me. Careful and patient."

She nodded. "Like the Ant."

He sighed, as if some burden had been lifted from him. "Exactly. Now let's go eat."

As he opened the door and she passed through, she said, "Of course, I guess there'd be a big difference in the actions of a little old sugar *Tachahooie* as compared to a Fire Ant."

Through tightened lips, he said, "*Tajuska*, Gallagher, *Tajuska.*"

Grinning, she ran upstairs to wash her hands.

"**WHAT** about uzell?" willi asked, once Quannah and she sat at one end of the long dining table.

Quannah cocked his head. "Who?"

Ah, the great investigator had already lost one suspect. "The train steward, Uzell Speer."

"Gallagher, spit it out. What about him?"

Willi clucked her tongue. "Patience. In time we'll get all the answers we need about him and the others. Remember the—"

When his neck started turning red, she gave in.

"Uzell remained with us because he was sick and went right to his room after we arrived. I *did* notice how many people got off the train." Tapping his shirtfront, she said, "Oh, well, I'm sure you and Mr. Droskill would have figured that out. You two certainly don't need me to help."

When he didn't say a word, Willi fluttered her lashes and scooted her chair farther from him and out of harm's way just as Jasper Farley tromped in with an armload of firewood.

"Maybe," Quannah ground out, "the hotel staff can take a tray up?" Ignoring her, he peered at Farley.

The old man grinned. "Yes, it'll be nice when the rays come up. We all need some sunshine."

"No, Farley," Quannah said, "a *tray*, can you take a tray?"

"Yes, sir. Nothing like the month of May for sunshine.

I can take the rays. We'll gab more, Mr. Investigator, sir, but I got to get vittles on the table whiles they're hot or Sam'll help you scalp me. Told them other folks to clean up and come get the grub. They're sure slow or don't listen. Always plumb amazes me how folks don't hear a dang thing others are saying."

"*They* don't listen. Old man—" A prominent vein in Quannah's forehead turned purple.

Willi leaned over and rubbed a soothing finger across it.

"Remember the *Tachajewie*," she said.

"*Tajuska!* Believe me, *Winyan,* I've the patience of a leopard waiting for the kill. I've stayed still in the brush for over eighteen hours while waiting for two-legged prey to make a move. I've outlasted some of the meanest, most stubborn—"

"Uh-humm. But"—she waggled a finger in his face—"a feller advanced in years who should have your respect, a man who's hard of hearing?"

Quannah clamped his lips together, breathed deeply, and finally said, "Gallagher, pass the salt."

"Like me to rub it in anywhere?"

The other guests bustled in and took a few moments to settle themselves, which gave Willi a reprieve from whatever retort Quannah might have had in mind. She blinked, grasped Jasper Farley's arm, and asked, "Would you please ask one of the maids to scrub the bathtub? Guess, from the looks of it, it's been a while since that's been done, and I understand that you weren't expecting—"

"One of the maids? There's only the one, Odessa. I'll see she sets things right."

That great chore erased from her mental list left only

one thing on her mind. Who? Who sliced open the congressman's neck? Okay, perhaps Lassiter didn't want her
to snoop around, but there was absolutely no reason she
couldn't help a fellow being in distress. She smiled across
the steam rising from the *sopa de frijoles* and bit into her
jalapeño cornbread. She'd helped Quannah along with his
Uncle Sheriff Tucker to stop the Wicked Wiccan killer.
Of course, she'd sworn to herself to never get involved
in another investigation, but she could . . . be *helpful,* and
nothing could be more helpful to the skeleton staff than
taking a tray up to poor Uzell.

SHE received no answer to her first quiet knock on
room 103 with a missing zero. Thirteen? Uh-oh. She
banged on the door. Uzell mumbled from the other side,
and she took this for permission to enter. Kleenex tissue
lay scattered beside the bed. A bottle of All-Night cough
medicine, guaranteed to end sniffling, sneezing, aching
and any other yucky feelings associated with a cold, kept
company with a water glass on the bedside table. Twisted
bedclothes fell halfway off the bed.

Uzell's beautiful cocoa skin, now feverish, was
splotched, the curled lashes matted together with cold mu-
cus. One eye was almost shut.

"Thought you'd need a bite," she said. "There's bean
soup." She lifted the lid from the bowl. Steam poured out
and with it the room was permeated with scents of hot
peppers, garlic and pinto beans.

Uzell struggled to a sitting position. "Be thinking of
me? I be feeling sorry for myself, what you think, and
look what you be doing. Thank you."

He ate everything, sopping up the last of the soup with his cornbread.

A spasm of coughing and sneezing made her back toward a far corner. When he gained control, she approached, cleared away the dishes and straightened the bedclothes.

Uzell reached for the All-Night bottle and, using the small plastic cup provided, poured himself a dose. He gulped it down and made a face, then grasped the empty water glass.

Willi filled it from the tap in the adjoining bathroom. When he took the glass, their fingers touched. Well, he wasn't faking the high temperature. Why in Blue Blazes would he? Here she went again. Seeing something suspicious in the smallest details simply because some evil had slipped into Lilly's Victorian Establishment. A murderer had struck viciously. She touched her throat. *Efficiently* also came to mind.

The steward poured another dose of the medicine.

"Do you think that's wise?" Willi asked.

"I must be getting some sleep. It's being okay." He swallowed, grimaced and shook his head.

Willi raised an eyebrow. "Did you stay in your room after that first trip up this afternoon?"

Uzell frowned, nodded and leaned back against the pillows.

Yes, of course, Uzell had come upstairs as soon as he could, certainly, if she remembered correctly, before Congressman Andrew VanBauer went into the parlor. Why, Uzell might not even know about the murder.

His eyelids lowered, obviously growing heavy as the

double dose did its work. Should she tell him now or let him drift off into an easy sleep?

She had decided to let him rest, set the tray outside the door, but then remembered an arrogant ponytailed investigator who believed she couldn't detect because she was a woman. *He* wouldn't give up so easily.

She remained inside the room, slammed the door and winced at the resounding boom.

Uzell blinked once or twice and finally opened his eyes. "Being big noises in this old hotel, what you think? What being the cause of that noise?"

"Uh . . . the grandfather clock?"

"Okay. I be sleeping now."

"No, don't drift off yet. I need to tell you something important before I leave."

He yawned and pulled the blanket up to his chin. One eyelid drooped.

"Congressman VanBauer has had a horrible accident."

"Uhmm," responded Uzell. His head tilted to one side, he slid down into the warm coverlet and smiled.

She shook him.

"Wha . . . what . . . what you think?"

"*Listen* to me. VanBauer was stabbed to death."

"You be telling . . . telling what?" Uzell slipped from her grasp, turned over on his side and snored. A pleasant smile hovered on his face.

"Oh, blast."

Okay, Lassiter was right. With her questioning, she sent suspects into sound sleep instead of nervous agitation. Oops, there she'd done it again. Used that word, *suspect*. Well, why not? One of the inhabitants of Lilly's Establishment had killed Congressman VanBauer.

She shut the door of 13, not 103—since it had been unlucky for her—she'd not gained one bit of information—and scurried down the stairs with the tray. Her thoughts scurried, too. Yes, a person from the Amtrak was responsible. She frowned and dismissed Lassiter from the list of possibilities. Who all did that leave?

Uzell Speer, the train attendant, for one, but he was so sick. Could he have managed to sneak down from his room? And even if he could, would he have had the strength to slice through the congressman's neck and inflict the other wounds?

She ran her free hand along the bannister as she stepped down a few rungs and stopped.

Elvis.

Yes, the congressman's secretary, the man who didn't want to talk about his boss. Where had he been at the crucial time?

She paused, admired the glossy oak wood, walked down a few more steps and pricked her finger on a loose splinter. She absently sucked on the sore spot and frowned in concentration.

Where had Elvis been just before the congressman's death? Willi had glanced up the stairs when coming out of the downstairs ladies' room. Elvis and BeeBee, heads together, had been whispering. Certainly, that scenario left some unanswered questions not only on the personal level but also on the professional, given the fact of BeeBee running for office against Elvis's boss.

Okay, Elvis and BeeBee.

Catherine Noble? Didn't seem to be any connection there other than the woman being on the same train.

Ivon Paulklin, the shoeless socialite, disliked VanBauer

for some reason. She'd not tried to hide that fact, either, which could be a really smart move to cover guilt or proof that she had nothing to reveal.

VanBauer's bodyguard, Royce Droskill, finished off Willi's mental list. He was a protector, a retired Tarrant County deputy sheriff, but . . . but he had said . . . something important. Or perhaps, he'd . . . done one tiny thing, something to make her now think it had been important. Actions speak louder than words, Elba was always telling her.

Willi sighed and continued down the stairs. The ancient boards groaned. She *must* remember what he'd said or done.

CHAPTER
6

SHE left the tray in the kitchen and wandered back out into the empty hallway, walked through the parlor and tried to ignore *the* chair. She wanted a quiet place to seriously consider all the facts she'd gleaned. A narrow door in a shadowy corner of the parlor beckoned and, at her touch, creaked open to reveal a library–sitting room combination, probably poor old Miss Lilly's hidey-hole when she was in residence. Lavender and rose sachet hung in the air. A warm fire crackled in greeting. Willi checked the deeper shadows, then lifted up on the door, which kept it from grating as she shut it. She curled up in a chair ornately carved with the ever-popular dragons of the Victorian Age. Snow blew against the window, banking heavily on the sill, but deposited more softly as if *Waziyata* had lost his rancor now that he, along with the Snow Snake, had cornered victims inside. She shivered and rubbed her arms. The outside lights created a yellow wash on the inky sky and white ground. Be perfect for someone to hide in those shadows, to watch her from that holly bush or—

Enough. Stop that.

She shook her head, but nothing—neither mental fussing nor the comfort of the room—could halt her musings about the bloody scene and the person who had committed the horror.

Suspects galore: Uzell Speer, BeeBee VanBauer, Catherine Noble, Elvis, Royce Droskill and Ivon Paulklin. Someone from the train. An Amtrak assassin—no, a slinking Snow Snake, someone who now forced the innocent to look at each other as possible killers—had murdered the congressman. Which one?

Maybe Lassiter was right. She would imitate *Tajunska* the Ant and wait until one of those folks said the wrong thing or did something suspicious. Sure, and up to that point, she'd weigh each and every word or gesture . . . and stay focused on the grim possibility that one who smiled at her might slit her throat the next moment.

Rubbing her temples, she relaxed her head against the back of the chair, and mesmerized by the calmer wind, the crackling fire and the faded Victorian splendor, she imagined herself in that age of grandeur, one of a slower pace and predictable manners.

A great fire overheated the room. A faint sheen of perspiration rose on her upper lip. She smoothed her silken skirts overlaid with heavy lace. Firelight caught the crystals in the chandelier and the refracted shimmers made the floral motif of the flocked wallpaper move as if it were alive. Roses—red, pinks, and yellows—in festoons of greenery, perched on every available surface. She breathed deeply, enveloped in their scent. A spark flew outward onto the fringed carpet. A hound bounded out of the way to creep underneath a brocade-covered table that rocked, threatening to topple the pictures.

She touched photos encased in ornately carved wooden and silver frames. Sepia-colored men with mustaches and thick sideburns stood stiffly beside sepia-brown women with pompadours. One of the men, so much like her great-grandfather, leaned out of a frame and whispered in a singsong voice, "Oh, the snakes play at night . . . like the old ones do . . . like the ancestors do. The snakesssss . . . play."

Willi blinked and studied the pictures closely. Women clutched sepia-tinted children with high-top shoes and cotton pinafores. In the background, a Victrola scratched out "The Blue Danube." She smoothed her lace before fingering the ribbon holding the cameo at her throat. A cuckoo clock chimed.

High tea.

He'd arrive exactly on time. Sure enough, he deposited his cane and umbrella in the stand behind the rubber plant, straightened his vest, pulled out his chained fob and checked his watch with the cuckoo.

She smiled at him and admired his broad shoulders, his strong chin. Her breath caught in her throat. But something . . . what in the world was wrong with him? She eased herself to the edge of the dragon chair to peer more closely. He was much . . . darker than she recalled. No, it wasn't just that.

He turned his back toward the fireplace to warm his hands. Dear Mother's Saints! He sported an unusual pony-

tail. His face was . . . oh, my . . . decorated with . . . war paint.

Willi rubbed her eyes and blinked. Her lace disappeared and became her functional Picayune Western blouse and ankle-length blue corduroy skirt. Her cameo and ribbon became a tear-drop diamond on her gold chain. No pictures tottered on the table, which on inspection hid no cowering hound. She brushed her hair back as if swiping at the Victorian cobwebs. Her heart pitter-pattered. Talk about wool-gathering. But at least Lassiter hadn't noticed as he'd walked into the room. She stood and edged toward the window, where she leaned against the pane to cool her warm cheeks.

"Daydreaming again?" He followed her to look out on the white-blanketed world.

"Certainly not. Better things have kept me occupied."

"Like your visit to Uzell Speer's room. I didn't authorize—"

"I didn't think a kindness of taking a sick man a meal had to be authorized by you or anyone else, and I was not daydreaming."

"Methinks the lady doth protest too much." He moved closer, pushed back the velvet curtain, and said, "I can't much blame you for an overactive imagination. The hotel does remind one of classic times."

"You sensed it, too? That old-world charm?"

"Sure, I've felt something about this pile of lumber and rocks from the moment we got here."

"Perhaps not so much the outside as—" He turned where his eaglelike persona seemed so strong. "Many have stayed here. Some joyful, others frightened, sad. A few took up the blanket to the Good Blue Road."

"You lost me," she said and softly touched his arm.

"The Good Blue Road toward the Star Nation. They died here. You were feeling the presence of the ancestors when I came in, were you not, *Winyan*?" He glanced at her. "Listen closely, Gallagher, they have messages for us."

Willi whispered, *"Oh, the snakes play at night . . . like the old ones do."*

Quannah nodded as if the declaration made perfect sense. "Inside and outside it's a special place."

Willi smiled. He understood the ambience behind the decrepit building, understood the sense of history embodied within the hotel, and perhaps that was a sign he understood her or, at least, one facet. "I'm glad you see it the same as I do."

"Sure, just look down that craggy hill," he said and pointed. "See? Down there where the light barely pushes back the shadows?"

"Yes."

"If there were a row of shabby motel rooms right at the bottom and a tall sign, this place would be the gruesome image of the Bates's house in *Psycho*. We'd be standing in that old house on the hill where the crazy lived his second life out.

"And you know, Gallagher, you're right. It is sort of nice we finally see eyeball to eyeball on something."

She shot a look at him that she hoped he'd interpret correctly, but obviously didn't since he hadn't immediately dropped dead on the floor.

"Well, I'm not sure about eyeball to eyeball exactly because—"

"In fact, since we're in such agreement, maybe you'd

like to sit down and talk about the case with me."

"I thought you—"

He held a palm toward her. "We could touch base on whatever you chatted about with Uzell. Poor man seems mighty sick."

"Oh? You went to visit him, too? Well, he barely got his bean soup sopped up before he nodded off. He took a double dose of that nighttime medicine."

"Now, he must have said something about—"

She crossed her arms to mimic his usual pose. "Didn't even know about VanBauer's death. He'd been in bed since the moment he went upstairs. Now, don't push for more, Mr. Big Chief Investigator, because there is no more."

"No problem. Won't need to pester you one bit, because there's no reason for you to go taking trays to everyone in the hotel, right? No sticking your cute nose in to snoop where it might get bobbed off."

"I was not snooping. Taking food to a sick man can't be called—"

"Gallagher, relax. Stop worrying about why or who. Droskill and I—"

"Droskill? *He's* a suspect."

The prominent vein on Quannah's forehead forged a blue trail across his temple. "Suspect? He was a Tarrant County deputy sheriff." Quannah thumbed his chest. "Probably brought more bad ones to justice than you've seen on *COPS* or reruns of *Hill Street Blues*."

Willi uncrossed her arms and placed her hands on her hips. "Excuse me, but right now one previous sheriff of Tarrant County is serving time in a cozy little place called Huntsville, a number of Johnson County prosecutors have served time right beside past clients, and a Corpus Christi judge is being tried for murder, not to mention—"

"Am I intruding, sweeties?" Catherine Noble asked, peeking around the door.

Quannah stepped forward, grabbed her elbow and guided her inside. "Perfect timing."

"You'd never be an intrusion, Catherine," said Willi, eyeing the long black dress. Hades, Catherine Noble could at the moment have played Bates's mother. Willi scooted away from the window and the view of the hillside, away from the idea the hotel housed a similar maniac with the same genetic compulsion as Bates, a nutcase who wouldn't be satisfied with just one bloodied victim. Willi sighed. If she were considering birdlike Catherine as suffering from a Hitchcock dementia, Willi had better get help for herself.

"I borrowed something black from the maid. It was old Miss Lilly's," Catherine said. "Someone should show respect for the deceased, don't you think? It's the smallest of gestures, but one must do what one can."

Willi nodded and plucked at her sweatshirt. "Don't think I brought anything . . . uh . . . suitable."

"Oh, don't worry. I'm of the old school and can't help myself. Of course, I put a scare into the kitchen help when he saw me in this black lace. Sam—that's the cook— thought I was a ghost or Miss Lilly come to check on his work. I've been exchanging recipes with Sam. He's an interesting character, and you two must meet him. I'd almost talked him into sharing his enchilada recipe when we were interrupted by that Paulklin girl." Catherine wrinkled her nose.

"Ivon? In the *kitchen*?" Willi asked.

"My, yes. To complain about the peppers and the south-of-the-border cuisine. Said she simply could not tolerate that another day." Catherine formed a moue of distaste. "Thinks she can have anything she wants. Such a despicable and selfish outlook to have about life and others around you, don't you agree?"

Quannah stuck his hands in his pockets with his thumbs hooked outside and said, "Well, she's probably used to having her own way. The name *Paulkin* and *Electronics* go hand in hand. She's been in the society pages of half a dozen big-city papers in Texas. What did Sam say about her butting in?"

Catherine giggled and pressed her palm against the black collar. "Handled it quite well. Told her there was no problem. If she didn't like what he cooked, she didn't have to eat. He also informed her breakfast was going to be hot-sausage taquitos with salsa de chili. Jalapeños on the side."

"Well, at least he didn't threaten to serve her a cyanide cocktail," Willi said.

"Oh, my," Catherine said, "I should never have said that this morning. Under the present circumstances it might put me on the list of suspects."

When Quannah arched an eyebrow, Willi explained the exchange she'd had earlier beside the train track.

Quannah sat on a hassock at Catherine's feet, but still loomed over her petite form. "We won't hold it against you. There's no question of poisoning with VanBauer. Were you in the kitchen after we arrived?"

"Investigator Lassiter," Catherine said, and tilted her head to look up at him, "if that's your subtle way of asking my whereabouts this afternoon, it's not so subtle. I realize you must ask."

"Yes, ma'am, I do. Gallagher, see if there's paper and pen in that rolltop in the corner."

Willi pulled the top down. Paper embossed with *Lilly's Victorian Establishment* and a number of envelopes rested in one corner. She took a couple of sheets, placed them in a small clipboard with attached pen and started to hand them to Quannah. He nodded to indicate she was to stand behind Catherine.

Some nerve he had. *Don't butt in, but please be available for secretarial duties at the drop of an Eagle feather.* She sighed but dutifully scribbled the date, and when the cuckoo peeped out at the quarter hour, she also wrote the time. At least Big Chief couldn't say she didn't pay attention to the details.

Catherine took a deep breath. "When we arrived, I went directly to my room to take a much-needed nap. These old legs aren't used to winter sports like climbing up ice-covered hills. Of course, I know a nap isn't a very good alibi for the time that poor man was killed." She placed a tiny hand over Quannah's strong, brown one. "I'm just glad I wasn't the one to find him. My heart might have given way right then and there, but I'm sorry Willi had to be so distressed. Thank goodness you were right there when she fainted."

Quannah eased his hand away. "Did you know Van-Bauer well, Mrs. Noble?"

"As a matter of fact, I thought I knew him quite well at one time."

Willi opened her eyes wide and stuck out her bottom lip. Interesting.

"Explain, please." His dark eyes bore down on Catherine.

Willi could have been watching a hawk swooping toward a dove. He was so intense. When he got that look, she could believe he brought toughened drug lords and murderers to justice.

He repeated, "Explain when you knew VanBauer."

"So many years ago."

Catherine bowed her head and twisted the black material of the dress but finally settled her nervous hands with fingers intertwined, like feathers at rest over a tired breast. "He . . . Andrew . . . was a student. *Not* brilliant like the papers always say, but average. I suppose he had good PR people. Somewhat intelligent, as I was saying, but no focus. Half-finished one thing, then went on to another, until . . . until he joined the Debate Club and the Young Republicans."

She sighed and pressed her lips together. She caught the material between her fingers and bunched it, noticed, and straightened it again. "At first, I helped him with both groups, but he always seemed to resent my help. Nothing said between us. Just a feeling I got that he desperately needed guidance, but didn't want to accept it from me, personally."

Only the sound of Willi's pen scrabbling across the paper and the crackling wood made any noise. *Waziyata* had died down completely. A log in the fireplace split, one part falling almost off the hearth, and blue flames licked hungrily at the remaining piece. Quannah stretched out and, with his boot heel, pushed the wood back. Willi finished the last sentence and sighed. There was nothing joyful in digging up the deceased's past.

"Mrs. Noble," Quannah asked, "what happened?"

"What? Oh well, kids grow up. After Andrew's sophomore year Mr. Collins, the civics and boys' choir instructor, took a special interest in Andrew, and he drifted out of my sphere of influence. He was personable when we met. Always spoke. Polite, especially when school election time arrived, but not friendly like you'd expect after my spending so much effort on him. But we don't teach for our own self-serving needs, do we, Willi?"

"Hardly."

"Really?" said Quannah, standing and pushing back the hassock. He placed his hands in that thumb-hanging position from his pockets. "From reports in the papers, some teachers must be there for that or the money. Got to be a lot of teachers not doing their job considering the type of product—illiterate students—the state is turning out."

Pen lifted in midair, Willi glared and clamped her mouth so tightly, her teeth hurt.

Catherine smiled. "Oh, Investigator, Willi and I know you're trying to get our ire up to maybe trick us into saying something ugly and revealing. Won't work, young man. There are a number of factors to consider and one of those is the slanted reporting done in the name of news. If you had hoped to get me upset, you'll have to go train with your betters—or perhaps I should say the members of the B&B Club, all of whom do deserve to be poisoned in a particularly nasty way."

Willi, shocked at this vitriolic outburst from Catherine, rolled her eyes upward. She had some guts to make a statement like that after being worried it would place her in the lineup. It also sure seemed as if Catherine had some issues roiling inside that birdlike bosom.

Quannah pulled one hand from his pocket and opened it toward her. "B&B Club?"

Willi explained. "Bitches and Bastards Club—what a lot of districts call their local school board—which also includes the superintendent and his second-in-command. Stereotypical Texas jargon and, to give our local Nickleberry board members their due, not a true picture for the many serving sincerely for the good of all. Like any elected board, they take a lot of undeserved heat." Willi frowned at Catherine and shook her head. Something must have happened to elicit such a bitter response. Willi was just darned glad she hadn't had to teach in the same district, somewhere north of Tarrant County if she remembered correctly.

Nodding, Quannah asked Catherine, "Did you speak with VanBauer on the train?"

"On the train? No. Well, yes, but only in passing. It's embarrassing to admit this. He didn't even recognize me. I nodded and smiled, spoke briefly to ask him how things were going. He treated me like any constituent. A glare of shining teeth, a practiced answer for the masses and a quick nod. That was our only communication on the Amtrak." Catherine stifled a yawn behind her thin fingers.

The cuckoo clock chimed. Willi finally located its position above the mantel. The boom of the vestibule's grandfather clock added the final gong for the half hour. Eleven-thirty. No wonder her eyes had the grit of seven deserts in them. She yawned and her eyes teared.

"Forgive me, Mrs. Noble." Quannah extended a hand and helped Catherine to her feet. "It's late. We'll chat more tomorrow."

After he'd shut the door, he reached for the clipboard. "Thanks. I'm slow as Turtle when I have to concentrate on spelling."

She had her mouth half open and frown lines pulled her brows together.

"What?" he asked.

She blinked. "Just didn't expect Investigator Lassiter to admit to a weakness of any kind."

"Weakness?" His dark eyes glinted in the firelight. "Must have been that Texas schooling I had in college. Ruined me, that's what it did. Weakness? Where do you come up with ideas like that, *Winyan*?"

She smirked at him, yawned again and excused herself. Out in the cold corridor, she shivered. Maybe she should have waited and walked up with Lassiter. She headed up the stairs and was too tired to even mull over Catherine's interview. One of the yellow globes flickered and went out, leaving the upper hall in a sickly wash. She quickly shut and locked her door. *Tunkasila,* her teaching stone, she set carefully beside her new bottle of perfume, *Passion.* Humm. Probably wouldn't need either one tonight. She raised an eyebrow. Mixed blessing. No trouble, no crisis . . . but no one to wear perfume for either. She undressed after making sure she had a clean Turkish towel hanging nearby, placed her shower gel on the side of the club-footed tub, and stepped in, closing the clear plastic shower curtain after her. The tub ring was still there, but she was too tired to be squeamish. Hot water pounded her aching shoulders; steam rose in a fog.

Wonderful what sloughing off the day's dirt could do for the mind. She lathered up her gel, reveling in the aroma it produced on her skin. She bent down to wiggle soap bubbles between her toes, but when she rose to peer through the plastic curtain, her limbs reacted as if every muscle were on strike.

Hades, what . . . *who?*

A figure hovered.

Visions of *Psycho* flashed through her mind.

Willi whimpered. Vulnerable in her nakedness, her stomach lurched and cavorted back into place. Blood pounded in her temples. Water streamed across her neck, shoulders, down her stomach, past her shaking knees. She couldn't even reach her towel without showing her bare arm to the killer. The face swam closer. The silhouette raised an arm.

No . . . no, no, no!

Willi shut her eyes, bent her head back and screamed. And screamed and kept on screaming.

CHAPTER
7

PINPRICKS of hot water rained down over her hair and face. She closed her mouth, but the screams didn't stop. Now they came from the other side of the curtain.

"What the hell?" Quannah's voice, irritated, blurted out.

Willi opened her eyes. The figure had disappeared from sight. "It was just like *Psycho*—"

She grasped the edge of the flimsy curtain. Her knees trembled and she sat, pulling the shower curtain down with her, which gave her a clear view of the small room.

Quannah soothed an old woman in a maid's uniform. He took a large cleansing brush from her hand.

Willi hugged the curtain closer.

"Odessa, *señor,* Odessa Morales." A red wig tilted at a precarious angle to reveal iron gray hair. She faced Willi, pushed away from Quannah, and sniffled. "Better, now,

gracias. Madre de Ladrones, the *Virgin María* would
think somebody was trying to kill her.

"*Una mujer loca.* Where she gets this idea about old
Odessa I don't know." Odessa grabbed the cleaning brush,
straightened her red wig on her head and marched out of
the bath and into the bedroom. "She is the *loca* what asks
me to come clean her bath. Her—she's the one got problems in the *cabeza.* I don't break in nobody's rooms.
Me—I got keys. How the crazy lady think I clean her
room without coming in? *Loca, loca, loca.*" The bedroom
door slammed.

Willi, trying to stand, slipped and slid. "Damn you,
Lassiter, it's all your fault, and you know it."

"My—?

"Talking about Hitchcock, the Bates Motel—"

"*Winyan,* your own imagination—"

"I was *not* daydreaming."

He raised an eyebrow and reached over to turn the water off.

She slapped his hand away, handled the chore herself
and tried a second time to make it to her feet. She would
have if the shower curtain rod hadn't jammed on the edge
of the tub.

Quannah grasped the Turkish towel, grinned and held
it out toward her.

Her eyes narrowed to menacing slits. He laughed and
threw the towel in her general direction before walking
into the bedroom.

Willi persisted. "After VanBauer's murder, maybe you
shouldn't have been talking about psychotic killers." She
couldn't seem to shut off the flow of words, words she
knew were better left unsaid, words that would probably

make her look even more like a nitwit in front of Big Chief Investigator. "You're the one who put those thoughts into my head."

Hades, she wanted to do something of value in his eyes. Fainting at death scenes and screaming at little old ladies with cleaning brushes weren't going to convince him she might have the intelligence and wherewithal to help with this investigation. Well, she might be prone to . . . uh . . . daydreaming, and she'd concede that her curiosity got up about things that might not always concern her, but she was also damned good at finding out the most impossible little details that eventually added up to that one big picture. She just had to figure out a way to earn a few war bonnet beads, feathers—whatever. She dried off before she slipped into warm pajamas and a robe.

Barefooted, she stomped as loudly as possible into her bedroom.

"Such suggestions," she said, "would set anyone's nerves on edge."

"Someone with an overactive imagination, perhaps. Not just anyone. Although I think the killer got the only one he intended to kill, you lock up. Don't go outside until morning, and don't go imagining someone's trying to slash you to bits with . . . with a toilet brush. Makes you a might touchy, and that screaming doesn't do a whole lot for my honed senses either. 'Course, if you'd prefer I stay the night to protect you—"

"Not necessary. Maybe the murders are finished, maybe not. Perhaps the killer's one of those who has reason behind his madness. Wants to slice up everyone with a V or a G in their name. Crazier nuts are out there. Maybe, he's out to get anyone in authority—congressman, teacher

. . . lawman?" She held her hand on the doorknob. "You may leave now, Officer. I'm not so unnerved that I need a man to take care of me every minute. I'll be fine, thank you."

He grinned and sauntered out. "Guess I'll use my own advice."

She gradually eased the door almost closed. "Oh?"

He stared into her eyes—bored into her soul with the intenseness of his regard. "Ant has lessons for both of us. Just hope you're not so long in learning them you miss all the good things that might come. Daydreams can't compare to the real magic of life. Hard to enjoy that magic, Gallagher, when you're all alone." He shook his head and pursed his lips, then finally allowed a great sigh to escape. "You must be a lot like Shakespeare's Kate— out-of-balance, bossy, and opinionated—or your daddy could have got you married off years ago."

"Me, bossy? What about—?"

"There you go getting riled before I can finish. You got more quills than Porcupine." He pointed a finger and tapped her nose. "Even Porcupine has a soft side."

She slammed the door, picked up her perfume bottle and threw it against the door. *Passion,* in full strength, reeked. She covered her nose.

From the other side of the door, Quannah laughed. "*Winyan,* you really didn't need to go to that extreme to attract me. Even a shrew doesn't need that much ammunition to seduce a victim. A house of ill-repute on a hot day in Texas couldn't smell that strong."

His footfalls receded, but his words rankled. Damn him to hell for getting in her head again. It never hurt when Aunt Minnie kidded her about being stubborn and having her sights set so high no boy in town could find a ladder tall enough to reach her. She fluffed her hair dry with her fingers. Besides, she'd promised herself that one investigator was not going to make her feel a damned thing for him. She wrinkled her nose and tried to raise the window. It stuck, but she dared not call the ancient Odessa back so soon. She cleaned up the broken perfume bottle before she settled onto the window seat.

She clasped her teaching stone, pulled back the curtains and peered out at the world. Lit more from the coverlet of snow than any stars or moon, the earth seemed upside down, glowing in the wrong direction. Soughing winds whistled around the cracked window casements. She pulled her robe more tightly across her shoulders and shuffled her feet into down-filled house shoes. Leaning her head against the cold pane of glass, she swallowed.

Bereft.

Alone.

Tiny thoughts that left big holes inside her, lonely tracts she didn't really want to examine. She studied *Tunkasila*. Yes, the tiny rock from the Black Hills was just a surrogate for the Grandfather, the Great Spirit, the Creator that the Sioux believed manifested in all living things. Yet each time she held it, a great comfort stole over her as if a tenderness and compassion emanated and pierced the shell around her soul. Each time she'd truly needed guidance, she held the precious rock close until turmoil ended and her mind cleared. Seemed like right action always followed. Okay, action that led to other actions that eventually ended well.

She shook her head. Lassiter ought to understand how unnerving it had been for her to discover Andrew

VanBauer's corpse. The least she expected was a bit of sympathy from a representative of the law, some token of appreciation for her proffered help. But no. Quannah Lassiter's dark eyes held disdain, not sympathy, raking up and down her as if she were a quarter horse on the auction block and he'd discovered she was spavined. Even after they'd solved one crime together with his uncle, Sheriff Brigham Tucker, Lassiter viewed her merely as a simple-minded female, and one he obviously thought would cavort in bed with one wave of his Eagle feathers.

This musing was getting her nowhere but closer to emotional chasms she'd prefer to avoid. The scent of perfume was sickening, and she had the itchies to be on the move, to do something.

From downstairs the distant bong of the grandfather clock sounded the half hour. She peered at her watch. Only half past twelve. No telling what she could find out if she did a bit of snoop—uh, *checking* on her own, and she wasn't a bit sleepy. She might yet show Big Chief Lassiter a thing or two. She'd done so before and could do it again. Quickly, she changed into jeans and sweatshirt, but chose to keep the warm and noiseless down-filled booties. Scrounging in her bag, she found a small flashlight and headed out the door.

A draft wrapped itself around her legs. Bending down, she rubbed them. Maybe she ought to return and pull on a pair of hose beneath the jeans. Nope, not enough time. She turned off her room light, but left the door ajar to dissipate some of the odor. A beam of light swept across the hallway from a door opening. Hades, she should have checked to see which one was Lassiter's. A frantic flutter, like a hummingbird caught in midflight, filled her throat.

She tiptoed in the opposite direction from the light and hid behind one of the many collections of rubber plants and palmetto trees. Dust rose from the plant leaves. Grasping her nose, she closed her eyes and held her sneeze in long enough to foster an A-bomb explosion inside her brain. When she had the sneeze under control, she let air in and opened her watering eyes. Oh, that hurt, really hurt.

A click signaled a door shutting; a beam of muted light penetrated the shadows in the opposite direction. Maybe Lassiter didn't follow all of his own advice. Just like a man, but . . . he'd have no reason to sneak; he could go anywhere with impunity, and he would. So that hand holding the flashlight wasn't his, nor would one of the three hotel workers—Odessa, Sam, or Farley—be likely to sneak down the hallways.

The beam grew fainter. She followed, keeping her hand on her flashlight, but not turning it on. By the touch of the wood paneling, she maneuvered through dank, unused corridors, past mysterious doors, which she tried but discovered were locked. At last, she turned a corner and banged her knee on a high step.

She stifled her impulse to yelp and rubbed her knee. She blindly fingered the flooring in front of her. Good grief, the damned step had to be double the normal height. Must be in a really old part of the hotel—probably unused, perhaps an area not even planned for use since the contractors felt no need to readjust the step. There was a third floor then. What in the late 1800s would have been termed the servants' stairs, but that wasn't the direction the sneaking figure in front of her had taken. She would save that third floor for later exploration.

Her knee ached, but only half a dozen of the imaginary spiders seemed intent on dealing out more pain. To her left a flight of steps headed downward, but not to the first-floor foyer. With her luck there'd be thirteen steps. She bit her bottom lip and squinted. She counted twenty-six steps. Great—thirteen doubled. Did that negate the bad luck or make it twice as horrible? The beam of light headed downward again. Okay, there was also a basement.

The dank stairwell brought her down exactly eighteen steps and to a doorway that had to lead to a cellar. She waited a heartbeat and was about to turn the knob when the glow ahead shone downward again.

More steps? Hades and damn. To what depths did this descend?

Hairs on her neck stood on end. So, the night wanderer was heading past the cellar . . . to . . . what—a dungeon? A crypt?

Something scurried across her foot, she pulled her leg back, and a reinforcement of spiders attacked her kneecap, this time sending a searing message all the way up her thigh. A worse thought struck. In this part of the ancient building, spiders—real biting arachnids, with big hairy legs—could be a strong possibility. The light ahead disappeared; the person was descending into the very bowels of the building.

She strained to hear *Waziyata*'s moans, but the most eerie silence filled the stairwell. Wooden steps gave way to those of stone, treacherously uneven. They pitched downward *thirteen* times, twisted and turned, finally leading into an abyss—a cellar, dank and nasty with the stench of rat droppings and the moisture-laden air created by some unseen seepage.

- Willi placed a hand over her heart, pounding out *thirteen, thirteen, thir*— She breathed deeply. Fine, so there was a baker's dozen of the damned things. Somber, subterranean cellars weren't high on her list of favorite places either. Surely, this being the dead of winter any snakes were in hibernation . . . unless they were human . . . Snow Snakes.

Suddenly, the beam flashed on and off. Willi ducked behind junk on the cellar floor. Touching gingerly with her fingertips, she encountered cold coils and feathers poking out of mattress ticking. She stood up behind the bedsprings and torn bedding and strained to get an idea of where the night wanderer was.

Toward her right something slithered like a mere whisper against the chilled stones. Her teeth chattered, and she bit her bottom lip to try to stop them.

A scraping replaced the slithering. Willi searched for something—anything. She closed her fingers around an old iron skillet. An overhead light flooded the room. Buzzing emanated from the yellowed fluorescent strung from a contraption of swaying wires. She knelt behind the tatty mattress and prayed she was invisible to whoever shared the area with her.

She peered from her feather fortress and located the cause of the noise—a floor-length coat or cape worn by the person in front of her. A rich purple and silver, the hem floated across the frigid floor. The figure approached and bent over a table in the center of the room.

Willi swallowed. The body of Andrew VanBauer closed up in an extralong traveler's bag lay on that table.

The sound of a zipper opening rent the quiet air and sent an army of chill bumps across her arms and down her spine. She cringed behind the coils, not wanting to look, but not daring to do otherwise. The figure itself stiffened a moment, as if it, too, stood in shocked emotion. With gloved hands, he reached into VanBauer's breast pocket and had to exert some strength to pull a paper from inside. That slight jolt shifted VanBauer's corpse, the last thread of resistance broke and Andrew's head tilted precariously on the side of the table, his dead eyes staring into Willi's own disbelieving ones. The caped intruder gasped and jumped back, knocking against the table.

Willi tried to scream, but a hand brutally clamped over her mouth. She dropped the flashlight, which Quannah deftly caught with his other hand.

Quannah's voice whispered near her ear. "Not a sound, Gallagher."

Trembling from the cold and from fright, she still managed to nod her head and pried his fingers away from her face. She grabbed her flashlight from his hand. She averted her eyes from Andrew VanBauer's face and concentrated on the grape-colored robe.

Retching seized the fleeing figure, who ran up the stairs and flicked the lights off in the process. Quannah turned loose of her and followed. Footsteps echoed.

Using her flashlight in one hand, Willi raised the old skillet in the other and raced up the stone steps after Quannah, rounded a corner and collided with him. He twisted around, his boot sliding in the seepage. He half sprawled and half sat with one leg at an odd angle.

"Great Coyote's Balls, I'm in enough pain. Set the frying pan aside." His leather-soled boots slipped out from under the one leg supporting him, and he yelped and leaned his head against the stone wall. "Would you get that light out of my eyes?"

His loosened ponytail streamed in wild strands around his shoulders. The grimace etched on his face along with the anger flaming from his eyes boded no good for her. All he needed was the war paint and feathers, and she'd be looking for a circle of wagons.

He was not going to cow her again. She straightened her shoulders.

"Seems to me like a trained officer of the law, especially a Texas Ranger, would know enough to be careful on stone steps. By the way, the killer is getting away."

"Iya ye sni."

She tried to push past him. "We'll have a language quiz later, Lassiter."

"Hiya, hiya. No. Stop."

His voice rasped. He grabbed her wrist to pull the beam toward his ankle. "I've twisted it." He sighed. "And we've let that robed man—"

"Man! Could be a *woman* murderer."

"—*thief,* not necessarily killer. Anyway, I let the jerk get away."

"Maybe you have more lessons than I to learn from Ant."

"Han, hecetu yelo." He leaned his head back on the wall. "Maybe you're right. I hate to ask this of you, but I . . . need . . . uh . . . maybe, yes, probably will need . . ."

"Yes?" Willi smiled.

". . . your . . . help."

"I knew you would. And I'm good. I mean about talking to people, getting them to open up, say things they wouldn't tell their mother or their psychiatrist. I can be a lot of help. Might even be able to catch that creep if you'd release my wrist."

"I don't want any amateur help with the case, especially someone who'll scare the culprit away."

"I was stalking him. The head moving scared the one in the cape—not me. It wasn't anything I did."

Quannah held one hand palm toward her. "Woman-So-Full-Of-Texas-Cowpaddies, just guide me upstairs with your flashlight."

She swerved the beam into his eyes.

He blinked. "Are you going to refuse, obstruct justice?"

"No, Sits-On-His-Backside-Chief. You seem to be doing a fine job of that on your own."

He drew her down to chest level. Nose to nose with him, she placed her hand on his chest. Beneath her fingers, his heart pounded. Ancient anger of eons past shone through the dark pools of his eyes. Battles won and lost, revenge sought and abandoned, pride of The People radiated within his eyes. Hooded lids closed over his eyes for a moment and finally released Willi from their spell.

"Gallagher, can you do what's necessary?"

"Help you up the stairs? Sure, Lassiter. No problem. Sorry I didn't think to bring a splint and a decanter of Black Label, but . . . even though I'm not the *trained* officer, I did remember—"

"—the flashlight? Thank Great Eagle's Feathers you do have the virtue of being prepared." He sighed. "Squirrel Medicine isn't bad Medicine to have, *Winyan,* not bad at all."

He placed his weight on his foot and drew in a ragged breath.

"You really are in pain. I . . . I'm sorry, but . . . can't you bear it stoically, and we'll hurry, maybe catch a glimpse and see which door that cape swishes through?"

"Your concern warms my warrior's heart, but no hurrying. I've made enough mistakes by not following my own advice. Things happen in their own time. First things first."

"What are you babbling about now?"

"We can't leave him there," Quannah said, gesturing toward VanBauer's body half-teetering from its perch.

"Well . . . why not?"

"A number of reasons, but the one that immediately comes to mind is our *cousin.*"

He moved her hand so that the flashlight reflected into the malicious eyes of a rat on a crate near the corpse.

"*Cousin Rat* cannot be allowed to tamper with evidence."

"Well, I hope you don't think I—"

"Yes, *Winyan,* you must."

"Oh, no. No . . . uh, and did I mention my knee? Yeah, I hurt my knee on the way up, probably shouldn't really be bending or—"

"It seemed okay for me to lean on you a few minutes ago, but—"

"But nothing. Rodents attack, and . . . I'm not sure dealing with a . . . *rat* . . . or touching . . . uh . . . a body, well . . ." Willi gulped and turned away. "Not this girl."

"You don't have to do more than move his face a fraction or two and zip the bag, but if you can't manage, *Winyan,* if you would rather go daydream about some romantic castle in the—"

"I was not"—she muttered through clenched teeth—"daydreaming."

"Guess the realities of an investigation are too much for a mere *female*, one of tender sensibilities, and if your knee is—"

"Oh, my blasted knee is fine. If I've got to do this, then I've got to." She pulled away from his grasp.

She trudged as slowly as possible toward VanBauer's briar. Hades and blazes. She didn't like this one bit. Not one damned bit. At the edge of the light, the huge rodent, whiskers twitching, kept a beady-eyed watch while she worked.

CHAPTER
8

WITH Quannah leaning heavily on her shoulder, by the time she struggled upstairs to his room, she became nauseated, dumped him unceremoniously on his bed, and ran into the bathroom. Once there, she surprised herself by not tossing up the Mexican cuisine. Instead, she lowered the toilet seat, sat and leaned her head against the sink edging. Ah, cool porcelain. Wonderful. She would not let him see her so weakened. She trembled for five minutes. Uncontrollably. Down to her toenails and back as if she were filled with Jell-O wigglers.

"Whew."

Finding one body a day was her absolute maximum, and never again—*never*—would she allow one Quannah Lassiter, badge or not, to convince her to touch another corpse. Ugh! Quincy and Mike Hammer might handle more in a given twenty-four hours, but they also had the option to walk off the set. No overly critical investigator would have been watching their every move, either. Nope, that kind of adventure wasn't for her, and . . . that *cousin* . . . that twitchy-whiskered, salivating rodent . . . well, it didn't bear thinking about.

She arched her back and sat up to peer at herself in the mirror before splashing cold water in her face. What a gosh awful mess. Spider webs floated around her head. She managed to get most of the persistent mass removed from her French braid. Her skin was as drained as VanBauer's. She pinched her cheeks and bit her lips to bring a bit of color. At last her limbs stopped trembling. Another few moments alone, and everything would be fine. She wiped cold perspiration from her hairline.

"Gallagher?"

Now what? Couldn't he give her five minutes to get herself collected?

"*Winyan,* you *can* get the door open, can't you?"

She marched into the bedroom.

"Of course. You *want* your ice pack. You *want* me to do exactly what you say when you say jump and only ask how high. You want me to touch disgusting, rotting flesh, grapple you up a flight of twisting stairs, all the while listening to how you think I shouldn't be involved in your case. *Your* case. I ask you. Did you discover the slashed body? No. Did you zip up that body bag? Did you? Did you?"

He grabbed her arm, pulled her down beside him on the bed, and rolled her over until they both sprawled on the crumpled quilt. Her hackles rose, ready to do battle, but he put his fingers across her lips.

"Gallagher, you're out of balance. I'll admit, I'm not used to working with a . . . another person."

"A woman, you mean?"

"Well, a woman like you." He shifted onto his back, placed his hands behind his head, and continued. "And the last woman partner I had—"

"Yeah, your Uncle Brigham told me. I'm sorry."

He sighed and nodded. "Maybe I was a little hard on you down there, but—"

"A little hard?"

"Do we not bleed, if you prick us?" asked Quannah and winked. "Surprised I can quote Shakespeare, huh?"

"I would prefer a correct quote, *"If you prick us, do we—"*

"Gallagher, you can ruin a beautiful moment. I was just trying to say I understand you being upset. Truly."

She raised herself on an elbow and looked into his dark eyes.

"Well, I guess the Bard would be as happy with a paraphrase. Thanks for the concern. That's what really surprised me."

What she thought most surprising, but absolutely would not tell him, was that his touch and his misquote from Shakespeare calmed and soothed her, made her feel all was better in the world, despite a body downstairs and a raging storm outside the walls of Lilly's Victorian Establishment. She pushed a strand of his raven hair from his forehead.

"Guess I'll get that ice." She eased herself off the warm bed and held her hands to the fire stoked in the bedroom fireplace, where phantoms of reflected light cavorted out and onto the walls. "Wish my room had one of these."

"I'll share anytime, Gallagher, if you don't harangue at me about the case."

"I don't usually shriek. Sorry." She peeked out the window at the black velvet night sky, the pristine coil of the dangerous Snow Snake seeming to constrict the hotel and everyone in it. She shuddered, and a tiny wire of ice twisted around her spine. "Sorry. I must have sounded like a fishwife," she said before edging toward the door.

He hefted himself to a sitting position and leaned against the ornate headboard. "Fishwife? No, more like an angry armadillo making a last gesture of defiance by baring its teeth against an eighteen-wheeler—maybe a necessary act to get a hardheaded Indian's attention. With some, you have to take a stand and set your boundaries or be taken advantage of. No hard feelings on my part, none at all."

"Good."

He patted the bed. "Come, *Winyan*. Sit cross-legged beside me for a moment."

"What for?"

He turned out the bedside light so the only illumination came from the fireplace. "Here, hold this and—"

"What's this?"

"A sacred Turtle rattle."

Willi sat and studied it. No bigger than her hand, it was a turtle shell attached to an intricately carved stick. When she twirled it, tiny stones echoed inside. Time-worn grooves made the rattle fit perfectly between fingers and thumb.

"Shush. Not yet." Quannah drew from his pack a small, leather-covered drum.

"You carry these things with you?"

"*Han, hecetu ye.* My mother gifted me with them when I was fifteen. She had the inner knowing that I would be often on the road and would need some Sacred Centering objects."

"Should I use your—"

"I will teach you with these and sometime gift you with your own."

"I am touched, really, and feel drawn to these, but maybe we should wait until after we've caught the killer and are out of this awful situa—"

"These, Gallagher, will help us get out of this situation. A deadly Snow Snake—one that has only the most murderous of games in mind—must be fought on all levels. We will heighten our intuitive senses. We will gather mental acuity and emotional strength through this centering ceremony.

"Eventually you will know the chants, which parts are for the men, which for the women. But I am not a purist and believe *Wakan Tanka*—Great Spirit—opens us all to all avenues no matter the parts we sing. In this ceremony you repeat the chant after me as you feel comfortable with it."

He took hold of her hand with the rattle and shook it to a gentle and slow four-four beat. When he turned loose, she kept on as he joined in a light counterbeat on the drum. She breathed deeply as the undulating flames wrapped shadows about the room, shadows that flitted and finally seemed to settle into a dance around them.

"The drum is the heartbeat of *Unci,* some call Grandmother, some Mother Earth. Turtle, too, represents a connection to *Unci* and all that surrounds, lives on, in, or above Turtle Island—Earth."

Willi nodded. Colors within the flames seemed more vibrant. Her nostrils flared as scents of woodsmoke melded with odors of freshly washed linens.

"As you chant, *Winyan,* energy from *Unci* comes through your body and is magnified. Through our chant we send this energy along with our requests out to *Mitakuye Oyasin*—All Our Relations."

He took a deep breath and intoned the lines of the welcoming chant to All Our Relations. *"Hey ya hey, hey ya hey."*

She mimicked him on those and the next lines. *"Yo hey, yo hey, yo hey."*

"You should feel the chant go through your whole body as I lead you in the *He and She Wolf Chant* taught by Brooke Medicine Eagle. It celebrates the union of female and male energy. We will need both, *Winyan,* to safely emerge from the coils of the Snow Snake."

Willi wondered why she hadn't floated off the bed. The laws of gravity, place, and time seemed suspended. A comfort settled around her, a rightness with the world she'd never before experienced. In a few moments she responded, *"Wowo wowo wowo wowo."*

Turtle rattle and drum in sync, Qannnah's voice came out clearly, *"Wo ya, yaayaa yaayaa yaayaa."*

Finally, Quannah ended the song with a strong *"Ho!"*

In the few moments it took to replace the sacred Turtle rattle and the drum, Willi's senses escalated, plunged downward and then balanced out. "Wow!"

Quannah laughed. "That was a simple short ceremony, but you were in the right frame of mind, so it was a powerful moment. Do you not feel ready to tackle the unknown, more acutely aware of your surroundings, prepared to come back down to the more mundane but with a belief that all will be revealed to you in time?"

"Yes to all the above."

"Good. So, since you're more aware, what strikes you most strongly?"

"I'm thirsty, and you need that ice pack."

Quannah laughed. "While in the kitchen could you get some bread?"

"Sure. Sam had some fresh from the oven and said for us to help ourselves." She turned the knob and said, "How about a couple slices of roast or ham?"

"Those will be fine, and one of chicken if it's there."

"Okay."

"If it's not too much trouble, maybe a dill pickle, chips, whatever?"

With hands on her hips, she asked, "About that setting boundaries with Armadillo Medicine . . . uh . . . perhaps . . . that's what the word *Winyan* means?"

"Nope, Gallagher. *And you know by now that Winyan means woman, referring to all the wondrous and irritating, magical and heart-rending qualities the word can signify, but always—always—respect.*" He stopped the flow of words with his upraised palm. "Enough said. You've already apologized once, and that's plenty. I was thinking, too, if that's homemade bread, a slice of cheese would be good with it."

She sighed and grinned. "How many sandwiches do you want . . . and just how high do I jump with them, not that you'd *ever* ask?"

"Don't know where you get these ideas. Two would be perfect."

"As in two for you?"

He nodded. "And the ice pack, if it's no trouble."

She walked out, executed a sharp flag corps turn, and stuck her head past the doorway. "Mustard or mayo?"

"Mustard . . . and—"

"What?"

"Forget the ice if it's in a walk-in freezer, okay? Be careful."

As she slapped mustard on the sandwiches in the cold kitchen, she grinned. Her cheeks glowed as she recalled Quannah's explanation of *Winyan*. She wrinkled her brow. What did the thief want from Andrew VanBauer's dead body? Whatever it was sounded like paper—crinkling paper. Maybe a will? No, that wasn't something everyone carried on their person. Willi glanced over her shoulder. Hades, every room in this building had more shadows than the Black Forest, more creaks than an arthritic crone, and more frigid drafts than Alaska. Oh, Good Lord, now she talked to herself in threes, sounding like old Elba. Well, Elba had been right on the mark with her prophesies of shrouds of white and problems with the law.

Willi shivered and frowned in concentration. Of course, a woman could have hidden in the folds of that cape as easily as a man, but the disguise would have been a clever camouflage for a man since one thought first of a femininely clad figure. She recalled the last case she helped Sheriff Tucker with where the Wiccan—not a good one, but an evil one—used a black cloak. Elba always said things came in threes. Was Willi to have yet a third encounter with a cloaked figure?

Might have been BeeBee VanBauer taking a last look at her ex-husband. Perhaps she still carried a torch for the man, despite what he had done to her in the much-publicized divorce. Maybe Catherine Noble wanted to see if in death he were more like the young pupil she remembered. Elvis, VanBauer's secretary, could have myriad grounds after having worked closely with the congressman. No reason came to mind for Ivon Paulklin to unzip the body bag.

Willi sliced dill pickles, making two sandwiches for herself as well, because there might be need for some extra energy before the wee hours were over. Lots of questions remained, and answers were somewhere in the old hotel. She paused as she put the pickle jar back in the refrigerator, again reviewed the suspects and shook her head. Enough.

Locating two types of chips and some cheese slices, she loaded down the tray, pushed everything to one side, added a couple of mugs—one with warm milk, another with golden pecan coffee for her—and headed upstairs. Small sconces lit her way to the first landing. One step screeched. The sound reverberated, echoed, and finally dissipated somewhere in the wainscotting. She held her breath, but no doors opened, and at least one of them should have because whoever had pulled a paper from VanBauer's coat pocket had to be awake, wondering if he'd be discovered.

Waziyata—the North Wind—whispered underneath the double doors in the foyer. That softer sound seemed a hundred times more menacing than the blast of his full wrath. Goose bumps trailed across her neck and arms. Her skin was taut with nerves, with the need to *do* something. She'd get Quannah settled with food and a couple of Excedrin PM, which, with luck, would make him sleepy.

Then she'd show him she could accomplish things on her own. One o'clock in the morning would be a perfect time for sneak—uh, investigating. It'd be hours before anyone else would be stirring. Even the twisted, sick prowler would pretend to be settled.

Smiling sweetly, she entered his room and placed the tray on the table between two chairs that sat in front of the fireplace. Somehow, he'd managed to liven up the embers and throw a log on for extra heat.

He said, "The fireplaces are the one thing I like about this old hotel." He lifted his foot sans boot and gingerly settled it on a low stool. She arranged the ice around his ankle.

"Better?"

"Some. It's an old injury that just got aggravated. Usually takes two, maybe three days more for me to put my full weight on it again."

She patted his shoulder. "Remember Ant. You taught me to be patient, so—"

"When did that happen? While you were in the kitchen?"

Smile still in place, she said, "Everything happens in its own time."

He glared at her, but finally grinned. "Deserved, well deserved."

Searching in the bathroom medicine cabinet, she located bottles of Tylenol, Excedrin PM and aspirin. She offered him two Excedrin PM caplets on her open palm. In the other hand, she held out his mug of warm milk. "Take these now," she said.

"Ugh. With . . . *milk*?"

"It's sugar-sweetened. By the time you've finished your sandwiches, you'll be able to rest."

"Good idea." He added, "Unless I'd be too sleepy to see you didn't flutter around and get into more trouble tonight."

That niggling thing called conscience wrestled for a moment with her baser instincts but lost out. "I'm tired, too."

He raised an eyebrow.

"Lassiter, would I lie?"

"No, you wouldn't, but I have caught you omitting a few pertinent details."

"Well, no sense discussing and fussing anymore tonight. I'm going to take my food and go to my—"

"No. Won't have it, you eating by yourself. Sit."

"Really, you'll rest better with me out of the way." She pretended to yawn.

"You could stay until I got drowsy. We might talk . . . about the *case*, about things Droskill shared about VanBauer."

"Oh? Well, I could stay until we finish our sandwiches."

He nodded but didn't seem inclined to talk at the same time he was eating. She gritted her teeth. Damn him if he hadn't hoodwinked her again with that old line about sharing tidbits on the investigation. Just didn't want her out of his sight until dawn. Well, those Excedrins would do the trick along with the milk and food.

She munched and studied his dark eyes for signs of sleepiness. She crossed one leg over the other, nervously twitching her foot. He had to drift off soon. Fine, she'd relax a few moments. She uncrossed her legs, breathed in deeply, smiled at him and yawned twice.

Go to sleep.

The brilliant flames—reds and blues, golds and greens—in the fireplace seemed to leap higher and higher.

She leaned closer to the veritable bonfire, a huge conflagration that sent sparkles out into the star-strewn canopy above the village. A soft ululant howl of a coyote rose. An Indian brave—no, more than a mere brave—a veritable warrior, a chieftain, danced in the firelight. Flames licked toward his swift feet encircled at the ankles with iridescent feathers. A lone drummer kept beat with the frantic tattoo his moccasins dealt Mother Earth. His bronze chest, under a thin sheen of perspiration, glinted as he swayed into the light, back into shadow, always keeping his feet moving with the increasing drum beat. Dried caterpillar cocoons tied in bunches around his knees rasped—a muted counterplay against the gourd players now joining the drummer. One wailed, "Hiya, hiya ho, hiya, hiya he." He waved a rattle of a Turtle shell. The Turtle shell turned bright red and the word HIYA appeared on it.

A wail rent the air as the Singer added words of the song in a Sacred manner, his voice vibrating between bass and tenor, soaring high and wide as Eagle's wingspan, dipping as low as Snake's whispered slide through grass.

In one heart-stopping moment, Drummer, Sacred Gourd players and Singer halted, and the Chieftain stood arrow straight with arms stretched heavenward as if transfixed by a vision beyond even the Star Nation. At last a maiden, dark hair streaming down her back, approached.

But . . . but the maiden was her.

He lowered one arm, opened his hand for hers and called her Hummingbird-With-Curiosity. *Somehow, that seemed as right and natural as the beadwork on her buckskin blouse, the oils anointing her soft curves, the pleasant warmth invading her as the tempo escalated.*

The Gourd Players created a haunting music with their instruments, created an ancient Earth waltz, created a Sacred Space for the lovers to dance. Hand in hand, Hummingbird-With-Curiosity moved in unison with Chieftain in a ritual of circling the fire. Gradually, the steps became more frenzied, and Hummingbird twirled so fast, a breeze created by her fluttering wings—the buckskin fringes of her dress—wafted against her cheeks.

Chieftain said. "High! Jump high!"

Hiii-hii-igh, *howled the coyote and the dried cocoons sputtered.* Hi-i-i-i-hi-high-Hi-i-i-i-hi-high.

"How high?" intoned the Singer.

"Wha—what? What do you mean, *how high?"* Her own twentieth-century voice startled her.

It must have startled Quannah, too. He tried to rise from his seat, winced and leaned back again. "Are you all right?"

She nodded. "Of course. Just . . . uh . . . thinking out loud." *Fool,* she chided herself. He finally went to sleep, and she'd awakened him.

"Come over here," he said.

"You just drift on back to sleep." *Now.* "Maybe you ought to get into bed and really snooze."

Warily, she approached to check the ice pack.

"No," he said, "sit in front of me."

"I can see your ankle just fine from here, thank you very much."

"Gallagher, do you argue about everything?"

She didn't want him upset. Better to give in gracefully, keep him quiet and be on her way. She sat down cross-legged.

Gently, he turned her away from him and unbraided her hair. She gasped, but remained still. Leaning over, he got a brush from his footlocker. He brushed until the long strands slipped through his hands like silk threads. She closed her eyes. Her mama used to do that, never rushing the process, taking pride in her long locks, always begging that she never cut her hair, a promise not made because the cascade would be down to her ankles if she didn't keep it neatly groomed at shoulder-blade length. Quannah wove the soft strands in and out in an intricate design.

"*Winyan,* in this firelight, your tresses are as shining as a bird's wing, probably a little bitty fluttery type."

She stiffened.

Get out of my mind, Lassiter.

That uncanny ability of his was as unnerving to her now as it was the first time he'd pulled thoughts from her, but she would not let him know it bothered her. "Maybe a little . . . hummingbird?"

"Nah, more like that big-eyed yellow cartoon that's always sputtering about some pussycat."

"Tweetybird?"

"That's the one."

She wanted to be miffed, but the moment of quietness, firelight, the touch of strong hands was too special, too magical to break away from. Totally relaxed, she was off guard for his next words.

"Guess you'll really have to help now," he said.

She pushed away from him, unwrapped her legs from each other and stood up. "More sandwiches? At this hour? I don't think so." Good grief, was the man a bottomless pit? Would he never go to sleep? She glanced at her watch. "It's almost two in the morning."

"I meant," he said as he motioned her to sit down in the chair facing him, "that we *must* work together. You'll have to be my feet until this swelling goes down."

"After all your broken promises of sharing information that never seem to be kept? What about amateur detectives who don't know what they're doing? Aren't you concerned over a female being involved in *your* case? How about Droskill, the retired deputy sheriff, who was to assist? Nope, this girl isn't falling for that line again. I won't help."

Quannah crossed his arms and narrowed his eyes. His jaw had sharper angles than a carpenter's T-square.

"*Winyan,* your Squirrel Medicine is okay, your fluttery Tweety—"

"—Hummingbird—"

"—that Medicine is good, but the bit of Porcupine you've got is damned irritating."

He gathered his hair back into a ponytail, tied it with a triple-braided leather piece, and sat up as straight as possible with one leg propped beneath an ice pack. All business now, he glared at her. "Has it ever occurred to you, Gallagher, that I didn't want you involved simply because I didn't want you hurt?"

Chagrined, she almost gave in to the piercing look in

his eyes, but at last, said, "No. You indicated just the opposite, in fact. I recall the word *fool* being used a number of times and *ineffectual amateur.*"

"If you're expecting an apology, you'll be waiting longer than it takes Turtle to cross the Atlantic. I did what I thought best for all involved, you included. That's what I'm doing now. I've got to have assistance whether I want it or not."

"So, why me rather than Droskill?"

"You're the only one in this place besides the octogenarian hired help who hasn't a link to VanBauer. You're also the only one with enough curiosity to overbalance good judgment." At her squeak of protest, he held his hands up. "That's not all bad. It got you onto the same track as me tonight. But, Gallagher, you must do things my way. Then you won't get hurt—and don't kid yourself—we're dealing with a dangerously sick person."

He hesitated as if about to add more, but shook his head. What was he keeping from her? Well, there'd be only one way to discover that. She mulled over what he offered. If she went about this on her own, she'd have no restrictions whatsoever, no one watching over her shoulder, and she could do what she wanted when she wanted. On the other hand, if she willingly helped Quannah, he'd be overbearing, expect to know her every step, challenge each idea, and keep her curiosity and imagination in check. Those two qualities she most relied upon would be denied to her if he had any say-so in the matter.

Peering at him from beneath lowered lashes, she caught sight of his wallet, which held his badge. Even though it was hidden, she envisioned it and all the authority it represented. She really had no right to interfere with the case. She tapped her foot and sighed.

"Okay, Special Investigator Quannah Lassiter, I'll help."

"Knew you would. Your sense of duty is the only thing that surpasses your curiosity, or so Uncle Brigham said."

"Where do we start? Don't guess we'll get much done tonight . . . this morning, I mean."

Quannah opened his mouth to answer, but his first words were lost in the caterwauling of loud voices in the corridor. Willi pulled open the door. Ivon Paulklin, fist raised to knock, stumbled inside, her lopsided red hair in the firelight shooting out purple and orange sparks.

Beside her, the congressman's secretary shook his head. "I tried to convince her," said Elvis, "that we should wait until morning to tell you."

CHAPTER
9

WILLI gritted her teeth. She *would*, come Hades or not, find that caped prowler, but again she sighed heavily while moving out of Ivon's path.

"Good God, yes," Ivon said, "he's tried to stop me from chasing the culprit. Makes me so damned . . ."

"Frustrated?" Willi asked. "Impatient?" She pointed her thumb at Quannah. "Ask him about *Ant*."

Quannah's controlled voice broke into the hubbub. "Explain. One at a time, please."

"I'm trying to," said Ivon. Barefoot, she did her best to stomp inside, pulling her silk robe tighter around her slender waist. The green hue made the redhead look like a tawny tigress slinking through the jungle. "My jewelry along with a great deal of cash has been taken."

Quannah leaned forward. "Since when?"

Here Ivon stopped to light up and puff one of her Turkish cigarettes to life, then waved the smoke in front of Elvis.

He flapped at the puffs. "Ivon, you are the most inconsiderate smoker I know. Lighting up in someone's room who you know isn't a smoker. You constantly kept your elbows on the table with that stench in everyone's face at dinner—"

"Well, good God, what . . ." Ivon glared and stubbed the cigarette out in a saucer. ". . . what the hell does that have to do with anything?"

Elvis ran his fingers through his ebony hair. "Sorry, nothing. If you'd just work some at being ladylike with the habit instead of like some longhorn in Dillard's glassware, you might . . . well, you aren't bad for the eyes, but that smoke is, and . . . that's not what—"

"Miss Paulklin, Elvis." Quannah's tone was warm, his eyes intense. "When someone gets killed, the act does strange things to the survivors. Nitpicking at each other and letting off steam about pet peeves is a sight more healthy than letting the irritations build like . . . well, like the murderer obviously did. Maybe once you recognize that fact, you'll have more patience with yourself and the others incarcerated here with you."

Elvis straightened his shoulders and looked Quannah squarely in the eyes. "Yes, I suppose being Indian you'd think smoking was sacred."

"Not *all* smoking. The social indulgence type of smoking isn't considered to be," Quannah said evenly. "When tobacco is offered in the right manner for a sacred reason, yes."

"Anyway," Elvis said, "as close as we can work it out, her diamond necklace—"

Ivon bristled. "Diamond and ruby neck—"

"Excuse me. Her diamond and ruby necklace disappeared about—"

"—the earrings, too."

Elvis shook his head. The namesake curl cascaded onto his forehead, and he grinned, pushing the hair back into place. "And the *matching* earrings disappeared about the same time Miss Gallagher discovered VanBauer."

Ivon, arms folded, said, "Don't forget the money. Over twenty thousand."

Willi whistled. "Not in cash?"

"What else?" Ivon jutted her chin higher. "I don't believe in credit cards any more than absolutely necessary. So, Investigator Lassiter, what are you going to do?"

Quannah stared at the ice pack on his ankle and nodded at Willi. "Gallagher, go help her search her room in case she misplaced the jewelry." At Ivon's squawk of protest, he raised his hand, palm toward her. "Patience, Miss Paulklin. First things first."

Willi stared intently at the ceiling and hummed under her breath the tune of "The Ants Go Marching."

"Elvis," Quannah said, "will search some other areas and report back."

Willi followed as Ivon marched down the hallway and around a corner. Just before they got to Ivon's room, Willi paused at the door from which she had earlier seen the caped figure emerge. "Whose room is this?" she asked.

"That's that bodyguard's room, Driskoll, Roskill or whatever. This is mine."

"Royce Droskill? VanBauer's bodyguard?"

"Yes. Didn't do the jerk much good hiring a bodyguard, did it? Are you interested in my missing jewels at all?"

"Coming, coming."

The scent of Ivon's heady *Opium* perfume and stale ashes permeated every corner.

"God-awful, isn't it? That maid, Odessa, refused to clean tonight. Said she'd had enough for one night. You just can't find reliable help these days."

"Uh, well . . ." Willi stuttered, not wanting to get into the housekeeper episode. "Where do you keep your jewelry?" she asked.

"Here."

Ivon indicated a tooled leather case, lined in the same shade of green satin as her dressing gown, then paced back and forth as Willi peeked inside. She let her fingers trail through pieces set with diamonds, others with emeralds, sapphires, and stones which she didn't recognize. "How can you tell something is missing? I can't believe you travel with all this jewelry."

"Hardly all. The seriously expensive family sets are kept in the vault. Daddy bought most of these trinkets for my birthday, school competitions, the beauty contests, Christmas. The missing ones were a Valentine's gift."

"My loves are Ariavapa breast plate jewelry, Navajo silver work and Lakota deer-bone chokers."

Ivon stabbed the air with her cigarette. "How god-awful. Well, we all have our weaknesses. I want my Valentine jewelry back and not because of their monetary value. Papa Paulklin wouldn't let Mother or his secretary choose them. He did. That's why I carry them with me and why they're more important than the family coffers of fine sets. Can you understand that, Willi?"

"Yes, of course, I can, but you act as if he'll never give you any more."

"He won't. He passed away May ninth. Same day as—" Ivon plopped down on the bed and crossed her legs, took a steadying inhalation of her cigarette and shook her head. "Everybody I loved is dead. And everybody I hated."

Willi waited, trying Ant's Medicine for once, hoping not to stop the flow. She touched a miniature picture frame and, giving Ivon a moment to collect herself, straightened makeup brushes and bottles atop the dresser.

Ivon blew rings of smoke into the air. "I hated him. Oh, how I hated that god-awful son-of-a-bitch."

Frowning, Willi asked, "Your father?" She peered inside a traveling coffeepot and a couple of canisters of tea on the lamp table.

"Good God, no. VanBauer."

Willi remained with her fingers poised above a set of coffee cups with the Paulklin business logo in gold lettering. "*Hate* is a strong word."

"Not strong enough in my case." Ivon swung herself off the bed in a fluid movement, sending the cascade of hair in a fiery swirl around her head. She ground her cigarette butt into the ashtray, lit another and puffed directly in Willi's face. "Not damned strong enough by a long shot." In silence, Ivon sat and puffed for a few minutes.

Willi stared out the window. *Waziyata* moaned rather than howled. Snow lifted in swirls and resettled. Moving out of range of the lit end of the smoke, Willi said, "Why? What did VanBauer do to you?"

Ivon stubbed her cigarette butt out. "Destroyed the two men I loved. Papa Paulklin took his antique Colt .45 and blew his brains out. The man I was to marry in two weeks chose a less dramatic way."

Ivon's lashes were wet with tears; she blinked and cleared her throat, grabbed her cigarette case, fumbled and dropped half the contents before she managed to get one between her lips.

"Here, let me," Willi said, flicking the lighter and holding it. "Sit. I'll make us a cup of tea." She laced both cups with plenty of sugar, scrounged around in a paper bag, and used a Kleenex tissue to hand over a bear claw cinnamon roll. "Go ahead. It's better than a taco and jalapeño salsa."

With one hand, Ivon tossed back her hair. "You heard about my fussing in the kitchen? Papa Paulklin would have been ashamed. Don't know what—"

"Like Lassiter says, murder does strange things to folks, and sounds like you've had more than your share of death especially since you're what? Twenty—?"

Ivon set the Turkish smoke aside, sipped and smiled again. "I'm twenty-three. As old as grave mold and just as dead inside."

Willi grinned at the overly dramatic comparison. "I still don't understand what VanBauer had to do with—"

"The murders? That's what they were, but nothing was done." Ivon leaned her head back and closed her eyes.

"Congressman Darren Stiltiman. He was on a subcommittee with VanBauer that dealt with gambling law inequities, prostitution, pornography, something like that. One of those committees where you don't really have to do a lot except show up for meetings. Darren changed overnight. He stopped saying the sweet things you expect, didn't send gifts, ended a friendship with a best buddy. I marked it up to prenuptial nerves."

"What happened?"

"May ninth."

"I don't understand," Willi said.

"The day of the wedding. Believe me, the shakes had hold of me, mainly because of the fear that Darren, despite his reassurance, would stand me up at the altar. I came downstairs early to show Papa my gown. He—" Ivon's features crumpled like the Kleenex clutched in her hand. She breathed in deeply and steadied herself. "After handing Mama a letter, he . . . uh . . . shook his head and walked into his trophy room. I thought he was overcome with emotion at seeing his only child about to leave . . . or . . . or that Darren had called the whole thing off, and Daddy just couldn't bring himself to tell me. Mother hugged me, and as we walked arm in arm upstairs, the shot rang out. We called the Stiltimans as soon as the ambulance arrived, but Darren wasn't able to come comfort me."

Ivon whispered and Willi had to lean close to hear the last words. "He'd drunk himself into a stupor and wrapped his car around a utility pole." Ivon cleared her throat and in her usual cynical tone said, "Good God, the rest of the week was a blur. Another few days when Mother and I had stumbled through the funerals, everything had been neatly shoveled into a dustbin and there wasn't any kind of stench around VanBauer. His letter explained that VanBauer had set out to ruin the family through a series of disgraces. Mama wouldn't ever let me read it and told the police there was no letter. The only fact she mentioned made no sense. She said Papa would rather not live than see me marry Darren Stiltiman." Ivon sighed. "Why? What had Papa found out? Darren and Papa's deaths are connected in some way to that committee of VanBauer's.

For eighteen months I've been trying to prove that."

Willi touched Ivon's shoulder. "As horrible as it was, can't you see the possibility that Darren came home inebriated after a bachelor party?"

"Darren's father was a drunk and a wife beater before he went into the wrong bar and got so soused he forgot where he was or where he left his car so he wandered around, bottle in hand. Went to a construction site and fell into a still-hot vat of tar. Darren, at nineteen, had to identify him. Darren *never* drank. *Never.*"

"May ninth? Is that when you started smoking those Turkish horrors, too?"

"How did you—?"

"Because you haven't learned to handle them, as Elvis puts it, like a lady, and somehow I see your father as the type who would have demanded such etiquette. You brandish them about more as a sword—a shield between you and the world. You don't really enjoy them—in a sacred manner or otherwise."

"Haven't we turned god-awful philosopher?"

"Sorry. Absolutely uncalled for."

"Forgiven. Any ex–English teacher who can end a sentence with a preposition can't be all bad. Thanks for letting me talk. You'll report that the jewels aren't here?"

"Yes, but you can't blame this theft on VanBauer."

"I would if I could."

Willi washed out her cup, dried and placed it back beside the coffeepot. She poured a second cup of tea for Ivon before emptying her ashtray.

"Willi?"

"Yes?"

"You believe Elvis really thinks I look like a Texas longhorn?"

Considering the socialite—all twenty-three insecure years of her—Willi placed her fingers underneath Ivon's chin and tilted her face up. "No, I think he sees an attractive young lady who's just enough of her own person that she's getting under his skin in the nicest way."

"Like you get under Investigator Lassiter's?"

"Hardly. I don't possess enough Ant Medicine to impress him."

"Good God, what is—?"

"Another night—morning—whatever. It's time I took *Tunkasila* to bed."

"I don't even want to know."

Willi grinned and walked out of the *Opium*-perfumed air. Between this stench and her own reeking room, Lilly's could be mistaken for an 1850s bordello. She peered up and winked at one of the cupids looking down on the poor little rich girl, a girl that might just have healed a bit tonight.

Willi headed back toward Quannah's room. Well, she hadn't located any jewelry but had gained insight into the one person she'd at first marked off as a possible killer. Certainly Ivon Paulklin had, in her own mind at any rate, a damned good motive. Now to figure out if what happened on the subcommittee did have any bearing on the murder in Lilly's Establishment. Willi paused to look back past three doors and frowned. Maybe Ivon was a practiced liar. Her bed hadn't been slept in. She could have been wandering around in a purple cape, but as Lassiter said, that didn't make the person a killer. Ivon might simply have searched VanBauer for some clue to her fiancé's death.

Willi stopped and backtracked. She stood in front of Royce Droskill's door. This was the door that had emitted light, the room from which a caped figure had emerged and led her on a harrowing escapade down to the rat-infested cellar. She knocked. He might be a sound sleeper. She banged louder. About to turn the knob and enter, she bit her bottom lip. Lassiter had told her to search Ivon's room, not Royce's.

But . . . she just *knew* a clue lay behind this door, and he hadn't actually forbidden her to go into someone else's room.

She nodded. With this argument ready for Big Chief Lassiter, she pushed the heavy door inward and peeked through the crack. Like Ivon's room, this one had a neatly made bed. Hadn't anyone gone to sleep tonight? She switched on the light to make sure. Nope, no one there. A momentary flash of Droskill on the Amtrak came to her. It hadn't been something he'd said that had peaked her curiosity. No, not at all. When VanBauer had waved Droskill's aid away, there'd been a look of disdain on Droskill's face for his employer. More than disdain. Loathing. Willi smiled. One more incident, though tiny, had fallen into place. She stepped farther into the room. Light from the hallway kept her from stumbling against furniture. A razor and a can of Gillette glinted from the bathroom countertop. Perhaps, he was in the bath. In the dark?

"Mr. Droskill?"

She almost stepped over the threshold when a sound overhead caught her attention. What in Hades was that?

A loud thump-a-thump came from the ceiling. Hairs at the nape of her neck stood on end. The monotonous noise continued.THUMP . . . THUMP-A-THUMP . . . THUMP-A-THUMP . . . THUMP! She turned off the light. A strangled moan cut off in midutterance catapulted her out the door. At least she didn't have to plunge down into the darkness of the subterranean hole of seepage. Heading up the stairs to the third floor, she paused every other step and listened carefully.

THUMP. THUMP-A-THUMP.

She clung to the side of the stairwell. Damn, and she'd left her flashlight in Lassiter's room. The air up here was dust-filled. She couldn't get her fingers to the bridge of her nose in time to pinch off the explosion. She sneezed. Afterward, she halted a moment. The rattling above continued. She took a steadying breath, moved one hand toward her jeans' pocket and caressed *Tunkasila*. Immediately, calmness surrounded her.

She eased open the first door she came to, and it squeaked in protest.

No light flicked on at her touch against the switch. The scuttling behind the next door, she attributed to mice, and raced on past. She saw a flash of white gown vanish into an attic opening and climbed the ladder in pursuit.

Willi shivered. *Waziyata* whistled around the circular inset windows, invaded the wainscotting and slapped against the clapboard. She scurried through a warren of tiny rooms, each with a single bed, a dresser. Sometimes a chair. These were hidey-holes for the hired help, obviously much more numerous in days gone by. She ran in and out of the cells, once catching a glimpse of a white gown.

Her foot gave way on top of a rotting floorboard. She edged around the section and tripped over a low stool. Dust rose in a cloud around her. She coughed and spat. She lay there a few minutes, testing herself for bruises and listening for faint footfalls, a swoosh of material, a ghostly murmur. Her eyelids closed. She'd just as soon lie here and sleep rather than chase more ghosts or caped figures tonight. Maybe Lassiter was right. She really did need to be more patient and let the killer come to them.

But no, that wouldn't do. Now she was *so* close. The cold in her bones might be numbing, but she had to go on. What was that? A lid closing? Someone hiding behind a stealthily locked door? She got painfully to her knees, then to her feet. Racing toward the newest sound, she paid no heed to dust or old furniture, to rotting wood or to her own labored breathing. One moment she skittered across a small bedroom; the next moment the world fell away beneath her feet. Dank lumber splintered around her ankles, waist, shoulders. She reached out into empty space. Her fingers caught on shattered floorboards, held only a second and lost their tenuous grasp on life.

CHAPTER
10

WILLI expected to crash through the attic to the floor of the next room, but she landed on the canopy of the bed below. A momentary horror of plummeting atop an unwary occupant made her groan. She choked on billows of dust. A piece of splintered wood scraped her cheek. Finally, the dank satin settled along with the dirt and debris. She opened her eyes and pushed rotted flooring off her back before crawling to the edge of the canopy frame and peeking underneath. She twisted herself to the floor much like an acrobat leaves the safety net. With her knees about as dependable as if they were melted marshmallows, she stumbled across the room to grasp the door handle. On the third floor again, she took a moment to get her bearings and whimpered. She reached into her jeans' pocket for her calming stone and yelped against the sharp pain. A glance down revealed little in the poorly lit hallway, and something . . . something was wrong with her right eye. She shut it, tried to focus with her left, and wished she hadn't after seeing the five-inch-long wood sliver piercing in near her wrist on the thumb side, going deeply underneath flesh, muscle, and veins to come out near the tender web between ring and pinkie finger. The wood was only as thick as quilting thread, but as far as she was concerned, such pain could be caused only by a Dracula-killing stake. Her stomach roiled, she forced her glance toward the ceiling and swallowed. Tears filled her lower lids to spill hotly over her cheeks.

Okay, she did not want to go into Lassiter's presence. She could just hear him growling about her Ant Medicine going south. He'd also be damned right on the mark. She slowly managed the stairway to the second floor. Maybe Catherine Noble could see to her injury. Willi wanted the comfort of someone wiser. Quannah's thoughts reverberated through her mind. *The Old Ones should be sought out for help. Those of more advanced age walk only a few steps behind those already in the Star Nation. They will impart their own wisdom as well as that of the ancestors on the Blue Road.*

But Willi had no idea which room belonged to Catherine. With no other choices remaining, she plodded slower than a Galapagos tortoise toward *his* room, and sniffled every other step.

WILLI stood as far in the shadows of the room as she could.

"What?" Quannah asked, leaning forward. "What do you mean you fell through a ceiling while chasing—

surely, I heard you wrong—a *ghost*? I knew one of these days you'd get those daydreams of yours mixed up with reality, and—"

"I do not daydream."

With her left hand, she pulled the hassock away from his bed, where he sat on the edge. He'd been asleep and his hair, with the exception of one wild tuft à la Alfalfa, hung in black wings beside his face.

"That gash," he said, "needs attention, not to mention the black eye. That scratch on your cheek, too. And why," he asked, "are you holding your hand behind your back?"

"A little blood is on it, and I don't want my jeans ruined."

Quannah eyed her from the waist down.

She crossed her legs to hide the worst rips and tried on a grin, which slid off at a lot faster rate then her mind seemed to be working. Somewhere in her muddled brain the words EVASIVE TACTICS blared forth, but for the life of her, she couldn't think of one. She allowed her head to droop until her chin touched her chest. Seemed like an awful lot of trouble to raise it again. She rested her hand on top of her leg.

"Gallagher? Have you fallen asleep sitting there? Gallagher, answer me."

She blinked and tried to look at him past her swollen lid, refocused through her good eye, but again the effort overwhelmed her. His form shifted hazily before her.

"Damn you, *Winyan,* don't you pass out on me."

Cold water hit her in the face. She gasped.

He set his glass back on the bedside table. "Sorry, but you were about to fall off, and I couldn't reach you." He frowned at her injured hand. "At least it's a thin splinter, but went all the way across your hand. Go get the alcohol, tweezers and bandages. And the pliers."

"Pliers?"

"There's a pair in the crime bag beside my shaving kit."

"Right." Numbed, she rose slowly and said, "Galapagos might be restful. I'll try there next winter break. Yeah, the Galapagos."

"Gallagher, don't go off into some damned daydream."

"Right." That word seemed like a safe response, one that didn't require much effort.

She returned with the supplies wrapped in a towel and clutched awkwardly in one hand. "The tortoise would definitely win any race with me."

"Okay, *Winyan,* whatever you say. Pull the hassock in front of the chairs by the fire."

"Right."

She slumped down and eyed his hobbling approach.

He grinned. "I know. Tortoise would win against me, too."

"Right."

She couldn't hold her eyelids open another minute. Breathing seemed to take too much effort, too. She dumped the bundle onto his lap.

He grasped her hand roughly, then more gently when he inspected what he was dealing with. "This could have gone through your eye—"

"Right."

"—or a vein or—"

"Get on with what you have to do. It doesn't hurt. Nothing hurts."

"You're dead-tired and in shock, *Winyan,* and perhaps that's best at the moment."

Taking one end of the wood tightly in the pliers' grip, he broke off as much as he could and poured alcohol over both punctures before gently pulling on the longer end. "Seems to be one smooth piece. I . . . I sure hope so."

She paled and blinked.

"Look away," he ordered.

The first inch moved from beneath her muscle, and every nerve in her hand came alive. Wide-eyed she yelled, "What in Blue Blazes do you think you're doing? You're going to kill me. Hell!"

"What happened to *right*?"

"Maybe we ought to stop, give me some painkillers, okay?"

"Only aspirin here." Another inch slid out.

"Holy Mother Cow, you've got to stop."

Sweat popped out on his brow, where the black wings separated, stuck, and twined in clumps like worms. He tightened his hold on her hand.

"I don't want it out. Don't want it out. Don't—JE-EEEZ!"

He gritted his teeth. "Another inch, maybe inch and a half, we'll be through."

"*Madre* and hell. *We'll* be through? We? What's this— ahhhh, ouch!—damned *we*?"

"Can't you just suffer quietly?" he asked.

"Stoically? Like an Indian?"

"Right."

"Turn me loose. Why are you getting that crazed look in your eye, Lassiter? You're not going to stop, are you?"

"*Right.*"

"Lassiter, wait. Wait. There are two inches left. You can leave two inches in, okay. Okay?"

"Right."

She relaxed. "Thank you, thank you. I'm so sorry I whimpered and whined, but I've never really been into pain, and—GOD ALMIGHTY HELL—you damned SAVAGE!"

"Got it all," Quannah said and poured peroxide over her wound. The antiseptic frothed. "This is to get the dirt out."

Back in glassy-eye land, Willi whispered, "Right."

He gave her a couple of aspirin.

"Go to bed, Gallagher. I'll think about your ghost story. Bright and early, before anyone expects anything tomorrow morning, we'll have a surprise ready."

She yawned. "What?"

"Be up and dressed by five. Make that six." He shook her shoulder. "You got that, Gallagher?"

She stifled a whimper, survived another jaw-popping yawn, stretched, and said, "Three hours from now, uh, six o'clock. We get down and dirty. Ought to be easy for someone from the Torture and Scalp 'Um Clan."

She stumbled toward the door and tripped over a corner of the worn rug. She barely righted herself by grabbing hold of the doorknob with her good hand.

"Gallagher!"

"I'm okay."

He eased down on the bed and leaned back on the pillows. He pulled his sock down. "See? Ice and being off it for a couple hours did wonders. Probably won't even limp tomorrow. Now, we need to get you well." Pointing a finger at her, he said, "No stops for curiosity's sake along the way. Straight to bed. And make it eight o'clock.

No one is going anywhere with *Waziyata* still whipping up the storm."

Fifteen minutes later she was showered and snuggled in her pillows, where she tried to sort through the evening's horrors from VanBauer's slit throat to the cellar fiasco and the THUMP-A-THUMP-A-THUMP chase, but came up with no feasible connection among those incidents and Ivon's missing jewelry and money.

She turned over to nestle into the down pillow and winced. Damned swollen eye. Enough scratches to cover three-fourths of her body, knee knocked to smithereens, and her hand throbbed. She tried to push the aches from her mind. If she could just concentrate for a minute, she'd have a vital piece of this crazy jigsaw.

After she had punched them into the proper shape, she sank deeper into the down pillows. At last the aspirins dulled the throbbing, and her mind took a hike into the welcome oblivion of sleep, that land of happy campers.

"I am not a happy camper," she growled into Quannah's ear as she handed him the crutches Jasper Farley had brought into Quannah's room. She rushed into his bathroom, grabbed the aspirin bottle and downed two tablets with half a glass of water.

"Mayhap this'll help him get along somewhat," Jasper said when she walked back into the bedroom.

She smiled at Jasper's use of *mayhap*, one of Sheriff Tucker's favorite words. Recognition showed in Quannah's eyes, too. A small thing, but her heart wrapped around the shared moment.

Quannah tried a circuit of the room, didn't stumble and

seemed pleased enough to smile at the clock, which indicated 8:05. "Punctual. I like that, Gallagher."

"Glad one of us is excited. It's cold in here. That
beastly wind is still blowing. Snow drifts are as high—"

"Whoa, whoa. In pain, huh? Is that what's got you an
eensy teensy bit bitchy?"

She raised her hand to wiggle her fingers. "It's sore,
but not painful." Damned if he'd know she was functioning on a double dose of Excedrin along with the two aspirin, which still hadn't completely stopped the constant
throbbing.

He narrowed his eyes as he looked into hers. "Not playing martyr? Seemed to hurt plenty last night. Thought
maybe I'd done some permanent damage."

"No permanent damage," she said, moving out of his
reach. "What are we going to do?"

Quannah motioned for Farley to come closer and yelled
into his ear so as to be heard clearly. "Jasper," Quannah
told him, "I want you to go get folks out of their rooms
quickly and escort them down to the parlor. Give them
no time to collect anything."

Jasper nodded and left the room.

"We are going to search rooms," Quannah said when
the old man had left.

"Fine, but—"

"For three items." He held three fingers up in front of
her for clarity.

"*I* can hear perfectly fine." She lowered his fingers with
a light touch from her own. "What three things?"

"Knives. Any knives. And that blasted cape. Ivon's
missing cache of jewelry plus dough."

"What about a white gown?"

"Anything suspicious point out to me. Anything. We'll search together. I don't want you traipsing across any more rotting floors."

Crutches beneath his armpits, he struggled to the door, threw one crutch aside and said, "Damned nuisance. Locked in by this blizzard. Bum ankle. Murderer could be in the room next door. Most accident-prone woman this side of the Rio Grande helping me. Great Eagle's Feathers, what have I done to deserve this?" He clomp-stomped into the hall.

She scooted off the hassock to follow him.

He said, "Let's go. Remember, we don't split up."

"Right."

"Gallagher."

"No problem. We don't split up."

CHAPTER
II

WILLI followed Quannah into Ivon's room, where the *Opium* scent still clung heavily. She jangled Farley's keys in her hand, winced at the soreness still evident and handed the ring over to Quannah. "I gave this room a good going-over last night, Lassiter."

"For jewelry. Great Spirit, do all you women mark the four corners of your rooms like Skunk?" He rubbed his nose.

"Odessa spilled a bottle. I think I'd have noticed a purple cape draped over the chair, money strewn about and certainly a bloody knife."

"And," Quannah said, chuckling, "you might even imagine one if you worked at it a little bit. You're right about one thing. None of those three items are here." He replaced a pair of folded pajamas in Ivon's designer suitcase. "Somewhere, *Winyan,* somewhere in this old hotel

are those three things, and we will find them. Let's try
Royce Droskill's room."

Once inside with the door closed, Quannah peered up
at the ceiling.

Willi, hands on her hips, sighed. "I did hear it."

Using his crutch, Quannah beat out a THUMP-A-
THUMP-THUMP on the floor. "Sort of like that?"

"Kind of, yes."

"You were extremely tired, Gallagher, and you are
given to—"

"Damn it to Blue Blazes, I *heard* it. There's nothing
here. How about Elvis's room next? It's right beside the
servants' stairway."

Quannah squinted into the darkness of the winding
stairwell before he opened Elvis's door. "It's a wonder
you didn't kill your fool self trying to maneuver up those.
Must've been even darker last night."

She frowned at his use of *fool* and said, "You going to
unlock this door before the next blizzard hits say in the
year 2200?"

"Gallagher, Gallagher, Gallagher . . . be patient."

She vented her frustration while going through Elvis's
bureau drawers.

"Wow."

"What?" Quannah shuffled over awkwardly. "You find
the knife?"

"Nope. Not the cape, the jewels or the money, either.
Look."

She pointed to a drawer full of briefs—vibrant blues,
reds, teals, tiger motifs, and leopard. She held up a tiny
one with zebra stripes. "Weird, huh? Elvis has wild
tastes."

"Remind me to take you on a search of a pervert's nasty den sometime, Gallagher. There's nothing weird *here*. The man just likes colors and patterns."

"Fine." She refolded the briefs and placed them with the others. "But it's unusual. Not too many men wear wild animal underwear."

"This is something," Quannah said, raising an eyebrow, "you're familiar with?"

"Well . . . I mean . . . you don't even see many ads for this kind of kinky colors. Would you wear such bright colors? Would you?"

"Why don't you finish this shaving kit and briefcase while I take care of his more personal effects?"

"You didn't answer, Lassiter."

"Nervy little wench." He set aside his crutch, pulled a half-inch of brief above his jeans' waist and grinned. "Leopard skin is my favorite, but red isn't a bad choice."

"Go figure," she whispered before opening Elvis's case.

A loud knock on the door made her look up. "Should I?"

Quannah nodded.

Jasper Farley stomped in and worried his right ear with a finger before he shook his head. "Mr. Investigator, sir, might be best if you was to come downstairs for a mite. Everybody has scattered theirselves from one end of this place to the other. Some insisted on sitting a spell in the kitchen, others in the dining room, one or two nested down in the parlor. I knowed you wanted them together and all, but they don't seem to pay me no nevermind. Never do listen to me. Never have, never will."

"By damn, when I deputize you, they will."

Farley grinned like B'rer Rabbit in the briar patch,

hitched up his pants and worried his other ear awhile.

"Yes, sir, Mr. Investigator, guess they might at that."

"Well, come on down with me."

"Yes, sir, it sounds good to me."

Quannah sighed, twirled, forgot to twist the crutch as he moved and winced. "Gallagher, continue here. I'll be right back."

He stomped out of the room with Farley close behind. "I'll go ahead and deputize you now."

"You ain't got no call. You think I'm the criminal? I thought you was—"

Quannah raised his voice. "Not Mirandize, DE-PU-TIZE!"

"Yes, sir, that's what I thought you done said."

Leaning out the door, Willi crooked her finger at Quannah. "Remember," she whispered, *"patience."* Slowly, she eased the door closed until she could no longer see the vein pulsing on his forehead.

She scrambled around the bed to lift one corner of the mattress at a time, but found nothing more than a few loose down feathers. She opened the closet. Two suitcases looked promising. Unlocked, they offered no resistance, but also no revealing clues. An old Victorian trunk with enough hardware to immobilize Houdini sat at the end of Elvis's bed. A quilt was folded neatly on top. Five feet long and about two and a half feet high, the luggage case put her in mind of the huge steamer trunks in black-and-white Charlie Chan movies.

Probably nothing but dust inside, but she had to look. Bending over, she threw the quilt onto the bed, lifted the lid and pushed until the rusty hinges caught and held.

"Blue Blazes, there it is."

A surge of electricity snapped through her. She'd found the first clue. Big Chief would be proud of her. She had to bend far down to reach the purple cape at the bottom of the trunk.

A burst of pain volcanoed from the base of her skull. Her knees buckled. A jolt in the middle of her back sent her over head first into the black interior and the silken cloth was pulled from beneath her at the same moment. The trunk lid boomed shut.

"No!"

She twisted around and beat against the lid, which sent a molten stream of agony through her tortured hand. She gasped for breath. Her heart fluttered against her ribs.

She wasn't any Houdini, had no keys hidden in her cheeks, and there wasn't . . . any . . . oh, dear God, there wasn't any . . . *air*.

That panic-stricken idea touched the edges of her mind like a butterfly's wings for the briefest of moments before flitting away along with consciousness.

Something in her rebelled. She fought her way back to lucidness, scrabbled upward, touched the trunk lid, and crumpled to the bottom. She clawed the surface with increased vigor, finally stabbing at what might well be her coffin as if she could force an air hole with a sharp fingernail. She whimpered, licked one finger and tasted the salty tang of blood.

Bile rose in her throat. Gasping for the last wisps of air, she hit the trunk lid with her feet.

"Lassiter?" she yelled.

The grandfather clock boomed out her death toll.

"Lassiter?"

She curled into the fetal position.

"Lassi—?"

CAYENNE pepper, roasting beef, freshly chopped green peppers and sweet onions. Those scents enveloped her before she could focus her eyes. She blinked. Steam rose nearby. When she turned her head, someone's face materialized within the vapor. No grotesque slash of red lipstick as she had expected. No plastic curtain. Not a knife in sight. Only Quannah's worried eyes peered at her from the other side of the steaming cup of hot tea he offered.

"*Winyan,* don't move quickly. You've got a bump on your head the size of a golf ball."

The drink, a strong blend of tea and roasted Brazilian maté, revived her. She pummeled the tattered sofa, where she sat in the corner of the huge kitchen. Sam, spatula in hand, and Catherine stood at one of the counters. Catherine approached to perch on the edge of the sofa.

"Feeling more like ourself, are we?"

Willi nodded and immediately regretted the action. She touched the base of her neck, winced and held out her empty cup.

"That's wonderful tea. I might just live again."

Uzell Speer moved into her line of vision, took the teacup and said, "Be living, that's what we all be wanting, what you think? You be giving each of us a big scare."

"Glad to see you up out of bed, Uzell. Maybe that's where I should be."

His brown eyes lit up, and he smiled while refilling her drink. "Glad to be among the moving again. Sam and Mrs.

Noble be telling me all manner of things be happening with the Congressman VanBauer." He handed her the steaming tea.

Willi sighed. She had also told him, but perhaps after taking the cold medicine, he just didn't recall all the details of her visit to room 103. She sipped gratefully and said, "The Brazilians know what's what. Delicious."

With the back of his hand, Quannah felt her forehead.

She pulled away from his touch. "I'm fine, no thanks to you, Big-Chief-Who-Says-Don't-Split-Up. Do you know what happened?"

"Just take it easy for a few minutes. We'll get to that."

"Take it easy? Sure. As soon as we find the jerk who knocked me out and stuffed me in that coffin."

She shifted to a better position to look him straight in the eyes. "Soon as the ache in my chest goes away, I'll tell you—"

"Why he knocked you out? I know why."

Willi took a deep breath and exhaled slowly.

Quannah stroked the side of her face and placed a finger across her lips as if silencing a child. "We were obviously getting too close to the jewels or the cash."

She shoved his finger aside. "*We?* I got bobbed about the head, stashed in a trunk and left for dead. *Me,* not *we.*"

"Thank Great Spirit," said Quannah, "you had plenty of air. Rather than face that someone is after you, I'd like to say you panicked, let that imagination of yours get the better of you, but the knock on the head says otherwise."

"This bashed head is not imagin—"

He raised his hands palms out. "Of course not." He

squinted his eyes and stared into hers. "Ready with that concoction yet, Sam?"

"Yep, *click-slurp-click,* nearbouts, anyhow. This'll make you feel perky *click-slurp-click,* in just 'bout no time a'tall."

She frowned at the strange clicks and slurps coming from Sam's poorly fitted dentures. Every few words and he'd slap his tongue around them to slide them into place. "What," she asked, "are you cooking?"

"Something near 'bout over a hundred *slurp-click* year or more old. My granny and mama done made batches up for us'un's many a time. Brothers and me *click-slurp* was always a-fighting and a-getting bunged up pretty near onct a week if'n not more."

After a while Willi failed to notice the strange interruptions in his speech. They had a special cadence that really didn't seem misplaced with his backwoods dialect.

"We gonna slop this on your noggin, and you'll be thanking old Sam come 'bout an hour or so, maybe less." He pushed the doughy mass into a plastic baggy, added ice, punched three holes in the middle, and made her lean forward while he placed the poultice on the knot at the base of her head.

"Now, you just lie easy on this here couch for a bit. That's it," he said as she complied.

Catherine fluttered up and out of the way. She stood by the butcher block full of knives, twirled them around, pulled them in and out, in and out. Sam came over to her, caught her hand and patted it. "Much obliged for the reminder, Catherine, much obliged."

He tapped Quannah on the shoulder. "That knife I told you about the other night, you remember?"

Quannah nodded.

Willi rose up on one elbow. "Knife?"

She glared at the back of Quannah's head, at the pony-tail hanging down his neck. "You never told me about a knife."

"Shush." He pushed her down on the sofa. "Go ahead, Sam."

"Ain't missing no more. Guess I'm getting older than the hills. Leastways, as concerns remembering things. Sorry. But I coulda sworn on my mama's Bible that this one here"—he wiggled one of the butcher knives in the block back and forth—"right in this very spot were missing first time you all done ate my vittles."

He clicked his teeth in place and grinned. "You all going to sure enough appreciate tonight's supper even more. *Chuletas con picante.* No better way to serve pork chops. Whew-whee! Taters with *cebollas*—onions—that is. Corn soup with jalapeños. Guess I better brew up an extry batch of iced tea. Ladies sure did get a mite thirsty last night."

Willi feigned light-headedness, which wasn't difficult to do, and placed a hand over her eyes. She understood why Catherine's face blanched.

"Maybe," said Quannah, "some buttered corn tortillas with that to take away the sting of the hot sauce?"

She uncovered her eyes. Catherine smiled.

Willi said, "Lots of butter, please."

"Who said I were serving anything hot?" His sigh, disgusted, let them all clearly know what he felt about their sheltered stomachs and blah appetites. A couple of extra clicks and slurps pounded the message home. He turned to the pork chops to marinate them in the chuleta sauce. She figured by evening the meat would be sending off smoke signals before any introduction to the cooking pan.

Quannah stretched and asked, "When was the first time you noticed the knife was returned?"

"Nearbouts when I heard you screaming *Gallagher* all over creation and back when you went a-looking for that pretty lady." A salsa-covered thumb pointed in Willi's direction.

Quannah's Ant Medicine seemed strong, and he persevered. "Who all," he asked, "was in the kitchen then or just before you discovered the knife?"

"God-Almighty near ever dang body in this place excepting that feller." His thumb indicated the direction of the cellar where VanBauer lay. "Madder than hell, all of them. Wanting coffee, tea. Wanting to know what's a-going on upstairs. As if anyone were a-telling me a thing around here afore it's half done with."

"Could you be more specific?" Quannah took out his notebook and pen.

Willi sat up on the sofa, held the remedy against her neck and leaned forward.

Sam washed and dried his hands before bending down to lift a plastic bin of onions.

"More?" Willi squeaked. "More onions?"

"Can't never have too many, can you, ma'am? They's good for the nerves, so's every soul here can make right good use of them." He peeled a dozen, laid them on the cutting board, and diced. The pungent odor wafted throughout the room. Her eyes watered, but not wanting to miss a word, she stared blearily in his direction.

"So," Quannah said, "who all came into the kitchen? Who all might have had access to the knives?"

"Some young filly in a green robe. A huntress to my

way of thinking. Seen them like that in army days. Coming to get their man or their man's paycheck. That kind of look about her. Determined. And she were a dang blame complainer from the word get-go. Didn't like my vittles."

Quannah nodded along with Willi. She said, "Ivon."

"That there feller with the curl on his forehead. Kind of a hang-dog look about him. Pasty skin. Ought to get in the sun a mite more, you reckon? Maybe some of my good eating will put some color into his cheeks."

"Elvis," Willi whispered and peeked at Quannah's notebook, where he'd written the same name.

Sam chopped the last onion, placed them all in a bowl, covered that with cellophane and handed it to Catherine.

She pushed the bowl into the depths of the restaurant-sized refrigerator. Before closing the door, she asked, "Is there anything else you need, Sam, hon?"

"Well, ma'am, now that you mention it, how about that bag of tomaters?"

She hauled out a huge paper sack.

He performed the same chopping operation. "That older woman—one what's been in the news. Come in here wearing a fur coat. Don't she have no robe? I figure on being took for a fool for thinking that. More likely, don't want to get it stolen like them jewels everybody's been jabbering about."

He nodded in Uzell's direction. "Him. Been mighty helpful. Got them all served easy like this morning. Appreciate that, son."

Uzell's Jamaican cocoa skin glowed with the compliment received. "That's what I be training for, what you think? I be happy to be doing now that the horrible cold be *almost* gone."

"In that case, get right over here and finish up these tomaters." Uzell wrapped an apron around himself and complied.

From the corner, Catherine chirped, "I was here, I'm sorry to say, among those pestering Sam."

Sam clicked his teeth and shook his finger. "Done told you, you ain't no more trouble than a kitten. And a lot cuter."

Catherine tilted her chin up. "You're kind. If we hadn't been roused so early this morning and force-marched downstairs, we wouldn't have had to put you to such trouble." She glared at Quannah as much as any flustered dove might at an intruding blue jay.

Willi said, "Really, Catherine, it couldn't be helped, and it was for your protection."

Quannah nodded. "True, Mrs. Noble. Sam, who else?"

"That's near about all I recollect."

"How about," asked Willi, "Royce Droskill?"

"Nope. He were probably the onliest one to do what Jasper asked. He stayed in the parlor. Well, now I'm guessing because of him not showing up in here."

"Excuse me, Investigator Lassiter, I be seeing the gentleman," Uzell said. "He be nipping in only for a moment for a cup. Sam, he being in the closet."

Sam frowned. "In the *click-slurp* closet? Oh, yep. Kid means I was in that there pantry. He's right. Guess that feller coulda been right here by them knives as well as the rest."

Quannah grabbed his crutch from the corner, heaved himself up, walked around the counter and reached over and pointed to a butcher knife. "Which knife was missing?"

"That big sucker. Yep, that's the one."

"Used it today?"

"Naw. Didn't touch it neither. Figured you might want to play detective. Can't say I ain't sorry, it being one of my most favorites." He handed Quannah a gallon-sized plastic bag and between them they placed the knife inside.

Sam peered at Willi, walked up to her, studied her head and removed the poultice. "How you feeling? Need a fresh one? Won't take a minute to fetch."

She sat up before standing on trembling legs.

"I'm okay for a walking accident victim. What's a bump on the head after knocking holy crud out of my knee, getting a black eye, and having minor surgery without a painkiller? I'm great. Just great."

Quannah touched the back of her head. "The swelling has gone down."

Sam clicked and slurped as he went into the kitchen. "Sure enough. What you all expect?" He returned with a bag of shelled whole pecans. "We might as well top them *chuletas* off with a *cool* pecan pie. And I'll make sure there's a good amount of butter on the table." He grinned at Willi and Catherine. "Now, I hate to be unneighborly, but if you all is going to be in here, I'm going to put you to work with this feller."

Catherine rolled up the sleeves of her silk blouse tucked into flattering mauve slacks. Sam didn't offer any resistance to her offer of help.

Quannah guided Willi to the parlor, no easy task with one side supported by the crutch.

"Where is everybody?" she asked.

"Once I knew you were breathing normally and in Sam's and Catherine's care, I finished the second floor. I sent everyone back to their rooms."

He seated himself across from her. The fire crackled. He laid his crutch down beside the chair. "Thank *Wakan Tanka* for faithful Farley. He's guarding the hallway."

She sat a few moments enjoying the warmth while eying the blast of snow against the window and the banked drifts against the sills. "Snow Snake," she whispered.

"The game," Quannah asked, "or the killer?"

"No, the killer and the one that's got us surrounded."

He leaned nose to nose with her. "We'll get him. Just have—"

"Patience?"

"I'll ignore," he said, "the sarcasm. You are all right?" he asked for what seemed like the hundredth time.

"Shaken, I admit. And maybe I did panic—a little bit."

"Makes two of us. Damn. I'm not going to be able to ever leave you alone, am I?"

Insufferable man. She glowered at him and sank back in the chair. "Oh!"

"What?" He jumped up, hovered over her. "What is it? What do you want me to do? Should I call Sam? Mrs. Noble? Spit it out, Gallagher."

"Gallagher would just love to if one ranting special investigator would alight somewhere else, preferably in the next county."

He sighed audibly and wiped perspiration off his brow. "You take me to new heights . . . and depths . . . each time you open your mouth, Gallagher."

"Do you want to know what I found in that blasted trunk or not?"

"I know. Nothing but stale air. I checked after we got you safe—safe being a very relative term when used in a sentence referring to you." He reseated himself.

"You didn't look carefully enough. I bent over . . . and—" A feeling of darkness settled around her for a moment as if the Snow Snake had suffocated her in feathery coils.

"Easy there." He placed a comforting hand on her knee. "Take your time."

"I bent over," she continued, "and the purple cape lay in the bottom. It was crumpled up. The next thing I knew, my head hurt like hell, I was sliding down and the cape was being pulled from underneath me."

The largest log was about to roll off to the side in the fireplace. She got up and kicked the offending oak back in place. The fire blazed, spitting sparks in all directions. She jumped back while Quannah brushed at her clothes.

"The venerable Standing Person is trying to get your attention."

"Excuse me."

Quannah nodded at the log. "The old Oak, even after cut down and considered as one of the Ancestors, even while serving us with warmth, can still give us messages. Maybe, *Winyan,* you're getting too close to danger and need to back away. I don't want anything to—" Inching his way to the edge of the chair, he gingerly tried standing without the aid of his crutch. He winced but maintained his stance, grabbed her arm and guided her to the door.

"Go rest."

He pointed to the cuckoo clock above the mantel. "Most sane people wouldn't be up this time of the morning."

"Darn right, Lassiter. And whose bright idea was that?"

"Guilty as charged. Every idea doesn't pan out. Go rest."

"I'll feel more like helping after an hour nap."

"Uh . . . no need to rush. Chasing ghosts, falling through rotting floors and being incarcerated in traveling trunks is bound to be rough."

At the foot of the stairway, he patted her on the shoulder and practically pushed her up the first two steps.

He kidded her about the idiot traipsing around in ghost garb, but she could tell he hadn't really doubted her about that nor about the cape. She lay down on her bed, but twisted and turned from one side to the other in such a frenzy that her pillow looked like an abused marshmallow. She got up to pull on fleece-lined booties and an extra sweater. She wouldn't even try to discover where the cape was now. Absolutely not. Bottom line, she'd stay off his case and enjoy herself as best she could until this ordeal was finished. Tromping feet down the stairs indicated Quannah had removed Jasper Farley from duty and lifted the confinement-to-rooms for everyone. She peeked out her door. *Friendly* would be her catchword for the day. She'd start by making a few morning calls. It'd be impossible to get in his way by just having a one-on-one chat with folks. Absolutely no harm at all.

CHAPTER
12

WILLI rather enjoyed sitting on Elvis's bed, despite the misgivings she'd faced upon entering the room and spying the trunk. Being here, first of all, made her feel as if she were getting back on the proverbial horse after being thrown. She had been brave enough to enter. Had Elvis been alone, her meager courage might have fled, but Royce Droskill hunkered down on the trunk, and BeeBee VanBauer, legs crossed and seated in the only chair, seemed eager to talk. Poor woman was probably suffering from media withdrawal. Willi leaned forward and voiced a question she'd worked up to through a roundabout conversation.

"Why did you divorce the congressman?"

"Old story. Took me years to find out what was going on. Womanizer." BeeBee stroked her ermine arranged on the arm of the chair. "Carrying on like that at his age. Disgusting old goat."

Elvis sat on the other arm of the chair.

"Found lipstick," Willi asked, "on the collar?"

"More or less. Roses ordered on our personal charge cards. Roses never received by me. Perfumes like *Opium* and *Jungle Gardenia*. Ugh. Expensive late-night dinners catered from the best establishments."

Droskill said, "You probably don't want to rehash all that again. I feel real responsible for you, Mrs. VanBauer, after letting someone sneak up and slit his throat. Some bodyguard I turned out to be. But despite the hard feelings between the two of you, if there's something I can do, you let me know." He got up slowly. It seemed to take a long time for him to get the kinks out of his joints.

BeeBee snapped her fingers. "Nonsense. Best thing you ever did for me was not to be there when justice—albeit not my kind of justice, but nonetheless deserved—was served. I'll hire you on the spot."

Favoring one hip, he edged toward the door and opened it. "Thanks a heap, but no thanks. Maybe after the investigation is over."

Elvis said, "Wait a moment. Here's your last check." He pulled a check ledger from his briefcase. "You did your job, Droskill, as well as Congressman VanBauer would allow. He'd often shoo you away when the situation was one where you should have been present."

"Old goat," BeeBee said, "had to control. Not to hurt your feelings, but the truth is he wanted you more for the publicity than as a guard."

Royce frowned, "Publicity?"

Willi nodded. "Of course, you won him lots of votes

in this state. You are a retired deputy sheriff. Just the sound of your profession sends a flood of patriotism through every citizen of the state. That disreputable hat of yours won him thousands of good old boys. Votes. You were in a number of his publicity photos in magazines, newspapers. Didn't they once interview you along with him on Channel Five?"

"Yep, guess you all might have the right view of it."

The revelation didn't add a sparkle to his eyes. His shoulders slumped as he slowly shut the door. Ivon Paulklin pushed it wide again as she entered.

"God, aren't we all cozy." Her green oversized sweater served as a dress over black stirrup pants. The three-inch heels gave her just the right height for membership in the Amazon Club.

Willi patted the bed. "Come and sit. We're just chatting."

"I prefer to stand." She took out one of her cigarettes, but eyed Elvis and stuffed it back in the case.

Elvis shoved his briefcase aside before he straightened the quilt atop the trunk. "Here, Ivon, this is more comfortable."

"Well, if you really don't mind. My room still reeks of *Opium*, which Odessa spilled, and downstairs stinks of onions and . . . worse."

BeeBee looked Ivon up and down. "Did you say *Opium*? Well, I see why you were hanging around Andrew at every stop on the campaign trail. Wouldn't think a young thing like you would want to rut with such a—"

Ivon jumped up and so did Willi, grabbing hold of Ivon's elbow. "Let's not jump to conclusions about—"

"Good God, don't link my name with that sorry creep. He ruined everything . . . he . . . everything." She sobbed and pulled away from Willi, ran out the door, slamming it behind her.

Elvis pushed the curl off his forehead. "Will she be okay? Should I go and—"

"No," Willi said. She told him and BeeBee about Ivon's double tragedy.

"So," BeeBee said, straightening her white fur, stroking it as if it were a favored pet. She sighed. "I owe Ms. Paulklin an apology. At least I'm in good company."

"I beg your pardon," Willi said.

"I'm no fool. Elvis and I were discussing this before you came. He's a suspect because he was most intimate with Andrew's legal and business affairs. I'm a suspect because of the high-profile divorce and the race for state treasurer. Now, Ivon Paulklin will be another possibility simply because she was wronged by that jerk."

Willi smiled. Now she was getting somewhere. She had to keep them talking, not that she was working on the case. Absolutely not. She would simply satisfy her own curiosity. That clarified in her own mind, she said, "I can see where you and Ivon might fall under the executioner's blade, but Elvis, being a secretary, wouldn't seem to have a strong enough motive."

"You're right. I don't." Elvis sat on the trunk.

"Well, I got this bop on the head in this room. Naturally, I did for a while think—"

"Ms. Gallagher, I'd never hurt you or anyone. Someone else came in after I went downstairs at Farley's request."

"Did you know the cape was missing?" A shot in the

dark, but what the hey, she had to keep the information coming.

"What cape?"

"The purple one."

"Don't know what you're talking about. I don't own a cape of any color."

Willi paused, thinking about his multicolored briefs. "Well, Lassiter didn't believe it was important, either." She eyed BeeBee, who looked as blank-faced as Elvis. The woman wouldn't be caught dead in anything other than her ermine. Willi shook her head. She wasn't giving up on Elvis. There had to be something to the fact that the cape was in this trunk in his room. Okay, she'd use the damned Ant Medicine and, like Quannah, approach from a different angle another time.

Jasper Farley tapped on the door and, at Elvis's bidding, came in. "Just me checking to see if you all folks might like some fresh coffee and cookies." He pulled on his earlobe and grinned. His eyes lit up with mischievous humor. "Mrs. Noble made them, not Sam. Mighty good, if I do say so." He started back out. " 'Course most folks don't listen to me. Never have and—"

"Wait." Willi grasped the doorknob, winced and pushed it open with her uninjured hand. "Come in for a minute, Mr. Farley. I have a question or two."

"Fine by me, ma'am. Is your shower out of order again?"

"No, my room is fine. Do you have any idea who our third-story ghost is?"

"Ghost?"

"Mr. Farley, I'm talking about someone in a white

gown who's been making quite a bit of noise on the floors above us."

"Investigator Lassiter said as you had a powerful imagination. Odessa thinks you do, too, what with you screaming at her and her toilet brush—"

"Just a minute." Willi glared at Farley.

He worried his left ear with his pinkie finger.

"This old hotel done seen better days, and the girl sure is a-showing it. Creaks worse than me and Sam put together. My hearing might be a bit off now and again, but my eyesight can't be beat. Might be best if you get some shut-eye. Maybe you won't be running into things in the dark and getting black eyes and such if you was to rest. 'Course don't nobody ever listen to—"

"Thank you, Mr. Farley."

"—me. Never have and—"

"One more thing."

"Yes, ma'am?"

"Have you lately run across a cape?"

Elvis shook his head. BeeBee grinned and stroked the ermine while the grandfather clock boomed out the hour.

"Well?" asked Willi.

"We got all kinds of caps in the storage room along with jackets and umbrellas and—"

"No, not caps, a purple cape."

"Oh, yeah, I seen one of them."

"Where?"

"Where? In here." He pointed to the trunk. "Came up to help Odessa set out the extra linens, but someone had that in there, so's I set the towels and such on the windowsill."

Farley left. Being patient had merely brought her full

circle. Well, not totally. But she still wanted answers. She glared at Elvis. Hands on her hips, she tilted her head.

"*Your* room. One of *your* favorite colors. You're lying, and I want to know why."

"I was in the kitchen drinking tea when we heard you."

"Sing another tune, Elvis. Your room is at the end of the hall, next to the servants' stairway." She pushed her dark cascade back over her shoulder. "You must have panicked when you realized Lassiter and I were searching for evidence."

"What evidence?" Perspiration kept his black curl plastered to his forehead.

"So you," she continued, "decided to come up the back stairs out of the kitchen, retrieve the cape and escape via the servants' stairs."

"You're making this up. There are no stairs from the kit—"

"Oh, yes, there are. I found them when making a midnight snack raid. They're inside the cavernous pantry of Sam's."

"That doesn't mean—"

"So you came up here to clean up any telltale clues, but encountered one small problem. Me. You knocked me down into that hellhole, but you salvaged the purple cape first, didn't you?"

Red blotches covered both his pale cheeks. He held his hands up. "No, you've got to believe me—no."

BeeBee patted his arm. "Anyone could have put that cape there. Why is it so important?"

Uh-oh. Open mouth, insert big toe with size five foot attached. That tidbit she wasn't supposed to reveal. In fact, she'd probably sidestepped around good sense about fifteen minutes back. "Something to do with VanBauer's murder."

BeeBee gave her a look she probably reserved for constituents who expected her to kiss their poodles. "We figured that much."

SHE knocked on room number 13 since the zero was missing. Uzell opened the door.

"Finished cutting onions?" she asked.

"Oh, do not go being disappointed," he said, eyes twinkling with humor, "because Sam may be needing more by the time we have the luncheon." He pulled out a chair for her.

"I be hoping you are okay, what you think?"

She touched the tender spot at the base of her head. "Sam's a miracle worker."

"That be making me happy. And let me say, you know, that you be deserving kindness after being so good to me yesterday. No one else thought about me, what you think?"

"No problem. Now that you're better, can I ask a few questions?"

"You are the investigator's helper, yes?"

"Uh, well, maybe . . . sort of, but I just wanted to chat."

"You being a curious lady."

"Well, a lady who is curious, yes. When we arrived, you helped Jasper Farley carry up some suitcases. What did you do then? Who did you see?"

"It was seeming so wrong to be letting the old man carry so much, so I was down again and then was carrying some more. Almost I was dropping them."

"You were so weak."

"No, but the big clock was striking so very loud, I not be expecting that loud noise, what you think, and that is when I almost dropped the suitcase. Then I be going upstairs."

"Okay, you helped Mrs. VanBauer. Maybe Mrs. Noble needed a hand, too?"

"Only on the train when her purse be falling opens all over the place. Pill bottles be spilling everywhere. My head is pounding, but I be helping her pick them up." He frowned. "Lots of medicine."

"Some folks do seem to carry a medicine cabinet full. Guess we will, too, someday."

"Another be using many medicines, too. The lady with the red hair, cut so." Uzell made scissor movements on the side of his head.

"Ivon Paulklin. She ought to be carrying Valium and anything else that would calm her down, but she probably wouldn't take them if she did have them. How do you know she has any medicine?"

"On the train she be taking many with her breakfast."

"Ah, vitamins, no doubt." Willi sighed and twisted a strand of dark hair around her finger. But you didn't see anyone downstairs near the parlor?"

"No. I be climbing into bed, and no one be seeing me except you bringing soup. Thank you. Maybe I was not saying it then?"

"You did. Well, you need to rest before Sam has you doing double time at the lunch table."

She returned to her bedroom, shut the door and gasped. Quannah, head back on one cushioned chair and foot propped on another, dozed away. Why hadn't he gone to

his own cozy room with a fireplace? She brushed a wisp
of hair off his forehead. Bone tired, that's why. Probably
didn't know what room he'd stumbled into. She definitely
had little bubbles of lost time here and there, which told
her in no uncertain terms that she'd better get some sleep
before she, too, fell into the nearest chair.

She scrambled into her disheveled bed, her head hit the
pillow and she instantly fell into an uneasy sleep full of
splotches of unrelated nightmares. Shadows and spiders.
A snake of pristine white writhing down a railroad track.
Pink eyes, malevolent and so cold, the snake hissed and
the hiss grew into a soughing wind that swirled snow
around her, crushing her in a cold, feral embrace.

She awoke and blinked at her watch. Two hours. Well,
she'd finally gotten her nap. Quannah, though his position
had changed, still snored lightly. Well, he probably
wouldn't be interested in what she'd discovered since he
didn't think her capable of keeping her wits about her.
She frowned and twisted the bedclothes, sat up and
straightened her sweater, brushed her hair and gently
shoved Quannah's foot to one side so she could sit in the
chair opposite him.

Quannah yawned and scratched his ear, but settled back
down to his soft snoring. She smiled at the vulnerable
boy's appearance he had in slumber. During their encounter with what the tabloids had termed the Wicked
Wiccan, a murderer in her hometown of Nickleberry,
she'd once encountered him asleep. Then and now, the
effect was strong, pulling her emotions into dangerous
tides. Her glance took in his broad chest, slender waist.
Just as she had a pleasant mental vision of a cozy tipi,

soft firelight, and softer buffalo robe beneath the two of them conjured, Quannah opened his eyes.

"*Winyan,* I guarantee you'll have more trouble than you can handle if you keep looking at me that way."

"Insolent redskin. Much you know about my thoughts." She bent over to straighten the legs of her blue jeans and hoped the action hid her warm cheeks.

"Redskin? Seems like that description applies more to you." He crooked his finger, beckoning her closer.

"No thank you." She stood up.

He winked. "One of these days, Gallagher, you'll be crooking your finger at me."

"Don't think so."

He yawned and stretched. "Fact. Something more than your daydreaming is going to happen."

"I do not—"

"Fine, Gallagher, fine. Find out anything while you were out interrogating instead of resting?"

"I chatted with a few folks was all. Nothing really important. I'm going to ask Catherine Noble a few questions."

"Oh? Just a chat?"

"Yes, exactly. I'm concerned about her health. This has probably been more of a strain on her than she's willing to admit. You are going to talk to Farley, aren't you?"

"Oh, I'm keeping an eye on things." This said, he leaned back and closed both of his.

She smiled, caught the door handle with both hands and slammed the door as loudly as possible. She stomped down the hallway, which didn't offer nearly the satisfaction she'd planned since she still had on her warm woolies. She found Catherine warming her hands before the massive parlor fire, to which Farley was still feeding logs. Catherine looked more like an overdone cooked partridge rather than a dove.

"Can't seem to keep these bones of mine warm," she said as Willi entered.

Willi chose a seat where she'd not have to look at the plastic-covered chair where VanBauer was murdered.

"How's your head?"

"Fine, thanks. Sam give you a break from KP duty?"

"Yes. He's such a honey beneath that brusque manner, don't you think?"

Willi shifted in her chair, crossed and recrossed her legs. When Farley left, she got up and used a poker to push a log back.

Catherine coughed and played with the crisp collar of embroidered bluebonnets. "You know, I had a third-grader once. Shamus Onderdonck. That child squirmed and inched his way from one side of his desk to the other, finally wiggling out into the aisle and back. A trip to the nurse solved the mystery. Pinworms. I'm sure that's not your problem. Perhaps you ought to just blurt out whatever it is that's bothering you. I'm a good listener."

"Guess I was obvious. I wanted to ask some questions, but I'm not sure how to begin." Catherine seemed ready to keel over and faint right now. Willi didn't want to push her to that point with the wrong statement.

"Questions about Sam and me? No, that wouldn't be it. Oh, you want advice about you and that striking man, officer Quannah Lassiter. Reminds me of Errol Flynn in his swashbuckling days. We need more strong men like him in law enforcement and tougher laws. Criminals should be shown no mercy. Death penalty ought to be it,

not all this parole and appeals and wasted tax money."
Catherine laughed behind her hand. "Doesn't take much
to set me off, does it? What's your question, Willi?"

"Remember the afternoon we arrived?"

Catherine closed her eyes and nodded. "I won't ever
forget that."

"You went up to take a nap . . . but . . . perhaps you
went into the kitchen first or maybe the parlor for a few
minutes?"

"Let me think." She smoothed the crease in her slacks.
"Told you on the train, didn't I, that one of my greatest
fears about growing old is that I'll be like my parents.
They survived to a very respectable age, but their memory
flagged. That's why I constantly exercise mine by mem-
orizing poetry. Robert Frost is my favorite. So, now I
know a lot of poetry, but . . . events from a day ago . . .
well, it's frustrating, but I'll try."

Willi sat down again. She narrowed her eyes. *Bunk.*
Catherine Noble was as clear-eyed and cognizant as a
Harvard grad on test day. Why in Hades would she try to
convince folks otherwise unless she had something to
hide? Her comments about cyanide, her vehement and
voiced dislike of some political figures, state and local,
belied the first impression of sweetness and light. Willi
prodded her to reveal more. "We all listened to Jasper
Farley rave about Miss Lilly, the founder of the hotel."

"Yes." Catherine smiled and her eyes lit up. "Jasper
and the train steward, Uzell, took my luggage up. I slipped
into the ladies' room next to the vestibule. The older one
becomes, the less one wants to guesstimate about such
matters as whether or not to wait or take care of matters
as opportunity presents itself."

"You were coming out when I went in," Willi said.

"Sorry, I don't remember seeing you, Willi. I went back into the bathroom to retrieve my handbag and literature from our visit with the state representatives. I have to give a report to my local chapter of retired teachers." Catherine frowned, small lines etching the worry above her brows. "Perhaps you were in a cubicle then. When I came back out, the grandfather clock boomed."

"So you stood in the doorway of the ladies' room, not the parlor door?"

Catherine nodded. "So glad I finally recalled. May I ask why that's so important?"

"Why? Because VanBauer was diced and sliced in those few moments by someone who had to go through the vestibule to get to him. That person also had to leave the same way, that's why."

"Well, of course, silly me."

Willi frowned. "I talked to Uzell and Farley. Farley thought he saw you coming out of the parlor when the clock belted out the hour."

"Good grief, you suspect me."

So much for handling the interview carefully. "No, no. I'm just trying to get everybody's whereabouts clear in my mind. I'm frustrated and was hoping maybe you'd seen someone with VanBauer."

Willi bent her head back, closed her eyes and sucked in her bottom lip. She counted to ten, straightened up and said, "Sorry, I really didn't mean for this to sound like an accusation. Of course, Farley was running about fifty different directions from last Sunday. He could have mistaken the exact time he saw you or anyone else."

Catherine patted Willi's hand. Her tiny fingers, despite

the heat in the room, were cold. "If he'd seen me, he'd have remembered one more thing. I dropped my purse."

"The clock frightened you, too?"

"Uh, no . . . just . . . age, I guess. My legs just aren't up to the task of uphill climbs through blinding snow. Anyway I gathered it all. I went up for my nap then, and I must go now to the kitchen. Sam probably doesn't really need my help, but he makes me feel like he does."

Sighing, Willi got up to stretch while distancing herself for a time from the retired teacher. As Catherine left the room, she smiled and patted Willi's shoulder. Catherine Noble was confusing. One minute she had not only her mental ducks in a row, but had a rifle's bead on them. The next moment, she seemed like someone's fragile great granny with a bent toward dementia. And now Willi had doubts about Uzell. He said he hadn't seen Catherine Noble downstairs, but remembered her dropping her case of medicines on the train. If the woman did that two times in one day, she really might have some issues, but of what kind Willi couldn't figure out. Either that or Uzell was so sick and disoriented he mixed up two different happenings. She couldn't believe that about this time yesterday, the Amtrak had been forced to stop at this out-of-the-way burg. She walked over to VanBauer's last resting place and shook her head. She blinked. Bending down, she peered closer. Beneath the plastic covering in a neat stack were crisp hundred-dollar bills. Definitely cold cash if they'd been long in this corner of the room.

CHAPTER
13

SHE got Quannah, brought him back to the parlor and pointed to the death chair. The plastic sheeting was crumpled up and askew.

"Right here. It's Ivon's money."

"Yeah, Gallagher, and white buffaloes are born by the dozens."

Willi shoved him aside. The only thing underneath the plastic was the bloodstained chair. She pointed her finger at him.

"Now, listen to me, Quannah Lassiter. You believed my tale about the cape being in the trunk, and it was gone when you got there. You didn't think I was some ranting and overimaginative sleuth in that instance nor am I in this matter. Stacks of hundred-dollar bills were right in this spot not more than three minutes ago."

"Why would someone place them there and then re-move them?"

"And don't forget the 'who' that should be tagged on to that question. Could be the one who placed them there was afraid we would find them during the search."

She batted those ideas and others around for what seemed an endless and certainly a fruitless time since nothing she said seemed to impress Big Chief. Quannah stomped off sans crutch and with very little limp to his gait. "Your ankle has improved."

"*Han.* Yes, I owe a certain lady with Florence Night-ingale instincts." He grinned over his shoulder. "Stay out of trouble for an hour or so if possible."

Her sweeter-than-honey smile in place, she shrugged her shoulders. The tumble into the trunk wasn't exactly her fault since she'd done precisely what he'd told her to do. She walked over to the window, pulled the velvet curtain aside and stared down the snow-covered hill. For the moment, the intensity of the storm had abated, leaving a pristine purity to the world outside so different from the evil stalking the inside of the hotel. *Waziyata* whispered around the casements. The blackened branches rattled in the wind. Great, guess those Standing People, the Trees, were trying to send her a message. The only thing that came to her as she stared out was a line from Robert Frost's poem. *Earth's the right place for love: I don't know where it's likely to go better . . . One could do worse than be a swinger of birches.*

She mused over the lines and the past twenty or so hours. Quannah said that the universe could offer many folks answers to questions and prayers all at once. She had never believed God *allowed* horrible things to happen, but she did countenance the idea that the Creator was creative and grand enough to use human weakness and foibles, when they occurred, to bring about some good. As Quannah and she both had said on different occasions and in various ways, "If one kept to what was right and true for others, good would come to them and to you."

She leaned her forehead on the cold glass pane. Could there be more than a train rerouting . . . and a killer that had drawn Quannah Lassiter to her side again? She and Quannah couldn't seem to find in the normalcy of everyday life the time to know each other. Was *Wakan Tanka* using the happenstances of a snowstorm, the murder—even *Waziyata*—to blow two wayward, strong-minded persons together for . . . ? She shook her head, stared at the Standing People again, listened to their soughing: *Earth's the right place . . . the right place . . . the right place.* She bowed her head in her hands and turned from the sight of what had become not twisted trunks and twigs, but welcoming and comforting arms.

How could so much have happened so quickly? She knew the train wouldn't return for a few more days. Tonight, the second evening in the old hotel, would surely prove more restful than the first night. Well, it could be if she and Lassiter could figure out answers to a few questions.

She idly drew intertwining letters in the frosty windowpane.

Sucking on her cold finger, she glared at the chair. Nothing could be accomplished standing here. Her scalp tingled. Lassiter hadn't told her to stay in one spot. He'd just said stay out of harm's way, something she'd man-

aged to do quite well since she'd found the cape . . . and
. . . uh . . . lost it. Turning from the curlicues of Q and W
etched on the pane, she left the parlor. Low-voltage electricity seemed to flow through her veins and some un-
fathomed source led her to the second floor. She stopped
for a moment on the landing. Where was she going and
for what purpose?

Taking the old adage of *follow your nose* to heart, she
stopped in front of the room she thought of as 13, listened
and glanced down the corridor. Uzell was by now downstairs helping Sam and Catherine in the kitchen. The open
door to Ivon's room revealed she'd made up with Elvis
and BeeBee. Their voices were easily heard even two
doors away. Where had Royce Droskill gotten himself to,
or was he just out of sight behind his half-open door?

One thing at a time. She tapped on Uzell's door, and
when silence greeted her, she peeked and slipped inside.
Why? The answer slid into place as easily as she slid
across the shadowy room. Uzell was the only one, other
than BeeBee, who'd had a personal encounter on the Amtrak with VanBauer. She liked Uzell. Maybe there was
nothing to that incident, but she'd feel decidedly better if
the slate were cleared. Perhaps she and Lassiter had
missed something the first time around. While she probed
into suitcases and bureau drawers, she hoped she wouldn't
encounter anything incriminating like one silk cape and
twenty thousand very mobile greenbacks.

Although this room had a fireplace, no embers glowed.
The cold in the room seeped around her. Outside *Waziyata* grew more insistent in his whispering, sometimes
coming through the crevices of the old building in a long
wail. She shivered and rubbed both arms. Opening every

drawer, looking behind each picture frame, and crawling under the bed to peer at the springs over her head revealed nothing except a lot of dust motes Odessa Morales hadn't bothered with in the recent past.

Willi sneezed. Scrambling upright, she sat on the side of the neatly made bed, grabbed a tissue from the depleted supply on the table and blew her nose. Where else could anything be hidden? The closet held nothing of interest. She checked the cushions of the two occasional chairs. No luck there. Giving up, she rose, bent to straighten the spread and spied something peeking out from the corner of the pillowcase. She pulled it out and studied the buff-colored business card, a calling card of one Congressman VanBauer, Republican. Flipping it over, she read the handwritten message.

For old times' sake—a private party. My room. To-night. Be there.

She replaced the card inside the pillowcase before she straightened the covers. Then she undid her work, pulling out the pillow, patting it down, pulling the pillowcase off. She thought something else might have been there, but she was wrong. For the second time she neatened up the bed. She surveyed the room, making sure she left it as she had found it.

Now, what to do with the information? She'd barely closed the door and started on her way downstairs when BeeBee, ermine thrown over one shoulder, left Ivon's room and headed in Willi's direction. Uh-oh, she'd rather no one knew about her extra visit to Uzell's room. She hurried to put space between herself and BeeBee and waited expectantly by the kitchen door, ready to scoot inside if need be. After a few minutes, Willi shrugged. BeeBee must have turned around.

Now, Willi wanted to find Quannah, get him up to Uzell's room to see the card before it, too, disappeared.

"OKAY, Gallagher, try the other one."

She pulled out the pillow and shook it. No card fluttered out. "Not five minutes have passed." This time tears of frustration gathered in her lower lids. She pinched the bridge of her nose. "I know you don't—"

"Yes, Gallagher, you may daydream—"

"I do not—"

"—but you can separate those visions and dreams from reality." He placed a hand on her shoulder and squeezed before handing her a tissue.

"Thank you, Lassi—"

"Ah, you've forgotten, that's—"

"I know. *Pilamaya ye.*"

"*Pee-lah-mah-yah yea* with the stress on the *lah*. You're learning." He nodded and crossed his arms. "So, somebody came in right after you, found the card, but thought it expedient to snitch the evidence there and then. I wish you had."

"At the beginning of our association, you indicated I wasn't to do anything without your permission. Believe it or not, I try to follow those instructions."

He raised an eyebrow in disbelief. "Except when you fall through rotting ceilings, tumble into trunks and run into *ghosts*."

"We both know it's a person in this hotel. That's just what I'm calling it until we know who."

"Exactly. See? You know perfectly well the difference between your daydreaming visions and reality."

His reassurances, important to her for some reason, made her smile. "Anyway, the back of the card had a personal message. *For old times' sake—a party. My room. Tonight. Be there.*

"Signature?"

"No signature, but if written on the back of VanBauer's business card, there would be no need." She sniffled.

Quannah sat on the side of the bed, pulled his leg up and rubbed his ankle. "Damn, Gallagher. I think this was truly a piece of the puzzle we needed." He pulled her down beside him. "Damned important."

"More than the cape? The jewels and money?"

"Yes, *Winyan*. Think about it. The jewels and money are Ivon Paulklin's. And the paper you saw someone taking out of VanBauer's pocket."

Willi snapped her fingers. "You know, I'm not sure." She frowned, wrinkling her brow. "Maybe someone was putting something into his pocket, but you didn't find anything, right?"

"We didn't look then because of my stupid ankle, but later I scrabbled down to check. I'd hoped you wouldn't have noticed my lapse."

"No matter." Willi waved away the incident with a slight movement of her fingers. "What did you find?"

"Nothing. Nothing at all in his pocket."

"Well, guess that would have been too easy."

"Anyway," Quannah said, "the purple cape is still a complete mystery, too. Probably someone who simply wanted to pay last respects without making an announcement about it. BeeBee would be my guess, despite what you've told me concerning her feelings. The card is the first clear link to Andrew VanBauer."

He stopped rubbing his ankle, got up and helped her remake the bed.

As she patted the pillow into place, she said, "That link points to Uzell Speer. Why would Andrew VanBauer send for Uzell last night when their encounter on the Amtrak made it plain Uzell feared the congressman, and Van-Bauer in turn held the train attendant in disdain?"

"What encounter? Witnessed by you and who else?"

Willi explained about the congressman ordering coffee. "Elvis was there, of course. Royce Droskill came in for a moment, but VanBauer shooed him away. Seems like one or two others walked through, but I don't recall anyone else who heard the whole incident."

"What about this scenario? Someone else is suspected of a foul deed, though not the murder itself. That someone desperately wants us to look in other directions."

"Ah, Lassiter, I see where you're heading with this. Elvis's room. The cape. But you said that wasn't important."

"As far as the murder goes, perhaps not, but you wouldn't believe some of the secrets folks think would cause the end of the world, and usually they're the silliest things. Elvis or someone who planted the cape there wants to get our minds off that discovery or off the money and jewels."

Willi snapped her fingers. "It would make more sense that VanBauer might leave him—Elvis—a note. After all, they could share a friendship as well as a professional relationship. When we discovered the cape was his, or at least in his possession, he planted this note to imply someone else was to meet with VanBauer last night."

Quannah stood up and stretched, putting his hands to the small of his back. "Could be. We need to consider BeeBee, too. If, and I'm saying *if* she were the one who came down to the cellar to pay respects, she wouldn't want anyone to know she still cared enough to do that. She could easily have hidden the cape in Elvis's trunk."

Willi snapped her fingers. "And she would certainly fit the idea on the card: Come *'for old times' sake.'* "

"Why not, Gallagher? Be surprised how many ex-mates try to see if the old magic is there . . . or if they can hurt each other just one more time."

"That's disgusting." Willi brushed the wisps of black hair out of her face. "I got caught between them in one of their heated moments on the train. Trust me on this one. They wouldn't touch each other."

"Okay."

"Okay? You trust me on—"

"You have an uncanny knack for reading people. That with your curiosity and your penchant for the truth is good Medicine."

Willi grinned. "Uh, so I am, uh, *lee-lah-wash-tay*?"

"Yes, Gallagher, *lila waste*. Very good. We'll continue to work with Ant medicine and somehow get rid of that flighty Tweetybi—"

"Hummingbird."

He grinned, tucked her hand through the crook of his arm, drew her close to him and headed downstairs. Her heart fishtailed as if it were coming up for sunshine.

"Just for the support, you understand," he said. "What with my ankle and your bum hand and head injury."

She drew back a little. "Uh . . . of course, I wouldn't

imagine anything else. The fact that you thought I might tells me something about *your Medicine*."

"Oh, and what might that be, *Winyan*?"

"Peacock."

"Peacock?"

"Yes."

"Thank you, Gallagher."

"Thank me?"

"Absolutely. Like I said, you have an uncanny knack for reading people. Not everyone would see that I try to camouflage the steely-eyed, sharp investigator side of me with that flashier, Stetson-wearing cowboy side. We lawmen have to be colorful and friendly to get folks to confide in us, but sometimes we use that badge like feathered-out tails. Give us our space, our territory." With more pressure on her arm, he turned her toward him and winked. "Generally the male peacocks are brighter than the female of the species."

She raised an eyebrow and sighed. "Also the most arrogant of the species. So, Chief-Peacock-Who-Knows-All, who took the card from the pillowcase?" She peered up at him after she had reached the first floor.

"Not Uzell. He was down in the kitchen while you were upstairs. He never left."

She reluctantly turned loose of his arm and tapped her nose with an index finger. "I saw BeeBee VanBauer coming out of the informal conference in Ivon's room. At the time, I wondered why she hadn't come downstairs. Why would she want the note back if she had planted it?"

"You were downstairs. BeeBee could have headed back to her own room. Elvis, also in Ivon's room—right?— could have retrieved the card."

"Why, Big Chief Peacock? Answer me that."

"Could be he figured the professional card could be linked to him, and he feared we might add two and two together faster than he wanted. Perhaps he even got a twinge of conscience. Why should he get some other poor bastard in trouble? That sort of idea. We definitely have to keep an eye on Elvis."

Willi did just that. Through the light luncheon Elvis talked with BeeBee VanBauer. After the heavier evening meal of the *chuletas con salsa* with all the trimmings, followed by the promised pecan pie, he was still in BeeBee's company. She didn't seem to mind one bit. After everyone had settled in the parlor, Elvis left her side to chat with Ivon.

Willi bent over Uzell, who sat in front of the fireplace. "What's that?" she asked.

He held up a wooden carving in the shape of an old-fashioned train engine. "Circa 1850s," he said. "I be making it for Mrs. Noble. She is liking crafts and such, what you think?"

Catherine leaned forward. "My father whittled me so many figurines. Friends, too, through the years have added to the collection. I've gnomes and elves, cars and a church house, mice and horses. Oh, just all sorts of oddments. They are most precious to me. This one will be, too, because Uzell carved it."

Uzell smiled, turned back to his work and concentrated on the cattle guard on the front of the engine.

BeeBee spent a few more minutes in admiration of the piece while Willi kept an eye on Elvis. She had to. Quannah lay back with his head resting on the top of the sofa, both eyes shut. She figured it was an *Indian* thing, this ability to keep an eye on matters while not actually having either eye open. Maybe he picked up vibes, heard telltale signs from what people said. When Elvis headed upstairs, she nudged Quannah.

"Hey, Gallagher, that's my ankle, and it is still a little sore."

"Oops."

She smiled. For once she had aimed correctly. Nodding toward Elvis, she motioned that Quannah was to follow the suspect. After all, so many things pointed toward him, they couldn't afford to let him out of their sight.

Quannah strode out of the room. A few minutes later, she caught up with him, yawned, and said, "Tonight, I have to get some sleep. Since that's all you've been doing, maybe you'll watch the culprit through the late hours."

"Excuse me." Sam edged past them, his lips tightly closed. Scents of onion and garlic clung about his clothes. He looked Quannah squarely in the eye and punched his chest. "Got a *slurp-smack-slurp* job for you'un, Mr. Invest-tee-gator."

CHAPTER
14

WILLI frowned. where was the *click* that accompanied Sam's cadence of slurping?

"Yep," said Sam, "I knows what a dang fool I sound. Can't be helped. One of them here is who done it. You got to put a stop to these goings-on. Hear, boy?"

"They who did what, Sam?" Quannah folded his arms.

"*Slurp-smack-slurp* took 'um. Right out of the glass."

"I see," said Quannah, raising an eyebrow as if Willi might clue him in.

She shook her head.

"It's my teeth," Sam said.

In unison she and Quannah asked, "Teeth?"

"That's right, *slurp*, my dentures."

"You want me to investigate a set of missing dentures?" Quannah looked as if a fog had settled over his brain. He pulled on his ponytail as if to get himself headed in the right direction. "And I suppose the ghost stole your dentures? Why not? I'd believe about anything at this point."

"You know about the ghost, do you?" Sam asked.

Willi grinned. "See? There is a ghost."

Quannah raised a hand. "Don't start that—"

Sam, in full sail, said, "Right off aside of my bed. *Slurp-smack.* Might very well be her. She's ornery that a way sometimes instead of playful." He attempted a gummy smile. "Likes her better, I do, when she's playful like. Anyways, I want you should find my dang teeth, Investigator. That's what I want you to do."

"I'll do my best, Sam." He patted the old man on the shoulder.

"That's all a body can ask. I'm taking mine on up to bed. Sure hope I got my teeth back in the morning, and I'll say a mighty big thanks."

She smiled at Quannah. "I'm sure you'll be successful with the hunt. Let's see. There's the missing money, jewelry, dentures and one *ghost*. Oh, yes, and one very ugly vicious snake. Nighty-night."

Even her insatiable curiosity gave way to the undeniable tiredness, and as soon as her head hit the pillow, she slept soundly. Giggling awoke her. Since she had been dreaming of a cat-eyed girl with dark braids entwined with feathers, she thought the giggles were part of the dream. Just as the maiden raised her arms to be picked up by an Indian chief with a decided limp, Willi awoke. She still heard the giggles. Not waiting to change from her pajamas, she grabbed her robe, raced from the room, hit her knee on the occasional table outside her door and swore. She glimpsed the white-clad figure. Definitely *the* ghost. It headed up the servants' stairs. Willi followed, but once on the third floor, she trod carefully. No more falls through rotting floorboards, thank you very much, if she could help it.

The third-floor corridor, dimly lit, of course, offered no help. She tiptoed to the first door, from where loud snores emanated, slow and even like a comforting tide. Probably Sam's room. Two doors down was Jasper Farley's quarters. Stopping outside, she leaned against the wood and put an ear to the door. Snoring here, too, although of a different quality. Higher pitched and more nasal. Bedsprings creaked and the sound abruptly ceased. She figured Farley must have turned over. About to walk away, she was held spellbound by the next noise from the room. Giggles. Muffled, but giggles nonetheless. An answering grunt from Farley.

She banged on the door. "Wake up, Mr. Farley. Someone's in there with you."

Jasper Farley, from the bangs and bumps heard, must have stumbled out of bed. In another moment, one bleary eye appeared in the crack of the door. Faint light washed out across the hallway.

"Did you see her?" asked Willi.

"Her?"

"The ghost?"

Jasper shut his eye and yawned. "Done told you not to worry none about that there lady in white. Ain't no ghost. Don't need to think no more on that, Miss Gallagher."

"But I heard giggles and saw her on the stairs."

"I'll fix that jiggle in them stairs tomorrow. I got to get some sleep now." The crack in the door and the light disappeared, but his mumbling was still audible. "Don't nobody ever give a listen to me. Never have. Never will."

She shrugged and left the same way she'd come, by the servants' back stairs. As she turned to go out on the second-floor landing and toward her bedroom, an icy draft hit her legs. The last time she'd felt such frigid air had been when she had crept down to the cellar. Had someone been visiting VanBauer again? Sure enough, when she located the cellar door, it stood wide open, barely swaying on its hinges as if someone had recently swung it back toward the stone wall.

Mindful of Quannah's mishap, she eased her way down each step, shivering as she came closer to the dark well where she knew one body lay in a zippered bag. Maybe she should have told Quannah before she entered here again. Too late now. Wind whistled outside and around the high-set windows. She pulled her robe tightly about her. Dim reflection from the snow shone across Van-Bauer's body. A shutter creaked. She jumped, made sort of a hop skip across the room, and skittered to a stop beside the death briar. *Waziyata* picked up speed with a vengeance, howled and moaned in its fury.

Another, more human wail joined the cacophony.

Willi's neck hairs stood up on end.

Yiiii-hiiii-yi.

She stopped breathing. It seemed as if a rubber band had tightened around her head.

Uncertain what to do when the eerie sound engulfed her again, she scrambled backward, stumbling toward the far wall to touch her fingertips to the rough edges. Wildly upward and to the sides, she let her fingers scamper over the cold stones.

Yiiii-hiiii-ye-ahhh.

A click sounded and light—weak light—lit the area

surrounding VanBauer's body. What the snow's reflection had not earlier illuminated now stretched before her. A bundle lay on the floor beside the funeral table.

That heap of clothes shifted and collapsed. Willi inched her way, one hesitant step after another, toward the crumpled mass.

QUANNAH, in the parlor, nursed a steaming mug of coffee and worried about that pesky *Winyan*. Yes, that woman who, if she didn't stop sticking her nose in where it didn't belong, might not survive this ordeal in Lilly's Victorian Establishment. Certainly wouldn't if she kept falling through rotting ceilings and into open trunks. He rubbed the back of his neck.

Oh, Great Spirit.

The simple words were a prayer. He was not prone to call on any but his own strength, but Gallagher was beyond his meager abilities, despite his showmanship to the contrary.

Oh, no.

He had that feeling again. Each time she'd been frightened or in trouble, he'd known. He didn't want to be a part of her psychic wave length. Great Spirit be his witness, he didn't, but there it was—that inner knowing about her and her thoughts. She was up to something again. He blinked his eyes and shook his head. Nope, he'd peeked in on her moments before. She'd been snuggled in the goose down pillows and giggling in her sleep. He tried to concentrate on what Royce Droskill had said.

"Yep, I felt plumb sorry for the kid." Royce rubbed the swollen knuckles on his fingers.

"Ivon Paulklin, you mean?"

"Yeah." The old watchdog hung his head. "Spoiled. Sure, like all rich kids, but she didn't deserve what happened to her boyfriend, that young congressman Darren Stiltiman." Droskill squirmed his bulk around to a more accommodating position in the stiff-backed Victorian chair, touched the dragons carved on the sides, and shook his head. "If I'd revealed what I'd learned, I might have stopped a tragedy. Blame myself. Damn it, in a position of trust like mine, though, first loyalty is to the congressman, and let me say right here, that's the way it was. Until—"

"Until?"

"Oh, the media mongers had hinted at so much dirt, but you learn to ignore them. When one of my own buddies told me it was dirt that deserved to stick, I felt it my bound duty to prove them wrong. 'Cause I was loyal to VanBauer, I was going to investigate myself and get that proof once and for all. And I ain't going into details, but because of that research, I can vouch that any way you look at it, stands to reason she might do some kooky things to get back at VanBauer. No real harm done as far as I can see."

Quannah eyed the old law officer. Best to let him think the subject was dropped about why Royce Droskill was looking into the personal affairs of his boss. For now, Quannah would stick to the subject of Ivon, perhaps work his way back around to the other insinuations later. So, he said, "No? She did no harm? She harassed him by following him everywhere. That in itself is unbalanced."

"Maybe. Then again maybe she was at her wit's end to get some justice. She wanted to make his life miserable.

That's what she wanted. Blemish his character and his political persona some way." Royce squinted one eye and leaned over and rubbed his knees with his arthritic hands. "We can forgive a kid crazy in love. Hell, just her way of working out her grief."

"Maybe she worked her grief out in a more final way." Quannah said. "She had means and opportunity."

"Hell, Lassiter, all of us had means and opportunity."

"Ivon also had motive."

Royce just shook his head in response, obviously not buying into the theory.

Quannah, ignoring the tiny spider of worry skittering up his spine, told himself to forget about Gallagher. He had to tell himself three times before he asked, "What was the link between the train attendant, Uzell Speer, and Congressman VanBauer?"

"Thought your lady friend explained that."

"I'd like to hear your version, too."

"First time I seen that Jamaican was on the Amtrak. When my boss and him had a word tussle, I stepped in, but VanBauer waved me away. Couldn't have been too important. Probably the poor man picketed against VanBauer's reelection, brought him bad press. He hated poor publicity. Would do anything to take care of media information."

"Is that," Quannah asked, "where you came in?"

Royce sighed, winked in a good-ol'-boy fashion, and admitted with a nod, "Yeah. I did a few things to keep the wrong kind of news—couple of megabuck deals—off the wave lengths and out of print."

"What kind of news?" Quannah's dark eyes smoldered

with the certainty that Royce Droskill hid an important fact.

"Ain't likely this is real significant."

"You're a lawman. You know better."

"Former lawman, but thanks for still including me."

"Spit it out, Royce. Anything and everything could prove vital." How many damned times had he said that in the last twenty-four hours?

The skittering spider of worry played along his spine. He rubbed his neck.

What was she up to now?

He wasn't going to run through this snowbound hotel and make a fool of himself again by looking for that troublesome woman. A vision of a pair of curiously dreamy, blue-green eyes danced in his mind. A cloud of dark hair floated around a heart-shaped face. He got up to walk the cobwebs from his mind.

"I've got to know, Royce."

"Yeah."

Royce turned his huge palms upward as if to say what choice did he have. "I'm not sure, you understand, but you can check out things with his secretary, that Elvis fellow, okay?"

"Got it. This is a hunch on your part, not fact. Let's play the hunch."

"Yeah, a little bit of gut know-how, some fact. He's a featherweight."

"Elvis?"

"Nah. Andrew Mr. Wimp-Wrist VanBauer. A real weak one when it comes to the ladies."

Quannah sat back down. "You're telling me the congressman was more interested in males?"

"Damn it all! This isn't easy. I respected that man and his politics. In the light of things I . . . discovered, I'd been telling lies to the media on his behalf for years, but I swear to God, I didn't myself know the real nature of those fibs."

"Okay. You thought he was a straight-shooting man in every sense of the word until you tried to prove those rumors wrong?" Quannah considered this shocker a moment. If true, no inkling had ever reached the media.

"Know what you're thinking," Royce broke in. "Reason nothing was known, he was discreet. Ain't never told the Paulklin kid, but I think that's why her boyfriend killed himself, and she must have found out some way."

"Fill in the gaps, Royce."

The old Ranger rubbed his knuckles again and grimaced. He sat on the edge of the chair. "The kid's boyfriend gets put on this committee with VanBauer. Now, this"— he held up a gnarled finger for emphasis—"is fact. VanBauer pulled strings to have Darren Stiltiman moved from another group to his. Checked it with one of my buddies who overheard the negotiations. Fact one, that's what I'm telling you."

Royce warmed to his theme. "To make a long story short, the meetings got later and later, just like the Paulklin kid said. Okay, then, here's what happened, and the kid don't know this. The members drifted off earlier and earlier. Except for Paulklin's boyfriend—that Stiltiman— and VanBauer." Royce raised his eyebrows. "See what I'm getting at here? Couple of times I took both of them to fancy hotels. VanBauer said for a fine gourmet meal and to discuss finer details of the program. I figured he was grooming the kid politically for a second-in-command."

Quannah nodded. "Could have been. No romantic liaison can be proven simply because they ate together in a fine restaurant."

Royce waved the statement away with his big hands. "Looky here. About the third time I took them late at night, VanBauer tells me to get lost. He'll find him a taxi. They gots lots to do. Stiltiman, in the meantime, has been promised the moon and stars in the political arena. Done heard all that while I drove them to these fancy places. To make a long story short, I get lost one night. For about an hour."

Royce narrowed his eyes and lowered his voice. "Listen to this here now. Listen, Lassiter. God's truth coming up."

Quannah rubbed his neck, glanced overhead and finally glared at Royce in an effort to concentrate. "Get on with the tale."

"I was bound and determined to prove to that nasty-minded compatriot of mine that VanBauer was just the brunt of a horrible media plot to mess with his reputation. So's I come back in the hotel. I was a free agent since he told me I had the evening off, right? Could do what I wanted, where I wanted. That's the way I seen it."

"Agreed. What happened?"

"Anyways to make a long story short, in that fancy hotel I went up like I was a going to register. Used to—like in this old place—you just signed your moniker, but now you got these sweet-faced babies tapping your life history into a computer. I answered all the questions and asked if my boss, Congressman VanBauer, had checked in yet. They ain't supposed to tell you room numbers, so's

I didn't ask. Sure enough. Little fool says he and the young congressman had come in at the same time to register. Separate rooms."

"Separate rooms? Then what the hell have you been rambling on for, Droskill?"

Veins stood out on Quannah's forehead. If he reached up, he'd touch a giant tarantula sitting on top of his head, squeezing his mind, worrying him with its hairy legs.

She was into something, maybe hurt somewhere.

"Damned—"

"Son, you got to learn patience."

"Sorry, Droskill. That wasn't directed at you. Go ahead."

"Little girlie talked to another customer. I turned that TV part of the computer around. Got the room numbers. Went on up. Now to make a long story short—"

"You were going to do that thirty minutes ago!"

"Anyway, rooms were three doors down from each other. Circumspect is what my old English teacher would have said. She's the type that'd purse her lips and say that kind of word out her nose, you know?"

"English teacher?"

Quannah figured his tarantula had to be of the blood-sucking species. What else could account for the rush of blood to his head? His insides roiled.

Undisturbed by this phenomena, Royce continued. "Anyhow I sat, oh, a couple of hours. Didn't read. No nap. Had both doors in sight." He paused for emphasis. "Young feller comes out of VanBauer's door. Never went into the room registered to him, I bet. VanBauer saunters out after a while. Me? I keep hidden behind them dang potted bushes, plants, whatever they always have in hotels.

"Pretty soon a little Mexican lady comes along. I show my gun and ID. She thinks she's got to do anything I say. Opens up VanBauer's room. Couple of drinks on the nightstand. Other things we won't go into. No papers in the wastebasket and no broads, in case you're wondering, stashed in the bathroom. In the young congressman's room there's nothing. *Nada.* I'm telling you facts. Guys will do crazy things in the name of gosh-awful almighty politics. That's what that young Darren Stiltiman did. Then regrets it later. Zippo. Wraps his car with him in it around a tree. End of the tale."

Royce got up, shook himself like a wet dog after a bath, and clapped his broad hand on Quannah's shoulder. "Might as well go looking for Willi. Knowed you was worried about her."

Quannah spluttered, "Gallagher? You've got to be kidding. She's sleeping, and if she wasn't, I'm not chasing after her, and I'll be damned if I worry about that woman. Where did you get such a fool idea?"

"Son, I know my grammar and my book education ain't what they's supposed to be for these modern times. Law officers now have degrees in literature sometimes, if that don't beat everything, but all of us develop a knowledge of folks and happenings. I got that *fool* idea the same way I had a feeling I ought to check up on VanBauer and Stiltiman that night." He grabbed his battered Stetson off the mantle. "Not all the hound dog's seeped out of these old bones, son." He clamped the hat on and walked out.

A distant scream broke the silence. Like a cloud dissipating, the worry shrank in size as his anxiety eased. At least he knew where Gallagher was—down in the cellar screaming ninety to nothing.

CHAPTER
15

WILLI stopped screaming by the simple expedient of biting down on the base of her thumb so hard droplets of blood appeared on the surface of the skin. Luckily, she hadn't chosen her wounded hand. Mesmerized, she stared at the drops of blood. Her world tilted at a precarious angle, righted itself, and moved in slow motion. An angry tirade erupted behind her on the stairway. A crazed Indian, with wildly flying hair and blood red eyes, wavered within her eyesight. His mouth opened and closed like a catfish. He grasped her arms.

"What in the world is wrong now, Gallagher?"

She pointed to the pile of rags on the floor. At least, that's what they'd been when she had first seen them, but they had moved, groaned before settling into the heap that the disheveled Quannah now bent over to inspect.

The wind created a frosty swirl around Willi's ankles,

but that was nothing compared to the chill wrapped around her heart. My God, had the Snow Snake somehow crawled inside her and claimed her lifeline? She fought for breath and shivered.

"It's BeeBee . . . ermine all bloody . . . thought it was just rags, but . . . is she . . . is she . . . ?"

Quannah took BeeBee's pulse. "Her throat's been cut. Face smashed, but she's alive. I don't think it's as bad as it looks. Help me, Gallagher. Damn it, snap out of it and help me."

"What . . . what do I do?" She knelt beside him.

"The cut isn't deep at all." He grabbed her hand to make her apply pressure to a pulse spot. "Press hard, Gallagher."

Quannah frowned and mumbled. "He hit her first."

"Who?"

"Whoever. Hit her hard in the face." He peered around the area. A few feet away was a corn pestle. "From Sam's kitchen, no doubt." Quannah held it gingerly in the middle before setting it on part of the torn mattress ticking.

"That's blood on the end?" she asked.

"Probably. He hits her with this. She struggles. He drops it and goes for his knife." Quannah lifted Willi's fingers away from BeeBee's neck. A thin line of blood rose to the surface, no more mortal a wound than the bite on Willi's thumb.

"See?" he said. "Not a deep cut at all."

"Thank goodness."

He pulled out a clean, white handkerchief, neatly folded, and applied it to the wound. "Got anything to hold this on?"

She pulled off the sash of her robe. By the time they

had the makeshift bandage in place, BeeBee's eyes fluttered and opened wide in fright.

"It's me, Willi. Investigator Lassiter, too."

Quannah took BeeBee's pulse again. "You're going to be fine, Mrs. VanBauer."

"Of course, I . . . I am." She had to try twice before the words were strong and clear. They created a wispy vapor in the glacial temperature. "Did you catch him? You didn't . . . let him . . . get away . . . did you? Who . . . ?"

"You don't know who hit you?" Quannah asked.

Willi helped BeeBee sit up with her back supported by one of the table legs. Andrew VanBauer kept a silent watch above them.

BeeBee sighed, touched her bloodied ermine and whimpered. "No, oh . . . look . . . my beautiful fur."

Quannah narrowed his eyes. "Mrs. VanBauer?"

"No, no chance . . . to see. Noise . . . behind me." She seemed to have trouble swallowing, reached up and touched her neck. "What's—?"

Willi patted her hand. "A few cuts and bruises, but—"
BeeBee groaned.

"You turned around and—?" Quannah persisted.

"Something hit me . . . twice. My face—" She gasped. "Broken nose? Why . . . would anyone do—?"

"No broken nose. And you're right. Why would anyone in this hotel do this to you, Mrs. VanBauer?"

Directing her look to the seeping stone floor rather than at either Willi or Quannah, she said, "I don't . . . know." Her eyelashes fluttered against her bruised cheeks. "I can't believe—"

"Okay, Mrs. VanBauer. Calm down. One more question and we'll see about getting you comfortably settled in your room."

". . . throat hurts. No . . . talk."

"A simple one. Why were you here in the cellar?"

"Go catch . . . him." She tightened her hold on Willi's hand. Anger came through her disjointed words. "Find . . . damned ass. Oh, what I'll have to go through . . . before facing . . . cameras again."

"Do you want to catch whoever did this?"

"So—?" BeeBee glanced at Willi and then at the disheveled Quannah. "Oh, okay. Came down because . . . because I found out about . . . *him* . . . sorry bastard." She peered upward at the zippered bag. "Came to . . . berate . . . vent anger. Stupid . . . I've been so—"

Willi spoke through her chattering teeth. "Completely different reason than your purpose in coming to see him last night?"

"What?"

BeeBee sat up straighter to pull away from Willi's support. She grasped her throat. "Never been . . . here before. Can't . . . talk . . . more right . . . now. *Please.*"

Willi thought her words held the ring of truth. So, if BeeBee VanBauer hadn't paid her last respects to him, who had unzipped the bag? What paper had they found and why was it important?

Quannah nodded at Willi. Between them they hefted BeeBee. Questions nagged at Willi all the way up the steps. Getting BeeBee settled took a couple of trips to the kitchen for hot water bottles, warm milk and toast. As Willi took a knife from the wooden holder and sliced the freshly made bread and buttered it, she worried about the questions like a badger fretting over its prey. She *would* find answers.

The trudge upstairs didn't help her concentration, and there was a hullabaloo going on inside BeeBee's room. Elvis, more white-faced than usual, peered down at the battered BeeBee. Ivon and Droskill stood in the far shadows.

BeeBee moaned and pointed at Elvis.

"You. All along. Not another *woman. You.*"

She waved a buff-colored card in his face. "This atrocity can't ever get to the papers."

Willi frowned. My, hadn't BeeBee's speech abilities improved after only a short time.

BeeBee continued to rant at Elvis. "Get out of my sight, you . . . you, pervert."

Willi set the tray down and grabbed the business card from BeeBee's fingers. She handed it to Quannah. "Here's the note on the back."

She glared at BeeBee. "From just where did you pilfer this?"

"This"—BeeBee waved her hands to take in the hotel and its clientele—"is a life-and-death situation. Your Indian scout wasn't doing *anything.* You *certainly* didn't seem to be *helping* him. I went snooping on my own. Damned good thing, too. That's what I found. That's proof."

Elvis raised his hands imploringly toward Quannah. "I don't know what she's talking about. I never saw that card before. Well, not the writing on the back, anyway."

Before the accusations were completed, he denied everything. "Hey, only time I've been in the cellar was to help Royce Droskill and you with VanBauer's body. I haven't been roaming around in a cape or otherwise. And to set the record straight, I'm not of a homosexual bent."

BeeBee sighed and looked dramatically toward the ceiling.

"Not," Elvis said, "that I've anything against anyone's lifestyle. Live and let live, but *that* wasn't *my* scene."

He looked toward the shadowy corners at Ivon.

Ivon swung her bright hair from her face and stepped into the light. "Of course not." She smiled and tentatively placed a hand on his arm. "Anyone can see you're not. If it had been true, I'd have been very disappointed."

"Now look," Elvis said, pushing his curl from his forehead, "If I'd wanted to do him in, I could have used my own handgun." Elvis groped behind Royce's chair, brought his ever-present briefcase out and opened it. "See?"

Quannah took the revolver. "A .44 Magnum, Smith and Wesson?"

"That's right," Elvis said. "Model 547. I've had it for years. Congressman VanBauer knew I carried it. In fact, insisted I get special training. Droskill can vouch for that."

"Yep," Droskill said, "Sure can. Went out on the range many a time with him. He qualified on small arms and the rifle. Think his favorite would be his Ruger Mini-14."

With a white handkerchief, Elvis wiped the moisture from his upper lip and hairline. "I had nothing to do with the congressman's personal life and didn't slit his throat."

Willi quirked up one side of her mouth. "Exactly what any sane person who doesn't like the stench of electrified skin—particularly his own—would say. You aren't stupid. What better way to draw attention from yourself than to use a means other than one so clearly associated with you?"

"The facts are, Elvis, that you had access to the knife in the kitchen," Quannah said, narrowed eyes glistening with predatory gleam, .

"And," BeeBee screeched, "that battering stone you used on me."

"Yes," Quannah continued, "the pestle. Certainly, as VanBauer's trusted aide, you could walk right up to him and surprise him in the chair, which would account for his not struggling. Motive? Perhaps, in time, we'll find one. Now, I'm wondering if you used another kitchen knife to attack BeeBee tonight after smacking her with the corn pestle?"

BeeBee pointed to the calling card. "This is what he was after. He left Ivon's room for a while this afternoon. I was standing at the door and could see through the crack. Elvis marched out of Uzell's room and went toward the bathrooms at the end of the hallway. When he came back, he didn't say a word." BeeBee rubbed her eyes. "I waited about half an hour and went to see for myself. He planted this in that poor man's pillowcase."

"No, I . . . I only went in to chat." Elvis swallowed and stared at Quannah and Willi. "He wasn't there. I went back to Ivon's room."

"Be that as it may," said Quannah, "there's still the question of the knife someone used tonight."

"Search me," said Elvis. His curl was damp with perspiration, which streamed down into his eyes. With the back of his hand, he wiped the moisture away. He repeated, "Search me."

Quannah and Royce Droskill took Elvis back to his

own room and did just that. The clincher came when they didn't locate a knife on his person, but did find a bloody one between the mattress and springs.

"Hey," Elvis said, "someone's setting me up. I've never seen that before now. You've got to believe me."

Quannah shook his head, borrowed another plastic baggy from the kitchen and sacked the evidence. Afterward, he locked Elvis in a small downstairs cupboard with only a cot and quilts for company. For all intents and purposes, the guilty party was arrested as far as hotel arrangements would allow.

Willi waited at her door as Quannah climbed the stairs. She wanted to reach out, straighten his wild strands of hair, touch his strong jaw, and kiss his bruised nose. She held out her hand to stroke his face.

He said, "Gallagher, go in your room. Lock it. Don't come out until I come for you in the morning."

Instantly, she withdrew her hand and bristled. "Says who? Big Chief to Pocahontas?"

"*Winyan* . . . just because one snake is caught doesn't mean you're safe from everyone." He sighed, grabbed her to him, and kissed her soundly, letting his lips linger for a final slow caress. Shocked, she didn't respond, but she didn't push him away either. He gave her an ambiguously meaningful look, shoved her into the bedroom, and repeated, "Lock your door."

She stood staring stupidly at the wood for at least a minute before she locked and chain-latched herself in. Her fingers played over her lips—lips still tingling from his touch. Quannah Lassiter's caress held more than any kiss she had ever experienced, a promise of things to come. She smiled at the thought, took off her robe and curled up in bed. In the dark she whispered *sweet dreams*, wondered if he got the mental message, and giggled. The Snow Snake was locked up. There'd be no more silent swish of blades, no more blood—just peaceful, sweet dreams.

"SO much for sweet dreams," willi said, eying uzell Speer and Quannah's woebegone expressions. She asked, "Are you sure?"

The Amtrak steward nodded.

Quannah said, "Gone."

Willi echoed, "Gone? Escaped?"

The sound of percolating coffee jangled instead of soothing. The scents of cloves and cinnamon hung heavily in the kitchen.

Uzell Speer, chocolate eyes lowered, said, "Yes, miss. I be telling the truth of this matter, what you think?" He set a pan of hot rolls, icing oozing over the sides, on the table. "Sit. You must be eating. Then the working can be going better, what you think?"

Quannah sat, shoulders hunched. He ground out each word. "My fault. He escaped during my watch. Thought I was rested enough to take the next two watches instead of having someone relieve me. I . . . I dozed off."

Willi grasped his forearm and squeezed. "Don't do this to yourself."

Uzell poured steaming mugs of coffee. He pushed one toward Quannah, held out a chair for Willi and placed the other mug in her hands. "Mr. Droskill be telling us this morning you had the killer sitting in the storage area. When I be coming into the kitchen to be helping with breakfast, the door is opening like you be seeing now."

Quannah stared at the empty cot. "And I was here— *right here*—sawing logs like some rookie."

"Stop that. Don't be so hard on yourself. You'd just come off a drug heist case where you probably didn't sleep days on end, then got pushed into this mess, twisted your bum ankle. Thank goodness, it's okay again, but hey, you were due the rest, and all you got was aggravation." Willi peeked around his shoulder into the shadowy little room. "He took the quilts."

As one, all three peered out the kitchen windows at the storm, which had turned into a true blizzard during the night. Now, the world outside was blinding white and ice as far as Willi could see. Snow devils twirled across the terrain. The back door crashed open. Willi jumped. Jasper Farley and Royce Droskill labored beneath two loads of firewood. Quannah and Uzell went to their aid.

"Shoot me for a monkey," Royce said, "if I've ever seen such a dang cold winter since I was a kid up in the Panhandle."

"Two more loads and we'll have her done," said Jasper. "Sorry about your prisoner. Uzell told us. Think he's in the hotel somewheres?"

"Maybe," said Quannah. He rubbed his hand over his face. His ponytail, neatly gathered at the back of his head, lay against his broad shoulders.

To the two men he said, "Come to the parlor when you're finished with the firewood. We'll do a search." He looked at the increased vigor of the storm outside the windows and shook his head. "I hope we find him inside."

"Darn sure better." Farley pulled his parka over his grizzled head and opened the door. With the bristling wind blowing flakes and ice through the door, Willi barely caught his last words. "Anyone not fetched up to shelter in this here ain't gonna last long. Specially a city fellow."

Quannah assigned particular areas of the hotel to one of four pairs: Ivon and Uzell, Royce Droskill and Catherine Noble, Sam and Odessa, Willi and himself. He said, "After your section has been searched and locked so Elvis can't find refuge in those areas, report back here. Be careful."

After an hour, a subdued group huddled in the parlor around the fireplace, which Jasper Farley had stoked up to a fiery blaze. In her dovelike way, Catherine Noble perched on the edge of a sofa beside Uzell. He reached into his pocket and drew forth the carving of the train and shyly handed it over to Catherine.

Willi leaned down to study his whittled masterpiece. "That's beautiful, Uzell. You ought to take it up and show Mrs. VanBauer when we're allowed to unlock her door."

"What you think? Yes, miss, I might be doing that."

On the other end of the sofa, Ivon Paulklin wrapped her arms around herself. Her cigarette dangled from two fingers. Ashes dropped to the sofa.

"God-awful. That's what my life is. Why did I let myself care even for a moment? So why can't I make myself believe he's guilty? I think he's been framed. Stupid misunderstanding, that's what this is."

She ground the cigarette to a stub in the ashtray as if it were responsible for all of them being here in the early-morning hours looking for an escaped murderer.

Royce sat down and sighed. He rubbed his knuckles before resting his elbows on his knees and allowing his hands to hang down.

Quannah said, "No luck, Droskill?"

With his hound dog eyes, Royce peered upward. "Worse luck. My kit was jimmied. He took my weapons."

"Which were?" Quannah narrowed his eyes. Willi walked over to stand beside him.

"My pump action, Laser 12 gauge."

"Laser?" Willi frowned and raised her hands, palms up.

"Yes, ma'am. It was a special law enforcement order only twelve and a half inches long and equipped with a laser aiming device that can pinpoint a target at night."

Quannah crossed his arms. "You said guns. What else?"

"My Colt Detective Special. Six-shot."

"Anything else?" Quannah's lips were compressed so hard a tic developed at the corner of his mouth.

"He didn't get my boot gun. A special type of 357 Magnum." Droskill pulled the pistol from his boot.

"Yeah," Quannah said, "I used to have one like that. The C.O.P." He took it and turned it for Willi to view. "Only one inch wide, but it has four barrels." He placed a hand on Droskill's shoulder. "Don't feel too bad. I was the dumb one. He also got his own .44 back, but not mine that I keep under the mattress. That's what I get for not truly sleeping, just dozing now and again for the past week. Damn, I should have—"

Willi put a finger across his lips. "At least, he's not in the hotel, right?"

"No," Quannah said, "he's not so far. Each of our groups has one other place to look, and we'll be sure."

Sam, smacking noisily, bustled in and wiped his hands on his long apron depicting red chilies on a green background. He stood to one side between Odessa and Farley.

While the others searched, Farley had laid the fires, but

now stepped forward. "What you want me to be doing, Mr. Investigator?"

"Got any kind of weapon?"

"Yes, sir. An old deer rifle."

"Stay in the foyer and the parlor downstairs in case we flush him out this way somehow. Don't take any chances. If you can, just get out of his way and let him go. Use the rifle only if you're directly attacked."

"Can do."

"You heard me? You understood?"

"Sure enough, Mr. Investigator. I guard the foyer and parlor, don't take any chances unless he threatens me."

Willi grinned.

"Oh . . . right." Quannah said, handing Droskill's weapon back to him. "You stay with Mrs. Noble and keep this ready just in case."

"That leaves Ivon and Uzell without a weapon," Willi said. "And Sam and Odessa."

"Oh, Good God, no it doesn't." Ivon fished a three-inch square, plastic box out of her purse. "It's an alarm. I pull this pin out, and we'll probably have an avalanche. Just come quick if you hear it, okay?"

"No problem. Odessa and Sam will be in the kitchen. They're through with the other areas. Lock the door, Sam." Quannah grabbed Willi's elbow. "Okay, this is the final look-see. Be careful and meet here in fifteen minutes."

It took more like a half hour, and the search proved futile as far as locating Elvis was concerned. Willi and Quannah had discovered an interesting trove, though.

"So, Mr. Big Chief," she said, "what do you have to say now?"

When she and Quannah stood before all the others again, he held something behind his back and pursed his lips. "Hey, now. Hold up there, Gallagher. I said from the first I didn't doubt you'd seen someone. Can't blame a fellow for ribbing you some about your term of *ghost*. I can see now why you might have thought that."

He pulled a white diaphanous gown from behind his back and held it up.

"This belong to anybody here?"

Willi peered at each person's face. Well, well, there was definitely a reaction, but not at all the one she'd expected.

Three folks' faces turned as many different shades of red as the flames in the fireplace. Leaning toward Quannah, she said, "Why do I get the feeling we're about to learn some more from Coyote—the trickster—who teaches with humor?"

"**WHO**," asked Quannah, "can explain this?"

He waved the gossamer gown in front of the assemblage.

Jasper Farley pulled an earlobe and shuffled forward. Sam smacked his lips on his dentureless gums and inched up beside him. Odessa blinked, adjusted her wig, but at last sidled alongside the two other hotel employees.

Odessa said, *"Los hombres son tontos."*

"Don't you," Jasper said, "go spitting that Spic at us. This here's your fault. You wouldn't listen to me, you hardheaded old woman. Never have and never will, that'd be my guess. Ain't that right, Sam?"

"Well, *smack,* being in the right and honest way of it, Farley, best we fess up maybe to our part, too." To Quannah he said, "Might be we're caught in the net, so to speak."

Seeing Quannah's fierce visage grow sterner, Sam said, "What I mean to say is . . . fish net . . . like we might be red herrings on a case, that's what I mean. This thing you're holding and us . . . well, we're not really important to what's a-going on here, and—"

"Hold on, Sam." Frowning, Farley nodded and dug in his left ear with his ring finger. "Uh . . . okay, then . . . maybe Mr. Investigator . . . seeing as how I'm your deputized deputy and all, we might take this matter into . . . uh . . . more private quarters."

Quannah eyed the three characters. He studied the gown in silence. At last, he raised an eyebrow in Willi's direction and motioned with his head toward the kitchen.

She nodded. "Might be best." She led them into Sam's domain and shut the door.

Jasper considered the toes of his work boots. "Guess I owe you an apology, miss. This here's your . . . uh . . . *ghost.*" He thumbed in Odessa's direction.

Willi took the gown from Quannah and waved it in the air. "Explain, somebody, fast. If this has something to do with the murder of Andrew VanBauer, we've got to know before heading out for Elvis."

"*Ay, ay, ay. No, señorita.* This, it does not have nothing to do with any killing. Eh, what you believe, huh? I go slashing up bodies with my cleaning brush?"

Shuffling up and moving Odessa aside, Jasper said, "I tried to tell you to pay no nevermind to the ghost. It didn't have nothing to do with the killing of that politician feller."

"Don't *slurp* see," said Sam, "what's the big fuss over a damned silly Republican. Democrat would be different. A loss to the world."

Odessa grinned at Sam. "*Sí,* you aren't so bad, *hombre. Aquí.* Here." Odessa pushed her hand in her apron and pulled out a baggy with a set of dentures. "These you can have back now."

Sam popped them in his mouth. "Should have knowed you had them. Jealous, weren't you, Odessa?"

Quannah slammed his hand down on the table, the veins in his forehead showing prominently. Willi, with tentative fingertips, touched one that actually rippled as if Quannah had metamorphosed into the Hulk.

She leaned over and whispered, "*Patience,* Lassiter, patience."

Hands on her hips, she faced the three employees of Lilly's Victorian Establishment.

All three now had mouths closed up as tightly as oysters guarding their worldly collection of sand.

She smiled and straightened Odessa's collar. "When I came upstairs the first night, Odessa, what were you doing in the attic?"

Odessa scratched the side of her head, which toppled the red wig to one side.

"*¿Quién sabe?*"

"*You* know." Willi stared into Odessa's black eyes. "You know exactly what I'm talking about."

Odessa shrugged. "The night you went *loca* in the shower?"

Folding her hands together and holding them tightly, Willi managed not to strangle the old biddy's scrawny neck. Quietly, she said, "Yes."

"*Sí,* I remember 'cause I was thinking then what you need, *mujer,* was an *hombre.* That's what's wrong with your nerves. And there, right there you got this fine-looking one." She smiled at Quannah. "In your room. I did everything I could to help you."

"What?" Willi gasped.

"What you mean what? Sure. Odessa knows what the *hombres* like. That's what I'm trying to tell you. I scare you, see? The man here—oh, he is so *guapo*—comes to rescue his *mujer*. I spray your bottle of perfume. Your scent, *sí*? So, you have the scene all romantic and set."

Odessa slapped her forehead. "And what do you go do? Throw the bottle at the door, break it." Odessa pinched her nose between forefinger and thumb. "Overkill. That's no way to get an *hombre*. I should know. Me? I got two."

Willi gulped and took a deep breath.

"You did the same thing for Ivon Paulklin, didn't you?"

"I am a romantic at heart. *Sí,* this I admit. Again, I mean only to spray, but her bottle is not a spray and slips from my fingers. Ah, you young girls, you know nothing."

Quannah pulled his fingers through his hair, loosening it from the rawhide thong at the nape. "*Señora* Morales, I'm not of a romantic bent right at the moment either. I'm all cop. Mad cop. Think of me as your worst nightmare— one of those card-searching guys on the border. One that never gives up looking for those who've snuck across and hidden in out-of-the-way little Texas towns like Lillyville. One who wouldn't mind kicking one old woman back across the *Río Grande*. This is clear to you, yes?"

"*Sí,* but who says I don't have my cards? *Mi tía,* she has them. I just got to send to Laredo to my aunt. *No problema.* This old woman no go back over the *Río Bravo*."

"Odessa," Quannah said quietly. "You know and I know where the truth of that lies. I'm not a border cop,

could care less if we call it *Río Bravo* or *Río Grande* . . .
and unless I'm suspicious, I probably wouldn't question
a *cooperative* Hispanic lady. For all I know, you could be
Puerto Rican or Salvadorian or Cuban, not from Mexico
at all. *Cooperation,* you *comprende*?"

Odessa adjusted her wig and bit her bottom lip. "The
night this *mujer* screams in her shower, that was the night
I visit Sam. The last night for a long time. We have a
little fight. I get even, that's what I do. So, I take his
dientes, but only for a day." Odessa pointedly stared at
Sam, turned her back, but she didn't miss a chance to
wink again at Quannah.

Willi sighed. Covered all the bases, Odessa did.

Jasper Farley squirmed. "Get through with the telling,
Odessa. They got to look for that fella."

Odessa smiled at him and patted her curls. "*Bien,* here
there's just me and the boys"—she waved her hand to
include Sam and Farley—"here alone most of the time
because, you know, the Miss Lilly, she is retired to the
farm out in the country. Is very lonely all year in this
place except for spring and summer when the *turistas*
come for the local craft fairs and ranch roundups. *Ay, ay,
ay,* but we are not *los muertos*—the dead ones, no. I like
both Farley and Sam. Most of the time."

Sam, wiping his hands on his apron, said, "Odessa went
plain crazy when I took some time with Catherine Noble."

"*Sí,* I got the hot blood, but you going to have a cold
winter, *hombre, muy frío.*"

"Now, Odessa," reasoned Farley, "don't seem right you
can carry on with the both of us, and we can't take a
chance at being with somebody else now and again. Ain't
like the opportunity arises real often hereabouts."

Before Odessa could argue her side further, Willi interrupted. "Why the sneaking around?"

"Porque," Odessa said, "I know they get jealous of one another."

"I see," Willi said.

Quannah braced himself with both his hands against the table, pushed away, and stood. "This . . . uh . . . has been interesting but I don't see it having anything to do with Andrew VanBauer's killing."

"Hold on, just a pea-picking minute, Investigator," Sam said. "I might have been wrong about us just being red herrings in your investigation."

"Those, Sam, are only in make-believe murder tales, not—" Willi began in her best English teacher voice.

"Well, ma'am, I know I probably misquoted myself about this and 'scuse me for interrupting, ma'am, but I'll forget if I don't get this out now. Tell him, Odessa, go on. What you done seen that night."

"What?" Quannah prodded.

"Me? I see someone else out playing ghost." Odessa scratched underneath her wig. "Purple cape floating. What I think is she—that Catherine—is after Sam, so me, I follow. Is dark in the cellar and these eyes don't see so well, but this crazy person unzips the bag. They puts something in . . . or maybe takes something out of the bag. *Loco.*"

"Was it a man, then, not a woman?" Willi asked.

"No sé. At least, I don't know at first." Odessa patted her wig. "Later when you are falling through the roof, I see the person, and he's carrying the cape. He runs into the young man's room."

Quannah pursed his lips, stepped up nose to nose with

the maid and tapped her on the shoulder. "Maybe you'd better call your aunt in Laredo."

A heartbeat later, Odessa raised her hands in the air. "Cooperation. That's what you say. Okay, here, this is what I know. That man who help Farley with the chores—him—he hid the cape. The *hombre* who has the sick hands."

"Thank you, *Señora* Morales. Farley, Sam." Quannah handed over the gown before he muttered, "Fine. Everything's fine. You three can go do . . . whatever you do."

"*Ay,* the way you think, I like." Odessa winked at him and patted him on the arm. "But during the working hours, we are all business."

Quannah nodded to Willi and they left the three to their chores.

She asked, "Are you all right?"

"Oh, fine. Everything's coming up blooming roses, Gallagher. *Great Coyote's Balls.* Cold corpse in the cellar. Near corpse resting in bed. One escaped murderer. Three looney tunes in the kitchen playing who knows what kind of kinky games. One aggravating woman who can't seem to stay out of trouble. Even Brother Coyote chasing his own tail could accomplish more with this zany group. Yes, *Winyan,* everything is just . . . fine." He brushed his hand through his hair, pulling more strands out of his leather tie string.

She reached up, soothed the stray hairs and replaced them in the ponytail. "You can't face those folks in there looking so disheveled."

"Don't fuss over me, Gallagher. Stop that."

"Done."

He marched off to the parlor.

Catherine, as usual, perched on the edge of the sofa. When Willi looked at Catherine's frilly blouse and crisp slacks, Willi found it hard to imagine the retired teacher with the likes of Sam, but then again some of the best couples were opposites. And she mustn't forget, Catherine Noble had her dark side, too.

Ivon opened a silver cigarette case, lit one of her filtered variety and leaned back with legs crossed, one shoe dangling. Uzell sat on a stool at Catherine's feet. Droskill, when Quannah stepped over to him, stood up and nodded.

Quannah crossed his arms. "What were you putting into the bag with your boss on Sunday evening?"

Droskill tipped the edge of his dirty Stetson up an inch. "Who saw me?"

"Willi did, I guess. Me, too, but Odessa Morales, the maid is the one who saw *who* you were."

"The maid. I was getting something out. Items I'm not at liberty to discuss. Be assured it has nothing to do with VanBauer's death."

"I'll be sure of that, when and only when, I know the whole story."

"Stop," said Ivon. She sat up and blew smoke into the air, which formed a halo around her head. She blinked her tiger eyes. "It was my god-awful stupidity." She sighed and stubbed her cigarette out. "I did a dumb thing. Might have worked."

She licked her lips and removed a piece of tobacco by using her pinkie finger. "I couldn't believe the bastard died on me. My one purpose in life had been to make his life miserable. I wanted so desperately to ruin his reputation, to ruin his name. *That* would have hurt him. Dying was too good."

She ran her tongue over her dry lips, lit another smoke and inhaled. Thus fortified, she continued. "I thought I'd cause a stink about the jewels and money. If those things had been found on him, I might have gotten some of the newspapers to pick it up that he was a petty snitch or kleptomaniac on the side. I wanted to make a small hole in his complacency, his *good* name. You two didn't see Droskill. You saw me hiding the money."

"Like I told you before," said Royce, "she's crazy sick over her daddy and boyfriend. Been keeping a fatherly eye on her, figured real easy why she did hide the goods on VanBauer. If I'd gotten you all to find everything, there'd have been no problem. I left the money on the chair." He pointed at the death chair covered in clear plastic. "I hid the jewels in one of the downstairs bathrooms. Shoot-fire, I figured you'd come across the goods and think the help did the stealing, but wouldn't prove nothing. That-a-way, Miss Paulklin gets all the goodies back and no one's the wiser. Everything's okey-dokey."

"Except for one small detail," Willi said, brushing her hair back over one shoulder.

"A rather important one," Quannah agreed.

Royce raised an eyebrow.

"Someone did steal the money from the chair," she said. "I found it, brought Quan . . . Investigator Lassiter in to show him, and the money had disappeared."

"What about the jewels?" Royce asked.

"No one's turned in any to me." Quannah asked the group, "Anybody see them in the downstairs bathrooms?"

Each one indicated a negative.

"Elvis took them," Ivon said, her voice catching and sounding more like the betrayed little girl than the fastidiously dressed socialite. "Makes sense. He knew he might have to run, found them, and decided to keep what might later be useful." She sighed. "I've no one to blame but myself. What a stupid thing to do."

"Where do you think he is?" asked Royce.

Quannah walked over to the window, where he lifted the heavy velvet curtain. "Out there, I'm afraid, and he's well armed."

He addressed the whole group about the next steps to be taken. "I'll be going after him. You all let the authorities know soon as the phone is working or as soon as a train comes down those tracks."

He was going for the final chase. Great. Just great. She'd risked life and limb to help him get to this point, but he was going to leave her here and take the glory of the arrest for himself.

Maybe.

Maybe not.

CHAPTER
17

WILLI plodded behind Quannah.

"Lassiter, for a man who just recovered from an injury to the ankle, you're setting some kind of record through this mess. Slow down."

The falling snow had subtly changed the appearance of the forest. Enormous flakes still fell, dense and heavy, but there was little wind now. The snow fused to the ground as fast as Crazy Glue, rapidly covering Willi's footsteps. The scene had an eerie quietness about it, far more unnerving to her than *Waziyata*'s loud wailings had been.

The only sounds were those of snowshoes, labored breathing and snatches of conversation between her and Quannah. Their words seemed so loud in the stillness, she had the desire to whisper. Her chest ached with the unaccustomed exertion of balancing on the snowshoes and carrying an awkward backpack.

"You'd better not give me a minute's trouble, Gallagher."

"Trouble?"

"I'm after someone who's murdered once and tried a second time."

"Wouldn't have gotten far, would you, if I hadn't come along with the snowshoes?"

"Nice of you to wait until we're hours away before letting me know." He pulled his parka hood up and over his head, effectively cutting off her vision of his leather-thong-tied black hair. He huffed with the exertion of lifting his legs with the snowshoes.

"And what," Willi asked, pushing her own dark curls away from her face, "would Big Chief Investigator have done? Sent the little woman back to camp?"

"Not without an armed guard. Let's hope Elvis doesn't realize we've got all the weapons and have virtually left the hotel at his mercy if he decides to return."

Willi stumbled over a snow-covered tree root. "Ouch! He won't. We'll catch him hiding somewhere."

"There'd have been no *we,* only *me,* if you'd not tried to sneak up on me so far out, Gallagher. This is no place for—" He stopped to take a deep breath.

"No place for a woman? I didn't try. I did sneak up on you when I was ready." There was no reason to tell him she had to mentally keep singing songs and reciting poems to keep him out of her head. Only when her brain grew weary of the self-imposed monologue did he turn and tell her to come out of the woods. She hefted the huge backpack into a more comfortable position. "Thought we were past that attitude."

Quannah merely glared over his shoulder.

Deciding to change tack, she offered, "You did get a line on Elvis at that farmhouse."

"Yeah. The couple said we're heading in the right direction—same one he took anyway. They'll let the authorities know soon as they can get into town."

"No phone at the house?"

"Nope. They're just starting out. Three youngsters no bigger than sparrows clinging to the young girl. Boy couldn't be twenty. Amazes me how some people let themselves get behind the eight ball so early in life." He stopped, bent over and placed his hands on his knees. He gulped in air.

Willi paused to get a good breath, too. She shoved her dark tresses over her shoulder and grinned. "I used to think the same thing every time one of my students ran up and showed me an engagement ring on her finger. They'd have a wedding invitation in one hand and stars in their eyes. All I could see was barefoot and pregnant, ignorance and poverty. But . . ."

"But it was worse?"

"For some, yes." Her words formed soft plumes of smoke. She rubbed her chest where the exertion of the past miles had created a numbing ache. "But the majority of those couples, ten and fifteen years later, have gone through college together, reared kids into their teens and survived. They have the invitations framed and on the living room wall. Stars still shine in their eyes. Maybe that couple on the farm are simply in love."

"Hope so." He grimaced, wiped flakes off his face, and narrowed his eyes in his search of the path ahead. "Great Spirit—*Wakan Tanka*—can turn the most depressing hardships into magical moments in an unexpected flash."

"Like that cardinal there against the snow?" The scarlet winged creature flew in a circle around them, finally alighting on a close branch.

"Yes, *Winyan,* this feathered friend is a good Medicine sign, one depicting passion for life."

"Of course," Willi said, "and sitting so beautifully against the white harshness, it's telling us that we're right where we should be in this pathway and what we run into on this path will lead to joy." Willi shook her head. "Where did that come from? It must be wrong considering we're after a killer. I—"

"*Winyan,* go with those first things to come up to consciousness. You may not understand until events confirm, but if this path helps lead to joy, so be it. That is the right message for you. Learn to—"

"I know. Learn to trust the inner voice. Seems to take a lot of practice."

"Years and years. Now, stand still a moment, Gallagher. Do you not, in this minute of space, feel all is exactly as it should be?"

"Well . . . yes, which doesn't make sense because look at all the turmoil going on—"

He grinned and raised an eyebrow.

She sighed and returned a smile. "Trust. Got it. *Trust.*"

"How much farther to reach the old mining town—dare I say, old *ghost* town?" she asked and pulled out two ski masks. "Is there a reason that concept keeps coming up and slapping us in the face—that *ghost* thing?"

"Ahhh. I believe, Gallagher, there's hope for you."

"Another three hours. Reach the old mining town about dark."

"Old ghost town, you mean." She offered him one of

the masks. "You don't think Elvis would circle around back to the hotel, do you? If he catches us out at night . . . well, he has that rifle, right? He could pick us off—"

"Stop playing the *If* game. It'll drive you crazy."

"Even in the daytime like now he could be out there waiting for two clear shots when we walk out of the woods."

"We'll hear or see him."

"You didn't see or hear me for three miles."

"But I *knew*."

"Oh, yes, but we . . . I mean we have this—"

"Mind connection?"

"Well, yes."

A smirk on his face and that damnable wink made her sigh. She should never have admitted she realized the link was there. Too late now.

The ache in her chest eased, and she moved out ahead of him. She said, "But we don't have that with Elvis."

"We are all linked, not only with humans, but with *Mitakuye Oyasin*—All Our Relations, the full circle of Sacred Life." He pulled his ski mask on.

"The *Me-Take-You-and-See*. Exactly, what—?"

"Me-tah-coo-yea Oh-yah-seen—*Mitakuye Oyasin*. This includes Two-leggeds of all colors, Four-leggeds, Finned Relatives of the waters, Winged Ones, the Standing People"—he pointed to the trees surrounding her—"the Crawlers who are upon and within the Mother Earth, and the Mineral and Stone People."

"Like my teaching stone, *Tunkasila*?"

He shuffled awkwardly by her side, hit a soft bank and lodged his snowshoe beneath it. Huffing, he pulled it loose.

"Yes, like that special calming stone. And the people of the Star Nation—those ancestors who have crossed onto the Good Blue Road, as well as the children of generations to come."

"You say them all as if each was a different race—capitalized or underlined or something."

"You do catch on to some things fast, *Winyan*. There is hope for you yet."

Quannah narrowed his eyes and pointed down an incline offering fallen trees as obstacles along with a crowded copse of living ones. "Ug-ah."

"Ug-ah?"

"Old Injun word means this-ain't-gonna-be-no-fun. Just shuffle. Don't try any full steps until we're out of this."

"No argument from me." She grabbed his hand. "I'll be careful. Tell me more about the links."

With his dark eyes—the only part of his face she could see—he stared at her—through her. "Keep moving, Gallagher."

About ten feet down the slope, he paused by a tree to rest, and said, "To all of these living things we have a connection, a way to communicate if we but open ourselves up to the possibilities."

"That makes us all as one."

"This is so."

"Then you're saying you have a mind connection to the criminals you hunt."

"Sometimes. When there is a strong current between me and the hunted, it can be fearsome on one level. Especially when flashes of their foul deeds become part of me. Other times, there may be only a tiny flicker that guides me to an important clue or pushes me to ask a question out of the ordinary."

"An awesome gift to have," she said between breaths, "especially for a cop."

"Teachers, too. You have an abundance of this gift, *Winyan*."

"Really?"

He nodded. "Remember your vision during the last case we worked on? The one with the two wolves? Wolf is teacher and protector of the tribe because of this special ability to sense things about to happen."

Willi grinned. "So when folks say we have eyes in the backs of our heads, I guess that's part of this . . . this *Wolf Medicine*?"

"Correct. All have this ability. Many never use the magic available."

"How do you live with this constant turmoil each time you confront a new case? It must be a *technospiritual* war inside you."

He winked at her, turned loose of her hand to move out in front, and continued to plow through the drifts. "It is, but I prefer that over emotional and spiritual death. You once told me yourself, Gallagher, there is never a dull day in your life. That's because you live—as one of my many grandmothers expressed it—*a little closer to the flame* than most people. So, keep your senses alert. Perhaps the Standing People or the Winged Ones will have an answer for us."

"Well, I'd just like to know one more—"

"Gallagher, that flighty, *twittering* Tweetybird Medicine is coming out in you again, and—"

"Hummingbird. That's hummingbird." She shivered

and pulled her parka hood tighter around her ski mask. He took off his shoes, added insulated socks, and said, "I have to admit, Gallagher, you thought of everything. How did you manage to lug both these backpacks so quietly I never actually heard you for three miles?"

"Extra blankets, socks and sweaters cushioned everything. However, now that we're wearing most of those, it may not be so quiet. *He* might be aware of us already."

Quannah raised his ski mask, sniffed the air and scanned the snowbound land. "No, he's not near us." She considered the place they were headed.

Twigger.

One main street with two- and three-story false-fronted stores built right at the edge of the road of mud or dust, depending upon the season. Sometime later the inhabitants bricked the main street. Her Great-Uncle Zeb Gallagher had mined coal to make a good living at Twigger. Smart enough to leave before the need for coal in Texas ran out, he'd gone into business for a fairly new company at the time, Shell Oil. Great-Uncle Zeb had made the right move.

As a youngster she had sidled onto an old-fashioned bar stool and drunk a cherry cola in one of the original thin-waisted cola glasses. Mama let her have two, each time with a fresh red-and-white-striped soda straw, before they drove back over the rough brick road to see the rest of the ghost town.

"Under normal circumstances," she said, huffing hard again, "I wouldn't have minded going back down memory lane, but chasing a killer through the boarded-up buildings of Twigger isn't my idea of a perfect winter outing. Es-

pecially since you have only your gun and Droskill's
while I have nothing."

She stumbled again, and tried to stop the clatter of pots
and pans.

He peered back at her and shook his head. "There's a
reason I didn't give you a gun."

"Why?"

"Because I don't want a slug accidentally to hit me in
the rear end. Because I like my head attached to my neck.
Because—"

"Fine, Big Chief." She sighed. "You've made your
point."

"Stop!" she yelled. "Time."

He halted so abruptly that she plunged into his broad
back, somehow tangled her snowshoes with Quannah's—
one atop his, the other below—and knocked him down
before she landed on her rear on top of him with the
backpack of pots and pans clanging in his face.

"Now that you have my undivided attention, *Winyan*—"

"Well, I didn't know you were going to stop on a
dime." She scrambled off him.

"Gallagher, Gallagher, Gallagher." His voice rose in ex-
asperation on the last repeat. "Elvis won't have to worry
about killing us. He has someone right here to do that for
him."

"Stop bellyaching." She glanced over her shoulder and
peered back up into the dark woods held prisoner like she
and Quannah by the white mantle—the Snow Snake.
Somewhere out there, perhaps even now observing them,
was another, deadlier two-legged variety. She shivered and
gasped. "I stopped . . . because . . . it's time . . . for us

to drink some liquids. Didn't they teach anything at the police academy or whatever you attended?"

"Yes. One of their warnings was not to take bothersome, know-it-all, daydreaming—"

"I do not—"

"—women along when chasing down a suspect."

"That's what I thought. You're irrational. Not in your right mind. Suffering from lack of nutrients. Here, drink this." She shoved a huge thermos toward him, but he didn't take it. "Healthaid, the drink to put minerals and vitamins back in the old bod. It's a mistake not to keep drinking in cold weather. You can die from dehydration just as easily in the winter cold as in the summer heat, Special Investigator Quannah Lassiter, *sir*." She saluted him.

"Love that limp-wristed salute. Just like a dumb old girl."

She slammed the thermos against his chest, frowned and tried to stand.

"How did I survive," he snarled, "before you came along?"

She lurched after him. "What survival skills *did* you learn on the reservation? Maybe this would be a good time to teach—"

In front of her, his stance suddenly changed.

Shoving his parka back and off his head, he turned expectantly in each direction. As if he were not close enough to the elements, he pulled off his ski mask. Like an eagle, his bronzed face pivoted. His nostrils flared. Eyes narrowed to slits.

Hairs at the nape of her neck rose. Electricity tightened her scalp. "He's here."

"Han, hecetu yelo."

"What?"

"Yes, *Winyan,* you are right. You, too, sensed his presence."

She sighed and pulled from his hold. "You think he's settled in for the night?"

Quannah shook himself. *"Han.* We'll do likewise. Or rather, you will."

"Okay, Big Chief. It's true, you know."

"What is?"

"Big Chief. When you sensed him, when your quarry came within range, you toggled a switch somewhere and became more . . . more—"

"Comanche."

"Yes, more Indian. You explained once why you speak Lakota instead of Comanche, but somehow that makes no difference to your . . . I guess you'd call it your Medicine."

"My mother chose three men to walk the trail with. With one she shared a child, with another the same tribe, and with another his language—Lakota. But certain *Medicine* doesn't come to us, Gallagher, for being born with more Indian blood than the one next to us. Everyone has special magical *Medicine* and *Totems*—some prefer to call *Angels* or *Spirits.* Some folks are aware of this magic the universe offers, others choose to ignore it even when it slaps them in the face." He shifted his stance and seemed to test the air currents.

"Slap them in the face?"

"Like your waking visions, your daydreaming episodes."

"You're always kidding me about—"

"Yes, that's that old Coyote Medicine coming out *again*."

"*Heyokah*. Yes, now I recall the Lakota word. *Heyoka* teaches through opposites, tests us by playing the devil's advocate and—as we saw back at the hotel—with humor."

"Perhaps my Indian bloodline has brought me to an earlier awareness of the *Medicine* offered by *Mitakuye Oyasin*, and the bit of Lakota language I use helps remind me of my connection to these gifts." He paused and sighed. "Gifts are nothing if not eventually shared. And Mother Earth is the place for sharing."

Goose bumps traveled across Willi's scalp. She whispered the line from Frost. *". . . don't know where it's likely to go better . . ."*

Waziyata wailed. A coating of ice crystals along a broken fence caught the last of the day's light. The quietness was a conundrum—full of sound like distant drums growing stronger until the beat flowed through her own limbs, burst into a fierce cadence in her heart. She placed a hand on her chest.

He grasped her by the shoulders and stared deeply into her eyes. "There are many ways to be Indian and to Walk in Beauty. Blood born is not the only path. You have Indian blood, and you are more aware for that reason, but anyone may seek the Sacred Path. The beat of *Unci*— Mother Earth—calls you tonight. She has called you before. These things your own heart must be open to, *Winyan*, and you will grow to understand. You've come such a long way already. *Lila waste*." He grinned. "That's *very good*."

At his unexpected praise, she grinned like a silly school

girl. *"Lee-lah wash-tay?* Really? That's twice on this trip you've given me due credit."

"Han, lila waste." Abruptly he turned. "Let's find some shelter, Gallagher."

For a heartbeat, she stood motionless, not wanting to let the moment go, not wanting the . . . the *magic* of life and that wonderful cadence to escape. Finally, she walked steadily after him, content to be out of his scrutiny and to enjoy her heightened senses. Each snowflake whispered against her skin; every star twinkled with wonderment. Wild fronds and weeds stiff with ice crackled beneath her boots.

Locating a section of wall covered with desiccated grape vines—some as thick as her arm—he set up camp of sorts on the leeward side by using discarded boards and the tarp that had been rolled at the top of his pack. The process of building shelter took some time since Willi and he had to continually stop and beat their hands against their legs to create at least the illusion of circulation.

When finished, the shelter was cozier than her room at Lilly's. She smiled and said, *"Lily wish-sh-tea."*

"Almost got it right. *Lee-lah Wash-tay."*

She nodded. "I'm a slow learner, but after I practice, I won't forget."

"Now, for heat." He started to leave the snug nine-foot by twelve-foot abode, but she grabbed his arm.

"Wait," she said. "This is one of those clanging things I've carried all day. Jasper found this and a big can of kerosene." She hefted a foot-square heater off one of the many hooks on her knapsack. "I remember going to the outdoor movies in the winter. They rented these contraptions at the concession stand. Blows really hot air and you can heat cans on the top if necessary. One problem, though—"

"You don't know how it works?"

"Farley didn't have time to demonstrate."

"Give it to me."

He had to take off his gloves, not nearly such a traumatic task within the shelter of four more or less sturdy walls.

"Ay-hi-ya!"

"What's that?" Willi asked. "A native incantation to the fire spirit?"

"As best I can translate: *Damned hot.*"

He winked and flicked a switch on the contraption. The smell of old popcorn, rancid oil and equally ancient space heaters inexplicably filled the air. Gingerly, he passed it to her by the handle, signaled her to wait a minute, and after donning his gloves, eased under the tarp flap. He hefted an armful of bricks inside the shelter. Shoveling a space clear with his gloved hand, he arranged the bricks in a square, where he set the kerosene heater on top. Enough room remained on the bricks to effectively create a ridge. She placed a battered coffeepot and pan there.

"Now, look what I did while you were scavenging some of Twigger's last bricks." A red kerosene lantern of the type often decorating barn doors cast a circle of intimate light in the small space. He saluted her effort with a grin and a nod.

"At the risk," he said, "of being a typical male chauvinist, I'm leaving you with the domestic chores while I scout around for Elvis before complete darkness makes the task impossible." He pulled a chain from around his neck and handed it to her. A huge whistle dangled from one end. "If you need me, blow this. I'll hear it even above the wind."

She nodded. "But, Lassiter, he has that gun. That rifle."

"I have skills to combat that. I've got to do this."

"Guess if I hadn't tagged along, you'd have already been out there hunting. Well, go on. I'll be fine even if I don't have a weapon."

He drew forth Droskill's and held it out to her.

"No, you keep both guns. I wouldn't know how to use one anyway. Elvis won't be able to find me the way you've hidden us behind this crumbling wall and vines."

He shoved the weapon into his boot. "That's true. Not one bit of light shows through. You'll be safe here. Would you mind getting a sandwich or something together?"

"I'll consider myself on *tipi* duty. You . . . you be careful. Do you want another drink of Healthaid? Keep that face mask on and your hood up around—"

"Gallagher?"

"Okay, no more fussing."

"Good."

"You might just want to take this flashlight, or—"

"*Winyan?* Your Tweetybird Medicine is—"

"Fine. Not another word. Go."

"*Pilamaya yelo.*"

She reached out and pulled his hood snugly around his head. With his face mask on, all she could view were his two obsidian eyes beneath his heavy lids. She shooed him outside before she removed her parka and sweater and lowered the setting on the heater. She scrounged in both backpacks for their evening meal. Farley hadn't been too particular about organization as he'd quickly thrown items this way and that.

She opened a can of beans and wieners and set them on top of the stove. Cutting cheese into bite-size pieces was a slow process until her fingers warmed up completely. She frowned at Farley's beverage choices: instant coffee or tea. When she discovered two dozen yeast rolls in a plastic baggy, she yelped with joy.

An owl hoo-hooed and another joined in the chilling chant.

Rolling out the two down-filled sleeping bags took only minutes. She nibbled on the cheese and a roll. With nothing else to occupy her hands and mind, she peered at the *tipi* opening.

Where was Lassiter?

And Elvis?

Perhaps Lassiter had already located the runaway and was bringing him back. But if Elvis sighted Quannah first . . .

The hooting owls grew in number. She frowned, having thought those raptors were loners. Their nighttime chorus picked up tempo, their squeals grew insistent, more like a pack of coyotes out for a kill.

Her heart skipped a beat. The cheese and bread formed a lump in her throat. She drank half a cup of tea and she still couldn't swallow right.

High-pitched wails rent the air. A swoosh of wings passed so close to the canvas covering, Willi could see the momentary indentation. She shut her eyes and imagined the owl with prey caught in its predator's talons. It screeched in victory while the mouse or rabbit screamed in its death throes. This was one of those times she wished for a less vivid imagination. Could have been the intended victim had escaped, and the assumed victory screech merely an agonized acceptance of defeat. Sure, cling to the fairy-tale version. But the scene kept replaying in her mind.

"Oh, no," she whispered, setting the cup aside. In his arsenal, Elvis no doubt carried his favorite weapon—a sharp-bladed knife. He could silently sneak up on Lassiter and . . .

"No, I've got to stop this train of thought." She swallowed and imagined her eyes opened as big as Gerber daisies.

Suddenly, the warmth, so welcome only seconds before, stifled her. She touched the chain around her neck and edged her fingers down to the whistle. Her heart beat erratically, not with the magical calmness of earlier in the evening. No, she would not, could not imagine one irritating, Lakota-speaking Comanche being hurt in any way.

She scrabbled in her coat for her teaching stone, but came up empty-handed. She'd left *Tunkasila* on her bureau at the hotel.

What could she do to help?

Her mind clouded with her fear. She would just step outside long enough to get air into her aching lungs, long enough to clear the miasma of panic. Yes, that's what she'd do and the sooner the better.

Air. She just needed fresh air.

She grabbed her parka and gloves and extinguished the heater. To douse the lantern, she reached out but halted. Out of the corner of her eye, she caught a movement and gasped. A knife blade—she didn't want to conjure up who was obviously holding it—pulled back the edge of the tarp.

Her world turned sickeningly cattycornered, wavered, and tilted again at a more alarming angle. Blood dripped off the tip of the blade.

She grasped the first thing to hand.

CHAPTER
18

WILLI gulped. The hand holding the knife wavered. The wind had caught the tarp and forced the attacker back a few inches. Willi held one of the extra bricks in both hands as if it were a discus about to be launched across the field. When the figure plunged inside, she used all the strength of both arms to land a resounding blow on the back of a parka-covered head. The knife dropped from limp fingers, the culprit buckled at the knees, fell down and over onto his back on top of one of the down-filled sleeping bags.

"Damn . . . you . . . Gallagher."

"Oops."

She managed that one syllable as she stared at the proud eagle she'd brought to earth. His hooded eyes shut. Behind her, the tarp flapped in the wind, wind that cut a swath through the shelter like a sharp knife through a wild mushroom, relentlessly quick. She turned to secure the corner, relit the heater and then attended to Quannah.

"But I thought . . . oh, never mind. Open your eyes. Do something."

Chagrined, she removed the leather thong binding his ponytail and washed the bump on his noggin, not nearly as bad as it could have been if his head hadn't been covered with the protective quilted parka.

Not knowing whether he could respond to her voice or not, she talked anyway to calm herself.

"Blast you, Special Investigator Quannah Lassiter! Why did you come into the tent holding a bloody knife like that? What did you think I would do? You didn't think. That's your problem." She eyed the bump on his head. "Wish I had some of Sam's poultice for you. You're hardheaded, though, so you'll be fine. You'll . . . be . . . fine. Those dumb owls. They're to blame. Oh, well, maybe my imagination did have a little . . . but I wasn't daydreaming, you hear me, Lassiter? Do you hear—?"

Continuing in this vein for some time, she finally lapsed into silence. He hadn't moaned. Hadn't moved. "You wake up. You hear me?"

She shook him. Taking his pulse, she breathed a bit easier. That seemed normal. She brushed the hair off his forehead.

"Please, wake up."

Tears pooled. When they swam down her cheek, she brushed them away and sniffed. "I can't imagine what I'd do without you." Lying down beside him, she covered them both with the other sleeping bag. The strong beat of his heart encouraged her.

"Lassiter," she whispered, "please be all right." She pulled back and looked at his face.

"I'm fine, Gallagher. Just didn't want to end your examination." He popped open one eye. "I had just killed a snake outside the tent. Can't imagine why one would be so far from its warm den in midwinter, but I've seen it happen before. Could be you called it to you with all that talk about Snow Snakes and—"

"You insufferable man. So you let me worry that . . . that—something . . . that . . . oh, you mangy excuse for . . ."

He grabbed her, pulled her down on top of him. "Repeat that, please."

"You mangy—?"

"The part about worrying . . . about me."

She had every intention of telling him the exact opposite, but his lips caressed hers, leaving her breathless and expectant. He found her ear, nuzzled aside her shoulder-long hair and whispered, "I believe I'll just play a bit of Ghost, if you've no objections . . . one of these days." Seemingly with great effort, he pulled back.

She reached up, held his head between her hands and lay a sound and long kiss on his lips, which he returned. He growled, "You'd better get into your sleeping bag and zip it up tightly . . . before . . . just . . . before . . . good night, *Winyan*." She obeyed, but it took forever for her heart to stop pounding.

In the early morning, she awoke, touched the empty spot beside her, and said, "Lassiter?"

She sat up. Where was he? Moving slowly, she located the lantern and lit it. A soft glow encased her, eased back the shadows of the space, but didn't reveal any passionate

Indian. She peeked outside. Daylight barely touched the pristine mounds of snow. The storm had abated, leaving an intense stillness, an eerie quiet.

In the distance, Quannah struggled under the weight of another man. Elvis leaned heavily on Quannah. Willi placed a brick to hold the tipi flap open. She added more kerosene to the heater and looked for something to eat. Finding the rest of the yeast rolls, she placed them near the stove to warm, added some of Sam's sausage patties, and cubed more cheese. She started the water heating and, with a blush warming her cheeks, straightened the sleeping bags at the moment the two men lumbered inside.

Quannah eased Elvis down on the bags and sat down himself, breathing in great gulps of air. Elvis fell back on his elbows and closed his eyes.

"I'm telling the truth," he said.

She raised her eyebrows in question. Quannah enlightened her.

"Found him holed up in a basement. Would never have located the place if I hadn't smelled wood smoke seeping through the door. Just looked like one of a dozen abandoned foundations. He'd started a fire to keep warm."

"And the guns?" she asked.

Elvis brushed his namesake curl from his forehead. "I don't have any. Only took mine. Thought I saw a bear, pulled it out, stumbled and dropped it down a crevice." He ducked his head. "Marksman, I am. Woodsman, no."

Willi asked, "What about the bear?"

"Well, it . . . wasn't exactly a bear. More like a really big . . . furry . . . loud . . . really huge . . . uh . . . raccoon."

She handed them both an extra-strong cup of hot coffee.

"Got sugar for this?" asked Elvis.

Opening a baggy full of sugar, she poured until he said, "Fine, thanks."

"Found him early this morning," continued Quannah. "I . . . I couldn't sleep."

Willi tilted her retroussé nose in the air. Nice to know he'd suffered a little, too. Guess other than that comment, he was just going to ignore those intimate kisses of last night. Fine with her. She could use what he'd once taught her about *Opposum* Medicine and pretend nothing important had happened.

"Well," said Elvis, "believe me, if I'd known food was here, I'd have beat you to it last night."

Quannah grinned and winked at Willi. Her heart fish-tailed at the light in his eyes. She frowned. What was the matter with her? One little smooch . . . okay, a couple of lingering kisses . . . from a wanderer such as one Quannah Lassiter meant nothing, absolutely nothing. She shivered and licked her lips. She was simply excited about . . . about apprehending Elvis, that was all. Her reactions had absolutely nothing to do with anything else. Right? *Right.*

She handed Elvis a plate of food. He sat up all the way and wolfed it down.

Again he asked Quannah about the delay.

"Got sort of waylaid . . . by a brick. Took me some time to come to my senses."

She handed him a warm roll wrapped around sausage.

He tickled her palm with his fingers as she turned loose. Clearing his throat, he considered Elvis. "Anyway, got back to you at break of light. Figured you'd be too weak to put up much of a fight."

"You're right about that. Too stupid to pack food or

water. If that young farm couple hadn't given me a meal, I'd be dead by now." He gobbled the cheese down and asked for more sausage. "Don't know why I ran in the first place. Yes, I do. I was in a panic. Would have been no trouble for me to do an imitation of *the* Elvis's trembling knees. Should have been plain someone was trying to frame me, but why?"

"Frame you?" she asked. "What are you trying to say? You didn't kill Andrew VanBauer or attack me or BeeBee?"

"Truth," he said around the remains of the sausage. "Should have known when someone conveniently left the storage room door open for me last night. They even had my parka and snowshoes close by. Figured the way you were snoring, someone drugged your supper drinks, Officer." He pushed his cup toward Willi.

She refilled it with steaming hot water, instant coffee and sugar. Pausing in midstance, she said, "Lassiter?"

"Gallagher?"

"What if . . . what if that's what happened? You being drugged, I mean. Now that makes sense." She set the hot water down. "You'd been catnapping. You'd slept fine the night before because you had taken things for your ankle. You really shouldn't and wouldn't have fallen asleep normally."

"You know, *Winyan,* you're right. I should not have doubted abilities tested many times over. It does make sense, which means—"

"Which means we'd better get a move on."

Elvis fingered his curl off his forehead. "And I swear, Investigator Lassiter, I didn't know about those other items in my backpack until I took them out after I found the old basement. Those things were planted, too, to frame me."

"What things?" she asked as the two men helped her pack items into the bags.

Quannah held up a bound group of dollar bills just like the ones she'd discovered underneath the plastic cover of the Death Chair. He also pulled out a set of jewelry matching the description given by Ivon Paulklin.

"I believe him," said Quannah. "Elvis is no fool. His whole job with Congressman Andrew VanBauer was spent in hiding a number of unsavory details from the press and revealing only the very best about the congressman. Takes a smart person to do that for so many years. He isn't *stupid* enough to keep these things on his person."

"So," she said, "he realized what an amazing amount of data had been gathered against him. Whoever did plant the money and jewels on him knew he might panic for that reason."

Quannah nodded.

She said, "So, Elvis, they took advantage of your one moment of weakness—they recognized the panic in your denials. You were used to covering up for your boss, but never thought to apply those same techniques to your own situation." She tapped the end of her nose. "But who?"

"They've all got motives," Quannah said.

An awareness enveloped Willi—a glow that had absolutely nothing to do with the coffee and heat-filled shelter. She smiled. For the first time, Quannah Lassiter was treating her like an equal, someone who had cognitive capabilities to match his own. It was, she thought, a better feeling than their kissing. Okay, almost as good. She finally said, "Yes, motives and opportunity. *Ivon*, *BeeBee*, *Catherine*, and *Royce*."

"What about that other fellow?" asked Elvis.

"There's not anyone else except for the hotel staff," said Quannah and Willi together.

"Yes, there is."

"Oh, Lassiter," she said, "he's right. Uzell Speer *has* to be included."

"You're right, although at the moment he seems the least likely unless you know something I don't."

She grimaced, thinking he was about to change from being a supportive man back into his Big Chief stance. "Well, let me consider. Everything has happened so fast. Seems like there's something in the recesses of my mind, so to speak, but . . . I can't remember . . ."

"We'll finish here. If something occurs to you, you can share it on the way."

She relaxed. "Oh . . . oh . . . okay. Sure."

Wasting no time, they ate the rest of the sausage balls and yeast rolls and finished the coffee. In minutes, Willi tromped beside the two men, and imagined they were all better for full stomachs and a strong purpose in mind. She stalked across the white world of laden snow to head toward Lilly's Victorian Establishment and a confrontation with the real murderer of Andrew VanBauer.

One horrifying thought goaded Willi into a trot. BeeBee VanBauer had been left abed, helpless against her adversary, an easy prey to the one who might think BeeBee could recognize him from the attack in the cellar.

Ironically, the stormy weather had subsided, but a relentless tempest exerted its way into her mind. A chilling blast of memories fought through the maelstrom and erupted. Ideas and past clues slithered into place for her and she shuddered. In a quiet voice she said, "I've recalled something which might be important, but I didn't think so at the time."

She told Quannah about the incident. "A cunning murderer, yes. He'd fooled all of us." In her mind's eye she viewed his confrontation with Congressman VanBauer while on the Amtrak. Blue Blazes, she had witnessed the electric shock of recognition cross his fine Jamaican features when he met VanBauer. Willi finished her tale with a question. "The congressman, in turn, had referred to them as *old friends*. What exactly did that mean?"

On mental point, Quannah tensed and edged as close as the cumbersome snowshoes allowed and said, "Guess we should catch *each other* up on information. For example, Royce provided new insight into VanBauer's lifestyle. I didn't share it with you before because I wasn't *sure* it had anything to do with this situation. I ought to listen to my own advice. Every detail is important. You don't know what it takes to admit this, *Winyan,* but I'm as guilty as you."

"So, BeeBee's wild accusations about another *man* weren't totally wrong?"

"Not at all. That might explain, too, why the congressman's card and the private note were in Uzell Speer's pillowcase."

Elvis lumbered up beside them. "I can just imagine what Royce Droskill told you, Investigator Lassiter."

"Well?" She stopped and faced Elvis.

"I suppose," he said almost reluctantly, "Royce Droskill discovered what I've tried to keep secret for years. Even before the VanBauer's marriage came apart at the seams.

BeeBee would have been much happier thinking another woman had lured him away rather than—a man. Certainly, even in these enlightened times, he wasn't willing to open his private closet, so to speak, before his political opponents. He wasn't stupid either."

Willi grasped the lapel of Quannah's parka. "Did the man not realize the time bomb he was sitting on? With the news hounds bent for every morsel of gossip much less real news, how could he hope to keep that a secret for long?" She frowned at Elvis. "I can't believe you imagined you could keep a lid on that forever."

"It's what I was hired to do, and I did it well."

"I see." She found it hard to stare him in the face, turned loose of Quannah's parka and clumsily clomped down the trail.

"No, you don't," yelled Elvis. "I'm not like him. Ivon's boyfriend wasn't either, nor was he anything great. She deserves better."

Willi paused and let him catch up. "I wasn't implying you had the same sexual predilections, nor would I have cared if you had. It's simply that I get angry at people like the congressman who don't stand up for who they are and what they are."

Quannah said, "Walk their talk?"

"Exactly."

She grinned up at Elvis. "Of course, I am sort of glad you have more interest in the female of the species since I happen to know of one young redhead who might be ready to bury the past and get on with her life. Seems she even expressed an interest in you."

His deep worry lines didn't disappear, despite her light words, and she shook her head and sighed.

Quannah grimaced. "Let's keep moving. You share whatever is causing that deep frown, and I'll tell you both all of Royce's story, which confirms Elvis's story and explains why young Darren Stiltiman took his own life."

By the time he'd finished, she understood far more about one Andrew VanBauer than she wanted. "Ugh. Now I wonder why we're so determined to get his killer. Maybe he deserved what he got."

"You don't really believe that, Gallagher, not for a moment."

"No. There would have been other ways to move out of VanBauer's path without taking his life. No one has the right to do that to another unless directly physically attacked."

"So?" Quannah asked, puffing with the exertion of the nonstop march.

"So, what?" she asked.

"Gallagher. Have you noticed lately that my patience is wearing thin?"

"Only lately? I've *never* seen you very *simpático* with Ant Medicine." She flapped her hands to increase the circulation. "Oh, don't get your war paint out. What I was thinking was so tenuous as to be practically useless."

"I'll be the judge of that."

She sniffed at the haughty look in his eyes. She counted to twenty under her breath just to make the point that she'd answer when she dadgum well pleased. If he thought a couple of sweet, mouthwatering kisses—no matter how earth-shaking—entitled him to special cooperation in any other area, well, he had another blasted thought coming.

"It's just," she said at last, "that VanBauer and Uzell

Speer had known each other in the past. Uzell hated him, refused to serve him on the Amtrak. Not blatantly rude, mind. He simply didn't show up. Instead, another attendant came to the diner. Don't you remember, Elvis?"

"Yes, now that you mention it. But believe me, so many do approach . . . *did* approach . . . the congressman that way. He didn't vote for the underdogs in this state. Definitely, a big-business man all the way. The only time he bespoke the democratic way was a few months before the reelection. Charisma, he had. They'd elect him time after time, even though his record showed how he voted on issues. You can't pick on Uzell, really. What I mean is . . . well, you all need to be careful. You thought it was me, too, remember? He wasn't the only one with a bone to pick. Mrs. Catherine Noble came all the way to Austin to see him in his office."

Quannah stopped a moment, bent over and placed his hands on his knees. "She's an elementary teacher?"

"Yes, sir. Retired and active on various educational boards. She'd been sent by a group demanding he change his stance on the upcoming retirement and insurance revenues for all teachers in the state."

"I suppose," Willi said, "he planned to opt for the cuts, not the increases?"

"Right."

"How did he field her request?" Quannah asked.

"Like always. Promised to think seriously about the problem and then vote according to the manner that would help the majority of his constituents."

"But?" she asked. "I did hear a *but*?"

Elvis sighed, sending plumes of frosty breath across the air between them. "His constituents were only the tycoons, the big companies with clout. He didn't plan to stay on one political rung of the ladder too long."

"And," said Quannah, "he knew who had the wherewithal to boost him farther along?"

"Yes, sir. And teachers, begging your pardon, Miss Gallagher, aren't the ones with power."

"Don't I know it." For a few minutes she shuffled and slid in the thick snow.

Quannah tromped behind her. "Be careful where you're going. Some of this is treacherous ice, not snow."

She flapped a gloved hand. "But back to Uzell. Perhaps Elvis is right. Maybe we're jumping to the wrong conclusion here."

She peered over her shoulder as she lifted one leg after the other in an ungainly maneuver. "Whaa—?" The sensation that half the ground below her had disappeared sent a nervous quiver of fear up her frame. She glanced down the hidden crevice.

"Ohhh . . ."

"Gallagher, damn you, *Winyan,* watch where—!"

KER-PLOMP!

One of her legs gave way, she landed on her backside, and shushed smoothly over the incline until her posterior met the first mogul. The impact sent her head over heels. She grimaced at the sounds of splintering wood and heavy breathing as if a bear were nipping at her rear and about to collide against her. One glimpse dispelled the vision. Instead of the four-legged bear, Quannah—the upside-down version—rolled over and over, a human snowball out of control.

She grabbed hold of a tree trunk and nearly wrenched her arm from its socket in the process. The snowball sped past her yelling nonrepeatable curses upon her innocent head. At last the flying missile stopped with a hard thud against a rock outcropping. *It* picked itself up and headed in her direction. She eased behind the tree, all eight inches of it, to no avail. Where was a really big Standing Relation when she needed one, preferably the size of the giant redwoods?

Resembling all the pictures she'd ever seen of the Abominable Snowman, Quannah lurched toward her.

"Blundering fool of a little idiot. She's trying to kill me. Damn, if I'm not after the wrong culprit."

"Gallagher! Where the hell are you?" He turned around, looked up the hill he'd so recently traversed. "Elvis?"

"Coming, sir." Gingerly, the secretary skidded and bobbed toward her. "Here she is, sir," he said and tried to halt his advance, failed and collided with Quannah, sending them both into a jumble of legs and arms, parkas and backpacks.

"Sorry, sir, my foot . . . uh . . . slipped."

From above the outcropping, she could just overhear them.

"I'm sorry, sir. I had just spied her." He pointed toward the tree.

"It's okay, Elvis. She has that effect on men. Hates us, you see. Me especially."

For the second time, he straightened up and helped Elvis to his feet. Between them, they had one good snowshoe remaining. Starting up the incline, he threw bits of splintered wood to right and left.

"Gallagher!"

Peeking from behind the tree, she waved. "Right here. I'm fine."

"Yeah. It usually seems to work that way when I'm around." He bent down to her eye level. "Why don't you get up out of that crouch, if you're fine?"

"Okay, I will. Now, remember"—she pushed him back with both hands—"Elvis is a . . . witness." Standing, she put both hands on her hips. "That was an accident. How did I know the ice shelf hid the edge of the hill? How did I know it would give way?" Briskly, she brushed herself off.

He held up the one snowshoe. "Both of yours all right?"

Easing the remaining one off her foot, she handed it to him. He held hers up against the one he had. "Great, Gallagher. These will be a perfect match for you. Two left feet." He threw them down.

Already halfway up the hill, she chose to ignore him. "What are you waiting for?" she asked.

Holding his head with one hand and rubbing his aching back with the other, he answered, "A shaman's last rites?"

His words sent a shiver down her back that had nothing to do with the chill air. Perhaps someone other than Andrew VanBauer would have need of such final ministrations. BeeBee VanBauer, for example.

Until Quannah grabbed her elbow, she didn't realize she had spoken the thought aloud. "You're right. We've got to hurry. For some reason, he tried to slit BeeBee's throat. Maybe, like all those in the political arena, she just can't tell the whole truth. Perhaps she had seen Uzell kill VanBauer."

Executing stiff steps like a prancing Walker thoroughbred, she made her way to higher ground before answering. "I don't think so. Remember the card found underneath Uzell's pillow? Right after I located the congressman's note on the back, BeeBee came into the hall-way. She could easily have grabbed it when I was downstairs, read it, came to her own hasty conclusions but kept silent, biding her time. Probably, she didn't hold any real animosity for anyone who'd do away with her worst enemy."

"Until," interrupted Elvis, "everything else pointed to me, she might have believed Uzell had killed VanBauer."

"True." Quannah snapped his fingers, producing no sound with the soft leather gloves covering his hands. "After dinner that evening, BeeBee did spend time hovering around Uzell while he whittled on Catherine Noble's train. If she'd dropped some hint of her knowledge of the card or even given Uzell the idea that she'd been searching in his room, that's all it would have taken for him to conclude that he had to do something about her and quickly." Abruptly, he halted.

"What do you think, Gallagher?"

"That he didn't have the opportunity."

"Everyone had the opportunity."

"Not Uzell Speer," she insisted. "Oh, I'm getting confused. I mean, he could have had the opportunity for the attack on BeeBee, but he didn't have the opportunity to kill the congressman. He was ill in bed. I took soup up to him myself. He fell asleep from the medication almost as soon as he scooped up the last spoonful."

"Maybe," Quannah said. "Catherine told you Uzell Speer was in the lobby getting the luggage for BeeBee just before he went to bed. Catherine Noble, if she had peeked into the parlor, might have discovered more—that Uzell just knifed Andrew VanBauer to death."

"Doesn't sound preplanned," offered Elvis. "None of

us knew we'd be staying over in Lilly's Establishment."

"True," Quannah agreed.

She stopped to catch her breath. The snow wasn't but about a foot deep, so the going was easier, but she'd had to match her stride to the men. She gulped in air and pushed a wayward tendril beneath her hood.

"We had about a half hour after the conductor notified us about our stopover."

"Your point, Gallagher?"

"Andrew VanBauer, admittedly, took his pleasure when and where he could discreetly do so. We know from Royce Droskill's account that Darren Stiltiman shared a bed with the congressman even though the young man was not of that persuasion and that led to his death. Now, what if VanBauer and Uzell had a past together like Darren Stiltiman and the congressman shared. VanBauer might have deemed it expedient to pass him a note, a special invitation for the evening."

"Gallagher, I hate to admit this, but that makes sense. The congressman got his kicks by pulling unwilling but pressured victims into his web."

"Sure," Elvis said, wiping his reddened nose. "There can be perverts who are straights, why not ones in the homosexual community? Sickening. It's ones like VanBauer that give them all a bad name, because he's the type that, despite PR men like me, will get in the media before this is all over."

Willi nodded. "By the time we climbed from the train and up to the house on the hill to the Bates Mote—I mean, to Lilly's Establishment, rage overtook Uzell. The past relationship must have been as you described or at least more pleasing for VanBauer than for him. Anyway, he—

Uzell—hated VanBauer and didn't want him in his life again. Maybe Uzell thought he'd pay VanBauer back for past indignities. Uzell's in his early twenties. Any past he had with Andrew had to be during his teen years. Volatile and unpredictable years to say the least. VanBauer may have misjudged his appeal for the teen just as he did in the case of Darren Stiltiman."

"Damn," Elvis said. "Then he thinks, like you all did, because I worked for VanBauer I had to possess the same sexual proclivities. He plants that cape in my trunk, puts the knife underneath *my* mattress and arranges for *me* to escape, thus sealing in the idea of *my* guilt."

"How could he have been roaming around that night in a cape?" she asked. "He was out, down for the count."

"Maybe, maybe not," Quannah said, pointing at the skyline above a ridge. Smoke curled in tendrils from numerous chimneys. "We're almost there. Let's hope we aren't too late to get answers."

"And," she added, "not too late to save BeeBee."

CHAPTER
19

SHE shuffled behind Quannah and Elvis as they ascended the last few feet of the hill. Over and over again, she mentally chided herself for her clumsiness. Analyzing the concept, she realized her bumbling antics had begun when she first met Special Investigator Quannah Lassiter. Their second meeting aboard the Amtrak hadn't been an improvement. Falling on top of him had set sequences in motion over which she had no control. Along with that, her emotions left her like a rudderless boat, letting her drift from acute annoyance with the man to euphoria, but she didn't mind. Everything had settled perfectly when they wrapped themselves together last night playing *Ghost* in the warm bedrolls. Staring at him now while he favored one leg and rubbed his back made her smile. Well, she never had wanted a blasé relationship. The one or two *almost* serious encounters she had nurtured in the past paled by comparison. Nodding her head, she settled Quannah's fate. His days were numbered, and he didn't even know it. That was not to say she wouldn't make the chase worth the end result. *Someday*.

QUANNAH climbed the first of the twenty-six steps leading to Lilly's Victorian Establishment. He paused and stared down at Willi and her blue-green eyes. She smiled and an ache coursed through him, opening a floodgate of emotions he'd never planned on developing. Nothing, he knew, would satisfy his spirit until Gallagher and he were at an understanding, and he wasn't sure he could survive the ordeal. By Great Eagle's feathers, he wasn't even sure what he meant by *understanding*. He was never quite in balance when she was around. A feisty spitfire hurtling him down a mountainside wasn't his idea of the perfect little woman. Well, it hadn't *been* his idea until now. He shrugged.

His uncle, Sheriff Brigham Tucker, had warned him long ago that no average woman would satisfy the strong spirit of this man of The People. Uncle was right. At this moment, Quannah wanted nothing more than to forget he was closing in on a deadly quarry. Instead he envisioned his lips caressing those smiling so mischievously up at him now. Shaking himself, he decided what her fate—no, her good fortune—would be in the future. Not that he wouldn't make the game of *Ghost* fun. Someday. Not yet. *Someday*.

* * *

ELVIS broke the tense regard between Quannah and Willi. "You think he's still inside?"

"We know," she said, "there's no place to go around here except where we've been. Somehow, I don't think Uzell would try a trek across the snow."

She tramped past the two men to push open the door. The heat of the vestibule and the silence of the building surrounded her. Sloughing her backpack to the floor, she walked into the parlor. Uzell Speer sat on the windowsill and stared out the window. The knife and the almost finished piece he whittled upon hung limply in his brown hands. He turned away from the window and looked at her. His dark curled lashes brushed his cheeks as he lowered his lids over eyes bleak and empty.

Quannah and Elvis pushed past her. Quannah said, "Go check on Mrs. VanBauer, Elvis."

"She is being fine," Uzell said. He hadn't moved other than to whittle a few more shavings off onto the newspaper placed at his feet. "The way you all be looking at me . . ." He shrugged.

Quannah unzipped his parka, took it off and laid it across the sofa. He sat on the other end, the one closest to the window seat. He motioned to Willi to stay behind the sofa. He leaned toward Uzell. "Want to tell us about it?"

"It doesn't be any matter now, what you think, huh?" Uzell shifted position. "I be seeing on your faces your knowing. Elvis is innocent."

Quannah had the raptor's look about him again, and he twitched his shoulders, moving ever so slightly, matching each change of Uzell's position with one of his own.

"When I was fourteen, my ma she was dying. Bad heroin. I was not knowing who my daddy is. Andrew VanBauer be speaking one day. I was picking pockets at his rally. Big bodyguard be catching me, what you think, but VanBauer didn't be letting them turn me in. He take me home, give me some schooling. All he be wanting he says is a son's affection. Young and not knowing what I be getting into, I be saying yes. Later, I learn the bad things, what you think, but in return, I be having a home, a *father* figure."

Uzell spat out the last statement, and whittled vigorously at what Willi could now tell was Lilly's Victorian Establishment, hill and all.

"Until," he continued, eyes covered with the sweep of his dusky lashes, "I was seventeen so I be staying. When I finally was getting a job, I stay away from him. Spent three years on and off in counseling. Never could be getting the dirty taste of him and that life out of my mind until about a year ago. That's when Amtrak be giving me a new chance."

"But this past weekend," she said, "you met Congressman VanBauer again."

"Yes. The bastard—I begging your pardon, miss—be sending me an invitation. Thinking he still owned me that way."

"And," said Quannah, eyes narrowed, "you proved him wrong."

The cuckoo clock on the mantel chimed, and the grandfather clock in the hall bonged agreement.

"Swear to all the gods, I don't be knowing the terrible thing that was possessing me."

In the silence that followed, only the distinct sound of

the clocks ticking caught Willi's attention. Her own breathing had slowed to a waltz tempo.

Uzell flipped his knife closed, pocketed it and stood up. He handed the finished wood carving of the hotel to her. "Be thinking you might be wanting a memento of where you two be learning to trust." His glance took in Quannah.

Well, Blasted Hades, she supposed their feelings had been that obvious to everyone.

Gingerly, she held the replica of Lilly's Victorian Establishment and said, "I don't understand, Uzell. You were too sick with fever to come down and do . . . murder."

"You were bringing me soup. I be remembering the kindness."

"So, how—?"

"Before I be getting in bed." He nodded and his shoulders slumped. "He be standing right there." Uzell pointed to the parlor door. "*Told* me to be coming in, to be shutting the door. I be remembering old days, bad days." Uzell bent over and put his head in his hands. "I seeing sparks—reds and blacks. I was being really sick already, but this other sickness be coming on me, too. So, what you think, I be going out to the kitchen and grabbing the sharpest knife."

"And?" Quannah edged to the forefront of the sofa.

"Even then . . . I might not have been killing. I even be starting up the stairs, but . . . he opening the door. He smiling and saying, 'I knew you'd come back.' Sitting in the chair, he be laughing."

He glared up at Willi. "Nice lady should not be hearing this." He closed his eyes. "I be remembering, 'Never, never, never again.' Then the red and black flashing be starting. What you think? I be leaving this room and be barely standing. I be stumbling into the hall, picking up Mrs. VanBauer's baggage, don't you know. Nothing else. Just the red and the black sickness."

Willi asked, "You saw Mrs. Noble in the vestibule, didn't you?"

"Maybe. I don't know. Yes, I be remembering. She be spilling all those pills and tissues from her purse."

"How," asked Quannah, "did you place the knife back in the kitchen?"

Uzell raised his head from his hands. Curled lashes glistened with his tears. "I be remembering . . . leaving it in VanBauer's side . . . right where I was stabbing him. In his heart. Then the red. I be seeing the red and the darkness." Uzell leaned back against the window seat's cushions.

"Sit up, Mr. Speer. Why did you also try to slit BeeBee VanBauer's throat?"

With visible effort, Uzell sat up and stared Quannah in the eye. "I don't be doing that. I don't be cutting *no one's throat*."

His words had the ring of unquestionable truth to them. Recalling her encounter with Andrew VanBauer's corpse, Willi, frowning, said, "Yes, Uzell, you did. Perhaps after the first shock of what you had done in stabbing the congressman, the vision has buried itself in your subconscious, but the congressman was almost decapitated."

Uzell raised his head to peer at her. Tears pooled and spilled from his chocolate eyes. "That be so horrible. I was not knowing I did that . . . blacking it out that's what I be doing . . . no better than him . . . so sorry."

Quannah sighed and shook his head. "Let's put you in

the storage room, Uzell. You might have allowed Elvis to get out, but there won't be any escape for you."

"I don't be letting no one out. I be thinking you finding out Elvis is the innocent one, so he is being in no real danger. Why I be helping him out?"

"Naturally," Willi interrupted. "If we chased after Elvis, you'd have time to escape."

"Escape? Where I be running to?" His brown eyes cast a woeful look toward the window and the snow beyond. "Besides." He tapped his chest. "This pain—who can be fleeing from his own heart?"

Quannah stood up and motioned for Uzell to precede him. "We'll get all the answers eventually. When you remember all the things you'd rather forget in that black fog. Right, Uzell? When you're ready to tell us the whole truth."

"I be telling you, I be taking a life. What is there to be lying about after this horror?" His shoulders slumped. Quannah led him away.

Sitting down in the chair with the carved dragons on the arms, Willi sighed. Uzell Speer was absolutely right. He'd made a clean breast of things. Why would he keep insisting he hadn't slashed VanBauer's throat? To think better, she pulled her legs up in the chair, curled in a comfortable position and tapped the end of her nose. BeeBee VanBauer had some explaining to do. Willi had read tales of criminals repeating themselves. Using the same MO. Perhaps BeeBee had tried a simplified version on herself—not too deep of a slash, just enough to allow them to think someone else had to be responsible. Therefore, someone else was responsible for VanBauer's near beheading.

Willi gasped and sat straight up in the carved chair. She considered the cold dragon's eyes. Maybe VanBauer hadn't been dead when Uzell left him. A vulnerable congressman could have been a temptation too difficult to pass up for one angry ex-wife and political opponent to boot.

Willi snapped her fingers. Catherine Noble wasn't as innocent as she appeared either. Anyone tough enough to beard the lions in the Texas State School Board would have the nerve to carry out anything she planned. She admitted to seeing Uzell when he left VanBauer. Perhaps she took advantage and—*Stop it.* Willi raised her hands above her, stretched and yawned. Okay, she was going into a fantasy world now. Nothing linked Catherine Noble in any way to the horror. *Face it. You like Uzell and don't want to believe it's him.* But he'd confessed. Maybe he couldn't face all the details of those few horrendous moments, but in time he would fess up about the details.

A log in the fireplace crackled and split to send little firecrackers of light toward the hearth rug. Willi jumped up to sweep away the sparks with the silver-handled whisk broom. The parlor door creaked open. Feeling defenseless with her back to it, she immediately rose and turned.

With red wig askew, fuchsia lipstick glistening, and the ever-present cleaning brush clutched in her hand, Odessa Morales looked her age this morning. She blinked and rubbed her eyes. One of her false lashes caught in the lower lashes, sticking and leaving Odessa with what seemed like a nervous caterpillar trying to hump the bags underneath her left eye. She twisted the pink skirt of her uniform and swallowed a number of times before speaking. "Hey, so I didn't frighten you, no?"

"No, Odessa," she said. How could she stay angry with the woman who had instigated thoughts of playing *Ghost* with Quannah? "Do you need to clean in here?"

"No, *señorita,* Odessa does this room about the middle of the afternoon. During siesta. Before the suppertime."

"Then you needed to see me?"

"Well, if that investigator who is so *guapo* is not here, you will do. He's got the eyes of the devil and God together, *sí*? He can eat *galletas* in my bed anytime, I was a little younger."

"I would think Sam and Jasper would be enough for any woman." Willi glared and put her hands on her hips. "What do you want?"

Odessa sniffed and waved Willi back into the chair. She sat in the one opposite and frowned at her feet, which didn't reach the floor. "Here's the deal. A lot happened the day this *loco* group come here, you know? So, Odessa"—she patted herself on her chest, sending puffs of Camelot powder into the air—"maybe she's a little busy to notice everything at once." She switched to the first person after getting this distasteful idea of advancing age out on the table. "*Sí,* I was doing the cleaning up while that poor man was sitting right where you are. Not that chair, though."

"Congressman VanBauer?"

"*Sí,* if you say so. When I left, I go clean the men's room. Uzell, he's the fellow been helping Sam in the *cocina.* He talks to this dead fellow, so he's not so dead then."

"You heard them from the men's room?"

Odessa shifted herself to the edge of the chair and with her toes was able to touch the floor. "You are getting the picture. *¿Verdad?* Before I close the door to *el baño de caballeros,* I see Uzell come in, you with me?"

"And did you return here later?"

"No, *pero,* but . . ."

"You heard something?" Willi scooted to the edge of her chair, too, and was almost nose to nose with Odessa.

"Sí y no."

"Yes and no? What does that mean? Either you did or you didn't."

"Odessa she is thinking to herself maybe you and the investigator believe Uzell did this thing to the newsman."

"Congressman," Willi corrected.

Odessa shrugged, which sent her wig far to one side. She used both hands to wiggle it back into position. *"Ay, sí,* the man in the news all the time—the Congressman What's-his-face. Uzell, he don't do this."

"But . . ." Willi protested.

"Pero nothing. Uzell comes in. This I see. I clean the men's. I come out to clean the lady's. I hear what's-his-face, big-shot *politico* talking. Now, *señorita,* he can't be dead if he's talking, *comprende*?"

"No, Odessa, he must have been alive. But are you sure it was VanBauer, not Uzell?"

"Señorita, listen to me. I ain't Sam and nothing's wrong with my sight. My hearing is *mucho* better than Jasper's. Uzell, he talks with a funny accent—Jamaican, he says. He don't speak the good English like me, *verdad*? Well, he can't help that. So, I know it's not him. Also I see him leave, *then* hear the big shot talking."

"Muttering to himself or was someone with him?"

"That's what I'm trying to tell you. *Sí*, another person is with him. Low talker so I don't know if it's an *hombre* or a *mujer*. My guess would be *hombre*. Maybe Uzell ain't the last one to see What's-his-face alive. *Comprende*?"

Willi nodded and swallowed.

Straightening her pink skirt and her apron, Odessa stood and headed to the door.

"Oh," Willi said, "thank you, Odessa. Thank you. Don't tell anyone else. You . . . you could get hurt. I'll let Investigator Lassiter know, but you don't say anything more."

"*Gracias.* For a *mujer loca*, you are okay. Odessa, she is not *tonta*. You can't survive in this world being stupid. You give that *guapo* cop a kiss from old Odessa when you tell him, *sí*?"

Willi's palms were slick with nervous perspiration. Blue Blazes, the Snow Snake still slithered within the hotel.

CHAPTER
20

WILLI found Quannah in the foyer and put her hand on his arm.

"I locked Uzell," he said, "in his room. Old Victorian grillwork blocks the window, and I have the key to his door. Sometimes my job can be the pits."

She walked with him to the dining room. "Sam's had Farley call us twice. I took long enough to change out of my snow gear and into house boots. Any more delays, I think he'll have our heads for supper."

When she had seated herself, she leaned across the dining room table and touched his arm and he entwined his fingers with hers. "I suppose," she said, "this must be the worst part of your job, but I may have worse news. We've got the wrong one again."

He put two fingers to her lips. "No, Gallagher. Now a little paranoia is healthy and certainly justified after what we've been through, but we've got a confession. I'm bushed. Not another word, Gallagher, until I've got a decent meal under my belt. Anything can wait a half hour. *Ant Medicine,* remember?"

Willi nodded. "Yes, you're right." Maybe she should calm down and think . . . think carefully before jumping to conclusions. That had happened twice already. The meal would give her a few minutes to get her thoughts gathered, and she could watch everyone.

The hotel patrons, including a white-faced BeeBee, drifted in one by one and seated themselves. Royce Droskill and Ivon, with Elvis at her side, shuffled into place as the grandfather clock bonged out the hour. Willi frowned at BeeBee. There was something wrong with her other than the bandage around her throat. Perhaps it was simply the absence of her ermine that made her seem so bereft.

Rich odors wafted in as Jasper Farley pushed open the bat wing doors. He set a steaming plate of enchiladas in the middle of the table. Following him, Sam added rice and guacamole salad to the offerings. Catherine placed crisp tortillas and baked apples nearby and took her seat.

Sam turned his head away in time to hide a yawn behind his hand. In response, Willi stifled one of her own and tears came to her eyes. She grinned and thought that obviously no one had had much sleep last night.

"I sure didn't," Quannah said, winking at her.

"Don't do that," she whispered back.

"What?" He splayed his hands on his shirt front. "Me?"

"Get out of my head, Lassiter. That's not funny." She tried to look stern, but her tirade ended in a giggle. "Later, I need to tell you about Odessa. She heard—"

"This god-awful weather is finally breaking," Ivon said, staring out the window. Ivon brought her attention back to Quannah. "How did you figure out who it really was?" He explained.

"Simply terrible," Catherine Noble said, "that in this day and time one mean-minded man could wreak such havoc. Just goes to prove that once a bully, always a bully. It's a shame that Uzell Speer must suffer. I don't think he should."

While Quannah elaborated between increasing yawns, Willi mentally ticked off folks. Odessa and her paramours hadn't known the VanBauers and had no interest in politics. Ivon's motive had been to discredit VanBauer, to make him suffer humiliation, not kill him. Ivon had no sleeping pills, only allergy meds in her bags, so she couldn't have been responsible for doctoring Quannah's food or drink the night of the escape.

For a few moments the only sounds in the dining room were the scraping of forks against plates, the crunch of crisply fried tortilla chips and requests for more water.

Ivon yawned and rubbed her eyes. "Good God, what's the matter with me? I've done nothing but rest. I guess we're all creatures of habit. It gets dark outside and we become like Pavlov's dogs."

BeeBee stifled a yawn of her own and yelped at the pain it caused her throat.

Knowing BeeBee better now, Willi *knew* without a doubt she was only getting back her own power by besting VanBauer in the political arena. She wanted to gloat. Like Ivon, BeeBee would get no satisfaction unless VanBauer were alive to suffer those proverbial agonies of defeat. Also, she didn't carry a cornucopia of medications around with her.

Willi's lids grew heavy, and she shook her head. She pushed her plate away after eating only a little Spanish rice. Opting to stand, she offered to go to the kitchen for refills.

Catherine waved her back down into her chair. "No, you're bushed. I'll go get the platters. You sit. I know you're dead on your feet after being out in the storm."

"Whee-yew," Royce Droskill said, rubbing his knuckles. "Believe I'm getting old. Can't seem to hold my damnblamed peepers open another minute."

"Maybe we're all in a state of delayed shock," Willi offered.

Slow-motion shock, if her senses weren't lying to her. Each person within her vision seemed to move within a distorted fog. She sipped cold ice water and vowed not to eat another bite. Why that thought even occurred to her, she had no idea, but Quannah said learn to trust her inner voice. So be it, she'd already pushed her plate back anyway.

"Hey, fella," she said, snapping her fingers before his tired eyes. "I need to tell you what Odessa told me."

"Uh . . . when . . . when did she tell you, Gallagher?"

"Just before we came in here, and it's important. I wonder where she is?"

"She never helps serve the meals, remember? And"— he paused to yawn and wipe the tears from his eyes— "can't this wait until morning?"

Catherine returned, carrying two heaping platters. Willi grasped one to help her. Why hadn't Sam or Jasper assisted? They shouldn't have left this to one of the guests.

When Catherine started to serve her, Willi held up her hand.

Everyone else took seconds, heaping their plates with enchiladas and rice.

Reseated, Catherine picked up the conversation. "Something has to be done about the bullies in the world," she said. "The Saddam Husseins. The Idi Amins. The Osama Bin Ladens. To terminate the development of such individuals is our responsibility, don't you think? I convinced Uzell to open up, tell his story of his three years of horror. Now don't get the idea that I'm narrow-minded. Homosexuality is a lifestyle I don't understand, but that's my problem, not those folks. People have a right to live like they want to live. As long as they don't hurt others. Andrew VanBauer wasn't just a homosexual, he was a perverted one. He chose partners who weren't truly of his lifestyle, just to torment and bully them because of his power." She paused. "BeeBee almost caught me trying to find some of his papers. I took his briefcase, you know. So, I followed her and tried to silence her when she went to see for herself that the monster was actually dead. I regret that my mission was unsuccessful."

Willi mumbled something appropriate. Or at least, she thought it was something appropriate. It was hard to tell with the miasma folding around her mind. Tiredness? Shock? Maybe a realization of the full truth. She tried to pay attention to Catherine's words. Catherine Noble was the only one left on her list of suspects who had the makeup bag full of drugs, who had been downstairs at the crucial time. And Great Hades, she was all the time expressing what horrible things ought to be done to politicians—local and state—and now the evil world leaders.

Willi looked down at her plate. She could hardly breathe when the fear of what might have been in her food came to her.

"Why—?" She croaked out the single word in an effort to ask why Farley and Sam hadn't come in from the kitchen, but she seemed for a moment paralyzed. She managed to grasp her water glass as Catherine returned once more to the kitchen. Willi drank two more glasses. *Dilute whatever she's put in the food.* She tried to kick Quannah but her leg wouldn't move.

Both the men's heads lolled. She could swear she heard snores from Royce. She attempted to elbow him, but every part of her moved in slow motion. Reaching a hand toward her water glass a third time, she grasped it, lost her hold but grabbed before the water spilled. On the second attempt she was successful. She lifted the water to her lips to drink thirstily. That was better. The mists receded momentarily. *Think, damn it, think.*

Catherine continued her tirade after serving another enchilada to Ivon and a dip of guacamole to Elvis. Ivon picked at her food before her fork clanked onto the table top. She blinked. Her head fell forward onto her chest. Elvis didn't react to this or the guacamole. With both hands in his lap, he stared at his plate as if this were the most activity he could muster.

Catherine patted his shoulder. "At first, I hadn't intended to do anything to Uzell. After all," she said, "I finished the job properly for him, didn't I? He's sound asleep now, you know."

Willi started to answer clearly. *No, let Catherine believe she was as sedated as the rest.* She garbled out what she hoped sounded like a stuporous answer. "Huh? Finished . . . job?" She mimicked Ivon's blinking.

BeeBee VanBauer was slowly slipping down in her chair. An inch at a time she disappeared beneath the edge of the table. No one else seemed to notice. Willi could expect no help from that corner. She wiggled her fingers and found now that her first panic had subsided, she could manipulate them fine. Her legs were another story. Under the table, she kept flexing her toes and legs, working the muscles, willing them to respond.

"Job?" she repeated.

Catherine answered. "I meant to behead the tyrant. No sense letting him go any farther, was there?"

"Uzell didn't . . . kill . . . Van . . . ?"

Willi ran a swollen tongue over her dry lips. Ivon suddenly lurched. She raised her head a moment and gave a good imitation of a blinking owl before she leaned back in her chair, mouth thrown open, arms hanging limply at her side. Quannah's cheek rested in his unfinished plate of enchiladas and Royce snored.

Willi kept her sentences strung out into bits and pieces, but wanted to say enough to keep Catherine talking. "You . . . intend . . . kill . . . us?" Her mind was functioning, but her arms seemed to get heavier. *Poco a poco. Little by little. Paso a paso. Step by step.* She would be okay. She hadn't eaten as much as the others for one thing, and she'd diluted whatever was in her system with water. She just had to keep her mind clear. The body would follow suit. To believe otherwise would plunge her into panic again.

"At first," continued Catherine as if she hadn't heard her, "I simply thought I would use those sleeping pills I'd saved. On myself, you see, because of the disease. Just like my parents, bless them. That forgetfulness. It's getting worse. The doctors said it would. That's why the insurance benefits were so important. But you can't reason with bullies."

"Hummm," said Willi.

Blue Blazes, Willi felt as if she could stand now if she tried, but she willed herself to listen. Catherine could have one or more of the guns or, at the very least, a knife from the kitchen. "Hummm . . . no," she mumbled to keep up her nonsensical side of the conversation.

"No, it's true. I am not old, after all, but getting up in years. Thought I was ancient until I met Sam. I want to live now. See other places and people while I can still remember my name and address. Of course, Sam, poor thing, won't get to be with me, but I'll find someone. You understand, don't you? I really was sorry you had to find the body. Most unpleasant for you. Well, for me, too."

Willi managed to keep one eye open and squinted in Catherine's direction.

Catherine picked up her napkin and wiped her lips. "The phone's working. I answered it on the first ring this morning, and I'm absolutely sure no one else heard it. So much easier to plan. A freight train comes through about nine tonight. The Amtrak passenger follows at nine-fifteen." Catherine folded her napkin.

"You kill . . . VanBauer . . . not . . . Uzell."

"Willi, I said that some time ago. That's why I used the sleeping pills in the enchiladas and rice. I'd saved up several months' worth simply because I don't like to take them. Doctors think that's all people over sixty-five are good for is to give us enough to feel like we're in La-La Land. That doesn't make us forget our aches and pains, our slow demise. Anyway, now you all will reap the medicinal benefits of those pills."

Pushing her chair back, Catherine got up. "I'm sure there's enough to keep you all in dreamland until early morning. I really don't want any more deaths. Death is for those wicked ones in life. You all . . . you all are just merely obstacles. By the time you wake in the morning, I will have packed, gotten aboard the Amtrak, and told my tale about the buses beating the train here. You all boarded the bus, of course. Yes, I believe that will work. I must keep things simple."

Catherine disappeared from her sight. Willi tilted back in her chair. When Catherine's cold fingers touched her neck, she jerked. Without turning her head, she couldn't see Catherine and unreasonable panic crashed through the clouds floating around her mind. After pushing back the plate, Catherine gently supported Willi's head in both her hands. She eased Willi down until her cheek rested on the table.

"You'll rest better that way. I've hidden all the weapons in case someone awakes sooner than expected. I've got Investigator Lassiter's gun with me. A little extra insurance never hurt a lady."

A napkin fluttered off the table and into Willi's one-eyed blurry line of vision, where it floated downward, downward to finally settle on the floor. Catherine's voice became an indistinct buzz with only intermittent words reaching Willi. "Yes, I must . . . of the shoes . . . be extra careful near . . . thirty-foot drop-off . . . down. Mustn't lose my footing. No problem . . . slow and easy, that's the way. No . . . rush at all."

Catherine patted Willi's shoulder. "You should have just had the guacamole, you know."

Try as she might, Willi couldn't seem to raise her head. The reason she should sort of drifted away, and she slept.

CUCK-KOO! CUCK-KOO! That sound and the bong-ing of the grandfather clock interrupted Willi's dreams of she and Quannah doing the Mexican Hat Dance in a bowl of frijoles, stomping around on the beans as if they were dancing on grapes. In fact, her head ached as if she'd overindulged in the fruit of the vine.

She moaned and with great effort turned her head, then wondered for a moment why BeeBee was snoring in such an unladylike position on the floor. In slow motion, Willi lifted her arm in front of her face. At last, she focused her eyes by squinting.

Nine o'clock. She eyed the dark outside the windows.

Something was going to happen at nine tonight. What was it? She pushed herself up. Her elbows felt like strands of cooked spaghetti. In marionettelike jolts, she got her chair pushed back and stood. Licking dry lips, she reached for her water glass and drank. When that didn't appease her thirst, she grabbed the pitcher of water and gulped its contents down, too.

There was something she had to do at nine, or was it at nine-fifteen? Stretching and yawning loosened the tight-ness of her muscles, too long in one position. When she glanced at Quannah with his cheek resting in the remains of his enchiladas, everything came back with clarity.

Catherine Noble.

Sleeping pills.

The freight train due at nine. The Amtrak fifteen minutes later.

Willing her limbs to move, she made her way to Quannah's side and shook him. "Wake up, damn it."

"Uhh."

She grabbed his ponytail and pulled his head from his plate. "She's getting away."

He opened one eyelid, which immediately closed. She got a quick glimpse as his eye rolled upward. Great. Only thing he was viewing had to be the underside of his eyelid. She dribbled water into his mouth, held her hand over his lips, and made him swallow.

"Lassiter?"

"Uhh-duh. Huh?"

Special Investigator Quannah Lassiter was out of this play. She'd have to stop Catherine Noble herself. Had the woman already stumbled down the icy hill to the train crossing, or would she wait until the last minute?

While considering this, she tried to awaken Royce and Elvis. Neither did more than moan. Going into the foyer, she grabbed her parka from the coatrack, pulled on leather gloves and shoved a ski mask over her head. If she could just catch up with Catherine, she knew she'd be able to overpower the old woman.

She opened the door. Icy air cut across her face through the mask. Pulling her head down like a turtle going into its shell, she faced the frigid aftermath of the snowstorm.

She should have changed from her leather-soled boots. She slid and stumbled down the hill, grabbing a tree trunk here, an outcropping there. Her knee hit the hard ice. Her torn jeans revealed a bloody gash. She couldn't feel the pain she knew she should. Halfway down the incline, she spotted Catherine in front of her, suitcases in hand.

An owl's soft hoo-hoo overhead sent a shiver down Willi's spine. Once he spotted his prey, he'd glide soundlessly until right above his victim, then he'd let loose with that bloodcurdling screech. Could she be so lucky with her encounter with Catherine when she caught up with her. Considering the noise Willi made, she gave up on the silent approach.

Catherine walked steady and upright in appropriate footwear.

"Wait," yelled Willi. "You don't have to do this."

Catherine turned to face her. Willi advanced closer and closer, keeping a wary lookout for the edge of the walkway. She had no desire to go tumbling over the mountain rim and down the thirty-foot side. She grabbed hold of a tree branch to pull herself along. The brittle oak wood broke off in her hand. When she was only a yard apart from Catherine, she breathed a sigh of relief. Thank goodness she wasn't going to have to grapple the old biddy to the ground.

"I really wish," said Catherine, "you hadn't awakened so soon."

"We'll talk back in the hotel." Willi's teeth chattered. "Where it's warm." Keeping a precarious balance, she stretched out her hand toward Catherine.

Catherine pulled Quannah's gun from her coat pocket and pointed it at Willi.

Backing up a step, Willi swallowed. Sweat broke out to leave her palms sticky even beneath the gloves. "You said . . . you said you'd taken a weapon. Now I . . . remember."

The owl hooted, swarmed close by Catherine's head

and shrieked. Catherine jerked in alarm. She pulled the trigger twice. The bullets zinged close to Willi's head.

Willi swiped outward with the oak branch, and the gun catapulted into a high arc and went over the incline.

A train whistle, distant but clear, trilled a warning farther down the track. Catherine's birdlike head tilted to listen. She smiled, seemingly resigned to missing her train.

Willi, mouth too cottony-dry to speak, nodded reassuringly. Her relief over the encounter left her with trembling knees. Finally, she managed, "Everything's fine. We'll . . . we'll go back to—"

Catherine stepped toward her and swung the largest suitcase into Willi's midsection.

"Ooomp!"

Willi lost her balance. The weight of the luggage carried her over sideways and backwards off the hardened path. She somersaulted over the edge. Out of control, her body gained momentum, bouncing off a tree once, scattering frozen snow and rocks in her wake. The edge of the suitcase hit her shoulder and head before it slid past her. She landed spread-eagled on top of the Samsonite and prayed she was as hardy.

Something was definitely wrong with her right shoulder.

Wrenched? Maybe.

Painful? Damn right.

Favoring her right arm, she scrambled up to the edge. By the time she'd reached the verge of the incline, her limbs shook uncontrollably. Deep gulps of air seared her dry throat and increased the ache in her lungs. Getting up on her hands and knees, she straightened her ski mask and checked the luminous dial of her watch. Five minutes until the freight train zoomed through. But twenty minutes until the Amtrak. She rested until her breath came more evenly, pushed herself up with her good hand and arm and inched down the other side of the hill toward the track.

Catherine sat on her one remaining piece of luggage.

"Sorry I had to do that, Willi. But I have to leave. You understand that."

"Catherine. When the Amtrak stops, I'll tell them the story here." She waved her arm to take in Lilly's Victorian Hotel. "The train staff isn't just going to invite a murderess to travel with them."

"I've been thinking about that while you slid down here. I have a plan."

"Oh?"

Catherine reached in her pocket.

Willi backed up. "You wouldn't . . . another gun . . . where?"

"Really, Willi, you must curb that overactive imagination." She pulled out the carving of the train that Uzell had done for her. Catherine said, "I want you to have this. Uzell would like that, too."

A warning whistle, long and urgent, rent the air. Willi peered down the track. The red glow of lights pierced the night sky.

"And your plan?"

Catherine stood up. "I can't abide prison, not at my age, you know. Our laws protect the bullies, not the liberators such as myself. No, you've left me no choice."

"There are lots of choices, Catherine. Come back with me. Maybe there will be leniency for extenuating circumstances or . . . or something." Even to her ears, it sounded false. The platitudes only brought a sweet smile to Catherine's face.

Another blare of the train's whistle sent shivers down Willi's back. Surely, the old biddy wouldn't . . . no, no one would willingly . . ." She refused to let the idea grow and advanced purposefully on Catherine. "Even if you did go to prison, it'd probably be a minimum security due to your age."

"No." Catherine stepped closer to the tracks. "It's best this way."

"Catherine!" Willi gulped, trying to keep the panic out of her own voice. Only seconds left to convince her. As she spoke, she inched her way closer. She just needed to be within an arm's reach. "Don't do this to me. I don't want to live with the guilt all my life."

Catherine threw the carving at her.

With reflex action Willi caught it. By the time she peered down, Catherine had picked up her suitcase, stepped over the railing and onto the track. Willi ran toward her, caught her sleeve. Catherine heaved the Samsonite overnighter at her. It hit her wrenched shoulder.

The pain seared through her shoulder and down her back to bring her to her knees. Tears streamed down her face. She kicked at the luggage. As she crab-crawled through the snow, she hunched up in an agonized spasm, but took a steadying breath before trying to move one knee in front of the other.

The train's bloody eye appeared, large and glaring. Like a banshee's warning, the whistle bleated in panic. The conductor braked. Sparks of fire spewed from the wheels.

Willi screamed. Her screams mingled with Catherine's.

And that cacophony of screeches—her own and the old woman's—reverberated in her head until only pitiful moans escaped her. She bent her good arm over her head. A pale glow came from the wooden train, its patina splashed with red droplets. Great sobs wracked her body. She collapsed on the blood-splattered snow.

Eons later, strong arms cradled her and a soothing voice said, *Winyan,* I'm so sorry. *Winyan,* it will be okay."

SOME three weeks later, February developed into an early spring in Nickleberry, gifting Mother Earth with early crocuses and budding lilacs. At nightfall Willi wandered in the garden-of-sorts behind the farmhouse. Charlie Brown, her dachshund, gamboled around her feet, chasing would-be villains from the area. He was most ferocious with a butterfly until it landed on his nose and he sneezed. She giggled.

"Thanks, Charlie Brown. I needed that."

Elba, as short and round as her familiar, Rose Pig, stepped out on the back porch and hollered. "That Injun man, Sheriff Tucker's nephew, is yonder." Her thumb pointed in the general direction of the living room.

As Willi went inside, Elba told her, "He's a damn handsome devil. Thirty-year-ago I wouldn't have minded being holed up in a snowstorm with the likes of him. Cozy-like, was it?"

Willi pointedly ignored the question.

"Fine, but the tarot deck don't lie. Stifled in white and in trouble with the law. You liked every minute of it. Uh-huh. Got to go. See you in the morn. Roosters crow early here. Earlier than Gabriel blows his horn, earlier than the dangblame blue jays, earlier tha—"

"Elba! Good night."

Willi walked down the hall, hung up her light sweater and paused at the living room entrance. His profile, turned away from her, still looked like a predatory bird. Had he forgiven her for her part in the tragedy? She'd practically driven Catherine Noble across those tracks into the freighter's path, had chastised herself again and again for not allowing the old woman to board the Amtrak. Quannah would have trailed her later, brought her to justice, not to a bloody death.

His strong fingers lifted the carving of the train from the mantelpiece. "You've kept it," he said, not turning. She nodded. She realized his sixth sense about her presence was still intact and this offered a needed lift to her spirits.

He faced her. "Gallagher. You haven't answered my phone calls or letters." He sat down on the low divan and patted the cushion beside him.

Opting for the chair opposite, she shrugged as she seated herself. "I thought . . ."

"Did you read them? The letters?"

She glanced toward the desk in the corner, knowing without seeing that the closed top covered a bundle of three unopened envelopes.

He shook his head, got up, moved a footstool close to her side and sat on it. He took both her hands between his own. "I wanted you to know I appreciated what you tried to do. Trying to catch her, I mean. Me? Looked like a fool on the report handed in . . . or would have if I hadn't put that *my assistant* had given chase when I was incapacitated. Thanks, Gallagher."

"But . . ."

"But me no buts, *Winyan.*"

Straightening her shoulders, she looked him in the eye. "She might be alive today if I hadn't chased her."

"Not really. We checked with her doctor. From what he said, she hadn't long to live. Parkinson's disease, not Alzheimer's as she feared. She was honest about the sleeping pills. She'd been saving them for herself."

"But she'd wanted to live. She told me so at the dinner table."

"Denial of the inevitable for a little while. Maybe six months. Also, she feared she might not be able to use the pills when the time came. Panic drove her to the tracks, not you, Gallagher, not you. It was the terror of living when she pictured what her last months might be like awaiting trial, knowing she'd probably not live through the ordeal one way or another."

"And Uzell?" It wasn't really a question. She knew the answer.

"Catherine knew she gave him a lethal dose. But, too, perhaps that's better. He would have ended up in a jail situation similar to the living hell he'd had with Van-Bauer."

The kitchen door banged in the distance. She looked up. Charlie Brown bounded into the living room, woofed at Quannah and growled.

"Come here, you *sunka cistila,*" Quannah commanded. *"Shoon-ka jeezes-tea-la?"*

"Yes, it means *small dog.* Be a different word if he

were still a pup, but I guess he's big as he's going to get?"

"Afraid so. His name," she said, "if you remember, is Charlie Brown."

"Charlie Brown, *what a clown*?"

"Didn't we," she asked, with the beginning of a smile tugging at the corners of her mouth, "go through this once before?"

"Yes, but let's do it again." He winked, grabbed her hand and pulled her up. "Charlie Brown, what a clown."

"So? I like Golden Oldies. You aren't civilized enough to know what those are, huh?"

"As a matter of fact, Gallagher, I could listen to Little Caesar and the Romans, The Tremeloes, Del Shannon, The Kingsmen. How many more you want?"

She motioned him over to the tape deck and opened a panel revealing cassettes. Below that, she pointed to LPs. "How about 'Silence Is Golden' by the Tremeloes." She opened her blue-green eyes wide and peered straight into his dark ones.

"Sure," he agreed and grabbed her around the waist. He nuzzled aside her hair and planted a kiss on her neck.

The first genuine smile in weeks brightened her face.

"Sure," he repeated. "And then we'll play this one." He handed her The Swingin' Medallions' "A Double Shot of My Baby's Love."

"Do you have a player up there?" He glanced toward the stairway.

When she raised an eyebrow, he said, "Just thought it might be more suitable for playing . . . uh . . ."

"Yes, Lassiter?"

He whispered, "Gallagher, let's go play *Ghost*."

"Patience, Lassiter, *patience*." She untied his ponytail. "You'll tell me again all the nice things *Winyan* means?" She left a burning trail of kisses up his neck and stroked her hands through his hair.

Quannah groaned. "Your touch has just destroyed any Ant Medicine I had left." His dark eyes peered deeply into hers and his breath quickened to match the tempo of her own.

"But . . ." she whispered halfheartedly, *"Winyan?"*

His hold around her waist tightened as he stepped on the first stair rung. "All in good time. It has many meanings, some of which should only be whispered gently against your ear in the dark."

"In that case, I guess playing *Ghost* might be . . . a valuable life lesson." She giggled and raced him up the stairs.